SUGAR

SUGAR

A NOVEL

DEIRDRE RIORDAN HALL

This is a work of fiction. Names, characters, organizations, places, events, and incidents are either products of the author's imagination or are used fictitiously.

Published by Skyscape, New York

www.apub.com

ISBN-13: 9781477829387
ISBN-10: 1477829385

Book design by M.S. Corley

LCCN: 2014956656

Printed in the United States of America

To all those who've stepped out of their own shadow.
For those who haven't, the sunshine awaits you.

Chapter One

"Move it. Outta the way, Sugar," my brother Skunk shouts as his orange soda sloshes out of the plastic Big Gulp cup. I'm not quick enough to avoid him as I plod through the living room carrying the laundry basket.

He plows into me. He could have waited or gone around me, but Skunk prefers to bulldoze. The duct-taped basket careens toward the tall bookshelf that holds Mama's porcelain-doll collection. It teeters. I imagine the dolls crashing to the floor and ghastly shards of broken, frozen smiles leering at me. Thankfully, the shelf rights itself. Only wet laundry spills onto the carpet, along with whatever's left of my dignity. I catch myself on the back of the couch. Dropping to my hands and knees, I pick up the sopping clothes.

He plops back into his divot on the sofa and resumes his video game. "Damn. You're always in the way," he mutters as shrapnel flies across the screen.

"Sorry," I say softly, more to myself than to him.

I lean against the doorframe, heavy with the truth. I am always in the way. I've known this for as long as I can remember. I'm the fat Puerto Rican–Polish girl who doesn't feel like she belongs in her skin, or anywhere else for that matter. I've always been too much and yet not enough.

A chocolate craving pulls at odd parts of my body—the slight web of skin between my fingers, the spot under my tongue, the place above my knees but below my thighs—tugging me toward the kitchen. It distracts me from the laundry and everything else I should be doing. I leave the basket in the living room.

I measure and mix, carefully following the directions on the back of the red box. I spoon the batter into my mouth and then, what's left of it, into the pan. After I set the timer for the double-chocolate cupcakes, I run to bring Mama her lunch. She asks for the saltshaker, a soda, and new batteries for the remote control. Finally, I carry the laundry basket through the living room—avoiding Skunk this time.

I struggle to slide the back door along its dirt-encrusted track, forcing it wide open. I step into the promise of sunshine. I hang the clothes on the line to dry. Today is Saturday, laundry day. After finishing the first row, I catch my breath.

I'm so out of shape. I scold myself. I wasn't always this way. No, that's not true. I haven't always had to do the laundry—that's the only difference. I'm a fat girl in a fat family—minus a dad. A dim outline takes shape in my mind, like a slim silhouette against the bright sun, empty and dark, lacking details. Fat Henry—my other brother, actually the skinniest of all of us, though not skinny at all—says we disgraced Dad when he couldn't fit in the church pew with us because we took up so much room. Maybe he left us because there was too much of us, or he was deported or sent to jail for doing something horrid. He's gone, and why? I'll never know.

I lean on the paint-flecked metal pole that supports the laundry lines. Sweat drips off my forehead and into my eyes. Nonetheless, I welcome the light, feeling it penetrating my skin, right into that place where the real me lives. My friend Brittany says I'm a skinny girl trapped inside a fat girl's body. All I know is I'm ginormous and everyone else in town knows it, too. I take another deep breath and dig into my pocket. There, I find a fun-size candy bar—chocolate filled with caramel. I stuff it into my mouth, ready for relief.

It's no secret that I love sweets. But every time I put something sugary in my mouth, I also taste a wad of guilt and embarrassment. I know that each bite of empty calories brings me one step closer to diabesity—a double-whammy affliction of type-2 diabetes and extreme obesity—which threatens Mama's life, but I can't stop.

The chocolate is smooth and creamy on my tongue. As it melts in my mouth, it relieves the chatter in my mind. Instead, milky-cocoa sweetness splashes through my veins like a dam bursting and saturating parched land. I feel adored and caressed by the confection. But, as quick as a snap, I'm shunted back to the present. The wrapper, crumpled in my sweaty fingers, reminds me that no one and nothing wants me here. I finish the laundry.

I guiltily think about Mama in her bed, unable to get around. But I shouldn't complain, not even to myself, about how all of the chores have fallen on my shoulders: laundry, cleaning, cooking, and shopping. With school starting in another week, I worry about how I'm going to keep up. Looking after Mama is a task requiring a general and an army. Skunk is no help. In fact, the last time I washed the floor, he stomped inside with muddy boots, then left a mess in the kitchen after he cooked a half dozen hot dogs, not leaving any for me.

I gaze out to the field bordered by the woods behind the house. Dirt bikes buzz in the distance. Skunk is sure to peel himself off the couch any minute and join them on the trails; riding is just about the only thing that gets him away from the TV screen.

"Sugar!" Mama hollers from inside, tossing me out of my moment of relative peace. I snatch up the laundry basket and trudge back into the house.

Skunk's glazed-over zombielike eyes don't veer from the animated gunfight as his fingers rapidly work the video game controller. The sounds of explosions mask the passing dirt bikes.

"Get me a refill," he says.

"Get it yourself. Why didn't you go see what Mama wanted?" I ask, this time out of his range of fire. Sweat prickles me with annoyance.

He picks up a ceramic figurine of an elephant off the coffee table and chucks it at me.

I fumble and fail to catch it. The trunk cracks off when it hits the floor. I bend over, the waistband of my jeans cutting into the flesh of my belly as I pick it up.

"Look what you did," I say.

"Look what you did, fatty," he says, without taking his eyes from the game.

"Takes one to know one," I mutter as I go down the hall. I know it's juvenile, but he's such a jerk. I try not to bicker with him, try to hold my tongue and all that, but sometimes—sometimes I could roar at him. I wish he'd go outside with the rest of the idiots on their dirt bikes and quads, chasing each other through the woods, and leave me alone.

I take the cupcakes out of the oven to cool. The pillowy tops invite a bite. I don't care that I burn my tongue. I get another hit of chocolate ecstasy. Then Mama calls again.

Piles of junk line the wall in the hallway. I turn to one side near the door to Mama's room in order to get in.

"You called?" I ask, licking a crumb from my lip.

"I dropped the remote control," Mama says, pointing one enormous arm anxiously toward the floor.

The TV is on a commercial, but it's two in the afternoon and she has her favorite shows that she must see. She hasn't missed a season in years, never mind the repeats.

"It's OK," I say, assuring her. "Are you comfortable?" I bend over to pick up the remote. Mama's heavy breathing hisses in my ear. Again, the button of my jeans digs into my waist painfully. I pass her the remote.

"Turn up the AC. And I need that pillow there behind my back," she orders. I do as asked, stumbling over a pile of clothes, a plastic crate filled with papers, and a fan with a missing blade.

"Can I get you anything else?" I ask.

A cough catches in her throat. The soap's theme song comes on just as her hacking dies down. She's had a cough all summer, but insists it's nothing and says she doesn't need to go to the doctor. At this point, I'm not sure how I'd get her there. I don't think she'd be able to get into the old Honda Accord I've been driving to the grocery store and am hoping to use to get to school. Last year, I took the bus and endured having marshmallows thrown at my head as the kids in the back offered to feed me, shouting, "Come on, Sugar, we know you like sweets" and "Catch one in your mouth," like I was some kind of sideshow attraction.

I also worry what the doctor would say. Last I knew, Mama weighed over five hundred pounds, but that was nearly four months ago, and I'm certain she's gotten bigger. Her knee gave out this spring when she missed the rotting step on the front porch. Aside from a couple of doctor's appointments, the last being when the doctor diagnosed her with diabetes, she hasn't gone out at all. Her physician warned that she had to lose weight, but, stubborn as she is, Mama defied his orders. Plus, where would she start? She isn't the type to get on a treadmill, there isn't a gym in our Podunk town, and she said that going on a diet is a form of torture. I have to agree.

We know she needs to lose weight, but unlike all those contestants on *The Biggest Loser*, Mama doesn't have a team of people to help her shed the pounds.

Mama takes a drag off her cigarette and her breath knocks in her chest. I count almost a minute before she stops coughing. Worry chews its way inside me.

"Are there any chips left? I could go for some with that dip you got," she says.

"I'll check. Chances are, Skunk ate it," I mutter.

I riffle through the pantry and fridge. Miraculously, there's still a bag of chips, and I find the dip, hidden behind a jar of pickles and sour cream. I dunk my finger in for a lick and then bring it to Mama.

Back in the kitchen, the cupcakes on the counter catch my eye. Mama and I each have our favorites—hers salty, mine sweet. But I'm lucky; I'm not stuck in bed like Mama.

A few minutes later, the sure-footed steps of the mailman cross the front porch. The creaky little flap on the top of the mailbox opens and shuts. I wait to open the door, not wanting to make small talk or to have to answer questions about how Mama's doing. Mr. Sheridan and Mama went to school together, and he always asks after her, but what am I supposed to say? He is active and fit—if he were my age, he'd probably be one of the kids who make fun of me. But Mama wasn't fat like me when she was my age, which she's always quick to point out. Anyway, I can't imagine anyone picking on Mama; she'd tear them up before the words had the chance to slap her in the face.

I glance at a family-photo collage my grandmother made, hanging crookedly in a dusty brown frame. After she died a few years ago, we moved here, where Mama grew up. In the black-and-white photo, I can tell the house looked groomed and neat back then. Maybe it's living under all our weight that's distressed it.

I see Mama in the past, smiling along with the rest of the cheerleaders on her squad. She wore a short white-and-green skirt, with the word *Blazers* written across her chest in gold, very nearly the same uniform the girls wear now. I guess I don't really care, but fitting into a skirt would be a treat. I know I'll never be one of them.

When Mama got pregnant with Fat Henry, she gained seventy pounds and never lost it. With Skunk, she doubled it, and with me, she lost track. She says I was the most difficult birth, and she named me Mercy because she prayed the good Lord would have mercy on her and get the damned baby out—fast. I guess there were complications and the doctor asked if she wanted a hysterectomy. She said, "Take it all! What good has it done me?" She didn't want any more babies, or even the ones she already had, and she never lost the baby weight. Now I'm just known as Sugar.

I gather the mail. A breeze passes through the silvery-green leaves in the birch in the front yard. It cools my arms. I skim through several bills. On the bottom, two envelopes bear my name. Auto-labeled on the first is *To the Parents of Mercy Bella Legowski-Gracia*. The return address is the superintendent's office of my school district, so I imagine it has something to do with the beginning of junior year.

Bella. The English translation is *beautiful, perfect*. It doesn't describe me at all. It was my father's donation, aside from my second last name, Gracia. I'm not pretty like the now-famous human-turned-vampire character, and I'm about as perfect as the broken elephant in the living room. Nope, Bella is a popular name for dogs this year, which better describes me. I shuffle the envelopes to bring the other one with my name to the top, continuing to let the breeze ruffle my long dark hair.

"Hey, Sugar!" someone shouts from the road.

I look up.

Brandon Thorne rides by on his bike with the seat cocked back. He wears his black baseball hat high on his head. His baggy shorts nearly catch in the chain each time he pedals downward.

Before I can escape from what I know is coming, he hoots for the whole neighborhood to hear, "Want some sausage?"

I slam the door. On the wall, near Mama's photos, a yellowing picture of my grandfather mocks me. He used to own a deli in town and became renowned for his specialty sausages. Only the letters *L* and *I* from the deli sign are visible. Among celebrity scandals, insta-media, and nine million other distractions, the kids in this town have retained this infinitesimal piece of information. My sausage-filled family history is coupled with sexual innuendos, and they can't resist teasing me, the fat girl, the granddaughter of the sausage guy. Of course, my brothers don't do anything about it. Although they're both big like me, they don't endure the routine taunts, the shoves, or the humiliation. Half the time, they're the ones dishing it out.

I lean against the door, safely inside. I look at the second envelope, pink, with my name—this time handwritten—on it. It reads *Sugar Legowski-Gracia* in a familiar bubbly script. A cupcake sticker seals the back flap. Before I open it, I march into the kitchen and pop a couple of the double-chocolate cupcakes into my mouth. I snap off a pudding cup from the pack in the fridge. I peel away the top. After three spoonfuls, I scrape the bottom of the plastic cup. I go for another and another. Before I realize it, I've eaten the entire six-pack of Boston cream pie–flavored pudding. Across the room, my cell phone vibrates.

I have one friend. Sorta. Brittany's name scrolls across the screen with a text and the words: *OMG. I was invited . . .*

I can't read the rest unless I press the button on the bottom of my phone. I ignore it, not wanting to talk to anyone at the moment. I frost the cupcakes, taking a few careful, but generous, licks off the knife. My tongue still stings from the burn earlier. My mouth itches from the sweet pudding and frosting. I root around in a cabinet and pull out an unopened package of cheese curls. I'd hidden them behind a pitcher and some bowls. I like sweets, but if I eat too much, I often need something savory to counteract the racing and rushing in my skin. I put one extruded puff into my mouth after another until my fingertips are orange and I'm thirsty from the salt.

Guilt creeps in as I survey the kitchen. Empty plastic cups and a cellophane bag with a hand-sized wrinkle from where I clutched it litter the counter. The discarded wrappers and empty cylinder of frosting stand like ruins. Regret submerges me like sludge.

I press my palms to the side of my head, wanting out—out of this body, this town, away, away, away. But there's no escape.

My brother appears to have finally vacated the couch. I grab my phone and the mail then plop myself down. I tear open the pink envelope. Inside is a card with brightly colored stripes and contrasting polka dots with the words *You're Invited to Hillary's Sweet Seventeen* in the center. On the back are details about the party, including the date, in two weeks exactly; the theme, candy; and that guests should bring bathing suits.

I reach for my phone, desperately craving another pudding cup despite the disgusting jiggle my belly gives when I move. Or breathe. Or exist. I tilt my head back on the couch cushion, wondering if it's possible Hillary is just being nice—which, in the last five years I've never known her to be—or if her parents made her invite the entire junior class. If that's the case, her guest list probably includes the entire senior class, too, since Hillary's boyfriend, Will Archibald, captain of the football team, is a senior this year. It's bad enough I have to endure taunts from the entire student population at school in another week. It doesn't appeal to me. Not really.

Once upon a time, Hillary and I were best friends. We played together, long ago, before the idea of cool girls, tight shirts, and lip gloss entered our lives—or, rather, *her* life. When she realized I was a fat girl and that wasn't going to change, and, worse, that having fat friends is unacceptable in certain circles, she drifted away. I didn't understand it at the time, but when the elementary schools in the region dumped us into the middle school, my status became as clear as the river that runs right outside our house. Which is to say, not very clear at all. For some reason, my size made me unwanted, a nuisance, and, specifically, about as desirable as accidentally touching a wad of chewed gum on the underside of a desk.

The major blow happened early in seventh grade, at lunch. I asked Hillary if she wanted to hang out after school. She stared at me as if I not only had three heads, but three enormously fat heads. The girl she sat with looked like she tried to swallow her laughter with a glug of diet soda. I started to walk away and heard Hillary whisper, "She's fat redneck trash. I don't know why she's talking to me." After that, the laughter flowed—and hasn't stopped.

Hillary's dad, Walter Prescott, was friends with Mama growing up, but he left town and went to college. Then, he earned a business degree and took over the family box-making business, pretty much the only source of employment in our town. Walter and Mama probably haven't set eyes on each other in over ten years, but he's always friendly enough when I see him around, though I can tell he's just pity-nice.

The Prescotts aren't rich—no one here is—but they have more money than anyone else does. When they bought Hillary a car instead of throwing her a sweet sixteen, she had an enormous fit. Everyone at school talked about how they were robbed of what was sure to be the one and only notable party during sophomore year. I imagine her parents caved, hence the "sweet seventeen."

I click on my phone and read the rest of Brittany's message: *OMG. I was invited to Hillary's birthday party.*

Me, too, I think suspiciously. Brittany doesn't think she's an outcast like me, but that's because she isn't fat. In fact, she's super skinny, I daresay too skinny. I've hardly ever seen her eat, but we only really hang out at school, and I wouldn't eat lunch there either, except that I get it free because Mama's on state-subsidized income. I can sorta see Brittany being invited, but why me? Maybe

Hillary and her friends want to humiliate me by throwing candy and marshmallows at me like on the bus. I text back: *Me, too.*

I pause before I hit send. If this is a joke, I don't want to seem enthusiastic and unwitting, like a pig going to slaughter. I add: *What's the catch?*

I lazily grip the remote control and flick through the channels, not really seeing anything distinct until I land on a show called *Cake Battles*. Just when it cuts to commercial, my cell phone rings.

"I totally can't believe it. I knew Hillary would eventually see how cool I am. I don't understand what took her so long," Brittany says breathlessly, naively.

Brittany doesn't realize she's a freak. At least I see myself for what I am.

"Yeah, but where's the fine print? Do you think her parents just invited everyone to make up for failing royally last year?" I ask.

"I'd kill my mom if she did that. So would Hillary," says Brittany. "No, maybe the summer changed her or something."

Brittany's mom is long gone. The one thing we have in common is our mothers would never throw us a party, period.

"I've known her my whole life. Doubt it," I say.

Brittany lives in the next town over, but because our high school is regional, we all converged when the lines between cool, jock, geek, freak, and fringe were drawn. We found each other when the PE teacher paired us up, probably doing the yearbook committee a favor, and named us the least likely to participate. The unit was flag football. Brittany is uncoordinated and doesn't give a care, and me, well, it's obvious.

"It's going to be so awesome. You're coming, right?" Brit asks.

"I'll think about it."

"Come on, Sugar," she pleads. "This is, like, our chance, y'know?"

I know an invitation to a party will not change how everyone sees me. I'm Sugar. The fat girl. End of story.

"What are you doing this weekend anyway?" Brittany asks. She frequently poses this question from the safety of the phone or in a text; it rarely results in an offer to do anything, from either one of us. I have to stay close to home in case Mama needs me, and I have chores. Brittany came over a couple of times, but I get the sense she thinks she might catch fat from the Legowski-Gracia residence, or that the house itself might just fall in and crush her bony little body. I don't bother answering her question about this weekend because I know it doesn't matter. We say our goodbyes with me promising to think about going to the party. As if.

My grandparents' house, now doing its thankless job of sheltering the third generation of Legowskis, is in desperate need of repair. The roof leaks, half the front porch collapsed last winter, and whenever it rains, Fat Henry says, "This might be the time we wash into the river." He doesn't care; he's rarely around anymore since he found a girlfriend and got a full-time job at the box factory. He mostly stays at her apartment unless they fight. At least he does his own laundry now.

I watch the finale of *Cake Battles*, which results in a confection inspired by the ocean winning. The first tier looks like the scales of a mermaid, almost luminescent in a green-blue hue. The second tier displays swirly tendrils kind of like an octopus, and the third is artistically dotted with edible pearls. A sugared seashell triumphantly adorns the top of the cake. Scenes of the baker's home by the sea flash on the screen. I think dimly about how I've never seen the ocean or ever really left this forgotten corner of New Hampshire.

The winning baker has tears in her eyes as she joyfully jumps up and down. I long for something sweet. Something to help me forget that the pink invitation on the cushion beside me isn't a genuine request for friendship. To dull the reality that I'm merely collateral in Brittany's life so she can make use of the texting feature on her phone, and that I'm a big, fat mess with chocolate frosting under my nails and a streak of orange cheese on my shirt.

I dig into my pocket for another package of chocolate, but can't squeeze my hand in. After I wriggle lower on the couch, I discover it's empty anyway. I look through the debris my brother left on the coffee table for scraps, but he's hoovered it all, as usual. Above the beaming congratulations coming from the TV, Mama shouts my name. I slouch deeper into the couch. Never, in all my life, have I felt anything close to pride, like the winning contestant cheering on TV. Mostly, I just know shame.

Chapter Two

On Sunday morning, the sky is veiled by clouds. It looks like rain. I roll myself out of bed and then down the remains of a box of Lucky Charms. I hurry up to get myself ready for church. Mama has long stopped going, but I head to the steepled building with peeling white paint week after week, hanging on to a thread of something like hope.

Skunk no longer attends Mass either, but that's OK—the less attention my giant family draws to themselves, the better. Occasionally I see Fat Henry, but he doesn't come every week. I take a seat toward the back and observe how the Prescotts neatly take up a single pew, their shoulders back and their chins lifted. I sink into myself, suddenly hungry. I stupidly wonder if I should try to catch Hillary's eye and get a sense of whether she meant to invite me to her party or if it was just an embarrassing accident that my name ended up on one of the pink envelopes. When she tosses her hair, I'm reminded that her repenting is about as likely as Mother Mary's tear actually dropping from her ceramic eye and landing softly on her robin's-egg blue robe.

After the homily, we rise for Communion. I have to stand on my tippy-toes to wedge myself out of the narrow pew and into the aisle. I catch a glimpse of some kids from school and worry they're all watching me.

As the wafer melts on my tongue, I suddenly crave bread. A long aisle of imagined white, potato, and cinnamon-raisin sliced bread stretches in front of me. Then, thinking about the cake on the television the day before makes my mouth water. A waterfall of chocolate cascades through my mind in a smooth wave ending in frothy bubbles. I almost crack a smile when I consider suggesting they replace the tasteless wafers with little round candy disks.

After Mass, I remain seated and fold down the little cushion to kneel. First, I offer a prayer in memory of my grandmother Busia, who I called Boo, and Granddad. Then I pray for my mother and my family, including my father, and finally myself. I'm not sure what to say, exactly. I mull over this not knowing, week after week, but then silence my thoughts when I feel like I skirt the dangerous edge of wishing for a change.

As I exit, the Prescotts stand in the doorway chatting with Father Caplin. Beyond them, the sun finally appears, spreading itself generously behind the clouds, glowing brilliantly in the sky and creating a backlight to the Prescotts' Anglo perfection. Hillary stands off to the side, her honey-blond hair flawlessly styled. On her slender frame, she wears a teal skirt with a black blouse. A gold cross dangles from her neck. I never realized how much she looks like her mother. This would be my opportunity to say something about the party, but I clam up. Instead, I offer a meager smile.

Hillary's lips form a flat line in response.

As I edge my way out the door, Mrs. Prescott calls, "Will we see you at the party, Mercy?"

I look back over my shoulder.

Hillary's glare is unmistakable. She gives a slight shake of her head to indicate not on her life.

I trip on the last stone step, but catch myself before hitting the ground.

"Oh, um, I'm not sure yet," I say over my shoulder, eager to escape the uncomfortable situation.

"You let us know. We haven't seen you in ages. It would be so lovely for you to celebrate with us," says Mrs. Prescott. She smiles at Hillary encouragingly.

Not likely, I think before giving a feeble wave, wishing it would wipe Hillary's glower off her face.

I trudge to the parking lot and get into the Honda. Now that I know that Mrs. Prescott, and not Hillary, invited me, I definitely won't be going to the sweet seventeen. I'm slightly ashamed that I'd even considered that there was a chance Hillary genuinely wanted me at her party. I scold myself for having the moment of delusion as I polish off a chocolate-chip-and-marshmallow granola bar in two bites.

I drive across Main Street to the grocery store, Od Town. The red letters used to spell *Food Town*, before the graduating class—a couple years ago—smashed the plastic and the lightbulbs in the first two letters as their senior prank. I wonder what prank the seniors will pull off this year. Skunk's in twelfth grade, so it's bound to be something horrible.

There's an actual supermarket about twenty miles away. But with the high price of gas, I stick to Od Town. Most of the items they carry are markdowns; some stuff is expired, though still mostly edible. Fortunately, their dairy, produce, and meats are passable because the prices are right. Though apparently not profitable enough to fund replacements for the broken letters on the sign.

Brandon cruises by on his bike. I turn my head in the opposite direction, hoping he doesn't see me. I wait until he's out of sight and then get out of the car. My arms, sticky with sweat, peel off the back of the vinyl seat. Doing the grocery shopping on Sunday is my routine, but I don't run into anyone else who is eager to remind me of how big I am by making me feel small—easier said than done in a small town. Od Town. Odd town. I snicker inwardly at how accurate the name is as I pass a metal fan at the entrance. Weare, New Hampshire—just north of here—is pronounced *where*, and it's an actual town. This is just *nowhere.*

From behind me, I hear snorting sounds and realize the fan blew the bottom of my dress—or more accurately, sack—up slightly. Brandon and another kid named Zeke laugh and make pig noises. My face grows hot and my jaw trembles.

"Hey, porker, can you spare some sausage? I know I can," Brandon says as he squeezes his crotch. More laughter.

I pull a cart from along the wall. With each turn of the wheels, it makes a terrible scraping noise and lurches, refusing to glide smoothly across the worn linoleum tiles.

Brandon and Zeke come closer, their squealing noises louder.

I try to ignore them. I hold back the tears that blur my eyes. I force the cart forward and down the nearest aisle. I want to get away from them, but almost more than that, I want to get away from myself.

The laughter fades as the boys, with the attention span of a couple of gnats, become disinterested and walk to the soda cooler.

My arms feel weak. I want to sit down. I lean against the handle of the cart and a sniffle escapes. I watch as one wet tear falls to my sandaled foot, and then another, followed by about a hundred more. My blurry ankles are swollen and pink. No wonder they laughed. In the locker room at gym, Alexis, one of Hillary's friends, called them "cankles," whatever that means. I just know it sounds ugly.

Alone in the aisle, tears blur my eyes as I stare, vacantly, at a wall of boxed meals that require just a boil and butter. I toss in a couple of packages that advertise *New Look, More Cheese.* Anticipation dries my eyes.

As I round the corner, an employee with a long thin braid running down the center of his back stocks a shelf. He catches my eye and holds up a plastic package.

"Twinkies, get 'em while you can," he says. "I guess they went out of business or something. I dunno. These things would survive a nuclear attack. Good thing to stock up on. You know, just in case."

I offer a half smile, hoping I look normal and not like I just cried like a baby.

"Yeah sure," I say. "I've never had one." The nametag on his shirt says Dale. And there is a little neon-green alien-head sticker on it.

He looks me up and down.

"*You've* never had a Twinkie?"

I nod.

"You hear that, Stubby?" he calls to another worker organizing the endcap. "This girl here has never had a Twinkie." They both look me up and down.

I shake my head no and offer a genuine smile.

"Come on, that can't be right," he says incredulously. "Sponge cake with creamy filling. Never?"

I shrug my shoulders. "Nope."

"Take two then," he says, handing them to me with an odd smile, eyeing Stubby.

I continue down the aisle, filling the cart with sandwich cookies and ranch-flavored corn chips, when his intention hits me. He didn't believe that I'd never had a Twinkie because the assumption is that fat girls love Twinkies. I let go of the cart and open the package, stuffing the first one in my mouth. My nerves instantly settle as I chew the soft cake and the sweet center lights up my tongue. It carries me away to a place where size doesn't matter, boys don't taunt me, and Twinkies are healthy, plentiful—they grow like lettuce—and everyone loves them and me. I inhale the second and toss the wrapper in the cart. Just then, Dale appears with a grin on his face, slamming me back to planet Earth.

"You're going to pay for those, right?" he asks.

I pick up the wrapper and shove it into his hand, banishing the tears of embarrassment that hang on to the tail end of Brandon and Zeke's comments. "I thought it was a free sample for big girls like me," I reply. With great effort, I manage to get the cart rolling again to continue shopping. Over my shoulder I hiss, "Watch out, I'm hungry."

Dale stands there in silence.

I spend the next fifteen minutes forcing myself to keep from crying or eating the rest of the Twinkies in my cart. Just before I check out, with Dale nowhere in sight, I grab a few more packages, partly because they were delicious, but also to make up for the ones I ate.

Back home, everything is the same except it looks like Skunk prepared a four-course meal given all the cookware and dishes in and around the sink. I put the groceries away and clean up. I check on Mama and bring her lunch. I plow through my Twinkie stash and, before I know it, I hardly remember what they tasted like. All that remains are my full belly and very empty heart. Preservative-filled tubes of sponge cake are a poor substitute for decency.

In the living room, Twinkie wrappers litter the coffee table. Although Dale claimed they'd survive a nuclear explosion, they didn't make it past me. Never mind having a sweet tooth; I have sweet teeth. Next time I'm at Od Town, I'll buy more, I promise myself. Or not. The sweet syrup running through my body makes me fuzzy, like I want to eat and not eat, cry and scream, go to sleep and run far away.

Hillary's invitation catches my eye. I rip it in half. Forget the RSVP. I turn on the TV and doze off to a cooking show as a kindly lady describes how to prepare something called bulgur.

"Sugar! Sugar! Sugar!" Someone shouts my name, waking me with a start. Mama. I hurry to my feet, rubbing my eyes awake.

"Coming!" I yell. You'd think I'm her maid as I try to shimmy past the piles of clutter in the hall. I smell smoke and not the kind from her cigarettes. When I push Mama's door open, a yellow-orange flame flickers on the floor next to the bed. Wearing an expression of angry terror, Mama feebly tries to jerk herself away to the other side of the mattress.

I grab a blanket to smother the small flames while I hustle to the kitchen to get water. It takes forever to fill the pitcher. I wonder if it's bad enough to call the fire department. I worry that if I did, they'd condemn the place. Then where would we go?

"I'm coming, Mama. Don't worry, I'm coming," I call to allay her frantic shouts. The noises she makes remind me of the squealing sounds Brandon and Zeke made at Od Town. I dump the water on the blanket and run back to the sink. I completely douse the fire after the third container of water.

Skunk thunders in through the back sliding door. "What the hell is going on in here?" he says, panting, struggling to catch his breath. His shirt, with the arms ripped off, rides up to reveal his ample belly. "I could hear you over by the woods above the dirt bikes. What the fuck?"

I look to Mama. For a rare moment, she looks embarrassed, but then says, "I don't know, something wrong with this lighter Sugar bought me. It's broke or something."

"That's what you get for shopping at Od Town. Idiot," he says, glaring at me as he grabs it from her hand.

I want to protest, but know it's no use. Not even being bedridden can stop Mama's utter refusal to be responsible for herself. She's stubborn beyond . . . I can't think beyond what, when my betrayal catches in an audible gasp. I quickly wipe the insult from my mind, stuffed with guilt. My job is to protect Mama, not ridicule her.

"I'm going to open these windows to get the smoke out," I tell Mama.

"Oh no you ain't. Then it'll let all the heat in. Plug in that fan," she says. It's missing a blade, but I do as told. There is no use in defying Mama. She may not be able to come after me anymore and give me a good beating, but she'll remember any disobedience, and when I'm least expecting it, she'll take a swat at me.

"Bring me a snack, will ya? And some soda—you did remember this time, right?" The comment is a warning because last weekend I forgot to get her more Pepsi. Skunk only likes colored sodas like Orange Crush and Mountain Dew. Mama, on the other hand, only likes Pepsi, so of course, stupid me, I forgot it, and she let me have it.

I follow orders. After I'm done, I go in the bathroom to rinse the film of biting ash from my hands and face.

As I dry my puffy cheeks, I look into the cracked vanity mirror. Skunk and Fat Henry had a fight a few years ago and broke it, and we never replaced it. The good thing is, if I turn and get the right angle, I look slender. I stare at this version of me for a long time, imagining what life would be like as a skinny girl. But I'm not and never will be.

The following afternoon, I make sure Mama is all set and leave for my shift at the Scoop and Sprinkle, the seasonal ice cream stand by the lake. I have one more week of work until school starts, which means only one more week of being keenly aware that everyone who buys a cone from me sniggers as they leave, thinking, *That girl helped herself to a bit too much of the rocky road.* It's not necessarily untrue, but the laughter and looks hurt. Again, I wonder what it would be like to be on the other side of fat. Maybe not skinny, but not fat either.

As I get out of the Honda, in the dusty parking lot, Brandon rides by and shouts, "Who stole the sausage?"

I shake my head and go inside to get sticky up to my elbows for six hours.

As I heap three scoops and sprinkles into a waffle cone for an impossibly lean little girl, I want to warn her not to eat it. I want to caution her of the dangers of breaking the seal with three scoops, which turn into a pint, which turns into a half gallon, but I hold my tongue.

When I pass the cone out to her she whines, "Mom, I ordered cookies 'n' cream, not cookie dough!"

No, she's probably one of the lucky ones who will be able to eat whatever she wants and have nothing to show for it—and get whatever she wants.

The mother looks at me imploringly. "Sorry. My mistake," I say. She passes the cone back through the little window. Although I'm sure she said cookie dough, I set it aside to eat after I finish with the short line of customers. I dish out the cookies 'n' cream for the girl. My coworker, a girl with an eyebrow piercing, picks up the rejected cone, sneers, and then tosses it in the trash, never taking her eyes from me. The hoop in her eyebrow looks dumb, but she's not wrong, not really. The shame of the truth stings like the dust from the parking lot when I lean out the window to pass the little girl her cone.

Later, as I count tips, I finish off the complimentary junior-size cone the owner permits during each shift. The only redeeming thing about this job, aside from the free ice cream, is that I've managed to save some money. About half of my earnings I chip in for household expenses since Mama's income is fixed and the state aid we get only covers so much, but the rest I've hidden away.

As my coworkers and I leave for the night, Gina, who I'm pretty sure is bulimic, bumps into me. With her hand on her hip, she says, "Um, excuse me, you're in my way."

It's true. I'd bent over to slide the broom and dustpan back to where they go, barring the way with my humongous backside, but she doesn't have to be rude about it.

"Sorry," I say quietly and press myself against the drinks cooler to let her pass. "I'll finish closing up." I smile apologetically.

She harrumphs into the twilight.

I sneak back in and grab a couple of brownies for the Fudge Sundae Special, then slip them into my bag. They'll be stale by the following day, and the next shift will have to toss them out anyway.

After I lock up and get into the Honda, I sit for a few minutes, watching the sun sink behind the trees. It shimmers between the leaves. I gobble the brownies and lick the remaining crumbs off the plastic wrap. I'll miss summer. Work isn't great, but it isn't the routine humiliation that I face at school, nor is it the constant harassment at home. In the dusky light, I can barely see my hands as I wring them, wondering why no one, in either of those places—or anywhere really—likes me. What's wrong with me? What's missing inside of me? I look toward the spot where the sun twinkled and winked good night; now it's just dark.

Chapter Three

Some days are more unendurable than others. It's laundry day again. After I've finally satisfied Mama, running back and forth from the kitchen to her room, I go out the back door. The sun shines hot as I hang clothes out to dry. Like always, the dirt bikes buzz in the distance. I'm thankful Skunk is out there, not in here, today.

Instead of retreating inside, I leave the empty basket on the back deck and take the short walk to our property's edge where the Henniker River, or more accurately a trickle of a stream, littered with trash, winds along and then skirts town. It's too shallow and rocky to swim in, but I slide down the bank, grabbing on to wispy saplings to keep from falling. I ditch my flip-flops and wade in. Lining the bank are the remains of a bicycle, rust-worn and forgotten, along with a couple of tractor tires and garbage.

In the spring, when the snow melts, the water rises. Then it's high enough to swim in, but it's also colder than a witch's tit—at least that's what my cousin Jerry says. He hates this river. As I wipe away perspiration from hanging the laundry, I long to take a swim, something I haven't done in forever. There's a county pool and the lake, but I don't dare put on a bathing suit.

I think of Hillary's party. *Bring a bathing suit.* No way. Last time I spoke to Brittany, she was still on about going, but I won't do it. Not a chance.

Birds call *craw, craw*, urging me to go in deeper, to shut out the noise in my head, the whisper telling me that I'm hungry, starving, that I need to be full. I think of cousin Jerry warning me about the water moccasins when I was still young enough to be fooled. I've never seen one—he was trying to scare us kids—but snakes are my least favorite critter with scales, so I'm careful. Jerry's cautioning on a day much like today, a decade ago, during a barbeque rings in my mind. "I swear on my right hand there is a whole family of them just waiting to sink their teeth into our ankles or arms or legs or hands. And I don't want to do no rescuin'. I ain't riskin' gettin' bit. Not for none of you." I think most of us believed him because we didn't want to see him lose his only hand—he lost the other in a mill accident over in Vermont.

The only difference now is that I'm alone and no one would rescue me anyway. I take my chances and slide down the rock I'm sitting on, plopping into the water. It pools around my unyielding belly. Maybe a snakebite wouldn't be so bad. It would put an end to this unforgivable wretchedness. I lean back.

Up the bank, my view of our sorry excuse for a house flickers between the layers of leaves and branches overhead. In the photos I've seen, it used to be straight and sturdy like my granddad when he was young, but with him gone, it's sagging and weathered. I wonder what will become of it . . . of me.

The cool water trickles and tinkles like chimes. I let my head go under and feel the rocky bottom beneath my neck and back. I open my eyes and, instead of the house, I see the sky beyond the trees. Big and blue. The sunlight dapples the green leaves. I wish for it to shine down on me and burn away my feeling of enormous insignificance.

I come up for air. The revving of dirt bikes pierces the relative quiet. I push myself up to standing. I pick my way over the rocks and back up the bank. I slip near the top, and my chest and belly stamp into the dirt. It smears my wet clothing and turns into mud from the chest down.

I hurry back to change, but I'm too late. Skunk and a couple other guys are on the back deck, chugging soda. Their laughter is immediate.

"What the hell happened to you?" Skunk asks. "I knew you were fat, but I didn't realize I had a hog for a sister." The other two join in his laughter.

I'm not good at comebacks. I always think of them when it's too late, but this time one comes to me.

"At least I'm not sweating like a hog," I reply.

"Sugar, you look like a hog, you smell like a hog, you sound like a hog," says Skunk, grunting and squealing like the guys at Od Town. "Guys, what you're looking at is a big, fat pig." He laughs dumbly. The loud cranking of a dirt bike breaks up their laughter. The three boys look sharply toward the woods.

"Damn. Who's that?" Skunk asks no one in particular.

"No way that's Caleb or Ford," says one of the guys leaning on the porch railing.

"Come on, this is our trail. If that's Dougie, you better believe I'm goin' to kick his ass." Skunk takes off on foot as if he's really going to catch the kid who's now out of earshot.

I roll my eyes as he tries to run but instead waddles after his slimmer friends. My inner laughter meets chagrin as I realize I must look the exact same way when I try to run, which, thankfully, is never.

I go inside to wash off the mud and shame. Brittany left me a text: *Where are you? One more day of summer vaca. Want to go into Keene to shop?*

Her invitation genuinely surprises me. I consider going as I dry off and then dig through my bureau to find something to wear. I could use some new clothing, but it's so hard to find anything that fits me other than at the plus-size section at Walmart. There's no way I'm letting Brittany or anyone else confirm that I actually buy my clothing at Walmart; it's bad enough for them to assume. However, isn't going back-to-school shopping what normal girls do? Could I try to be a normal girl, even for one evening?

I text back: *Want me to pick you up?*

I beat back the knowledge that her invitation is likely nothing more than her trying to sponge a ride. I turn to my closet and slide the door open. I push a few hanging items aside and pull forward a cache of garments I've hand-sewn. In the front is a vintage-style cocktail dress in dusty-rose lace. The front gathers at the waist and falls just above the knees. The back is open with two inch-thick straps on either side that come down in the center to a bow. I'm still astonished at how beautiful it is. I run my hand down the front, remembering that I'll never wear it. A secret part of me hopes beyond measure that my fat will magically melt away, and I'll be able to wear it to prom. Then, someone would have to ask me, and that's beyond doubtful.

I hang it back up and admire the second garment, a vintage-style tank dress with polka dots on the top. In the middle is wide red belting. The skirt falls to the knees in a whimsical pattern of coffee cups and donuts, but from a distance, they look like large circles complementing the polka dots on the top. It's a fun and flirty dress. But I'll never be able to wear it either, even though I made it with my own two hands.

When Boo, my grandmother, was still alive, she taught me to sew. It's the only thing I know how to do well. If I had a superpower, sewing would be it, even though I don't know how it would save the world. I could create capes and disguises, maybe? A part of me hopes that someday it will save me.

I slide the hangers over some more and pull forward a golden dress, also vintage style. It has a fitted upper body and then a skirt with an overlay of tulle that sweeps itself into gathered tiers, each dotted with a small rhinestone. It's something Audrey Hepburn would have worn. I'm about as unlike Audrey Hepburn as a mouse is to a gorilla, except for her hair. My thick, dark bangs, swept to the side, look like hers circa the early eighties, though my hair is long. My hair is the only thing I like about myself. When I think about all the things I don't like about myself, I push the dresses back, hidden in the depths of my closet.

My phone vibrates with Brittany's reply: *Cool. Be here in an hour?*

I take my time doing my hair and then put on a T-shirt and a pair of flared jeans that I read help balance out girls who are top-heavy. *I'm just heavy,* a voice mocks in my head. I slide on a pair of sandals and go downstairs to Mama's room to see if she needs anything before I leave.

"Get me my cigs," she says, pointing to the carton my brother brings by every week.

The acrid smell of burnt fiber hangs in the room. I want to remind her to be careful, but I'm afraid she'll snap at me.

"When will you be back?" she asks.

I'm not sure. "In a few hours," I reply. "Brittany and I are going to get some stuff for school."

Mama sneers at the mention of Brittany's name. "Good luck. You probably won't find anything that'll fit."

I don't need the reminder.

"Heat me up some ravioli before you go," she orders. "And, hey, bring me back something from McDonald's. Skunk promised to earlier, but he said he forgot."

Yeah, right. He probably ate it.

"OK," I respond, rushing to the kitchen. I heat the ravioli in the microwave and pour a glass of Pepsi for good measure. I quickly devour a few slices of bread and butter along with some leftover chicken. As the microwave beeps, I fill my mouth with M&M's, sticking the rest in my bag to eat on the way. I hurry Mama her dinner, hoping she doesn't need anything else from me.

I pull up in front of Brittany's double-wide and honk.

She comes out, tottering on heels I've never seen and wearing a pair of shorts that practically reveal her butt—or would if she had one. She slides into the seat beside me.

I look at her sideways, unsure about the purpose of her getup.

Snapping her gum, she says, "What?"

I shake my head, saying, "Never mind." It's none of my business. "Where to?"

"I dunno. I wish there was a mall nearby. The closest one is about an hour and a half away," she says. "I mean, I guess we could go there. When did you say you needed to be home?"

"I didn't. I don't know. It's pretty far."

"I'll chip in for gas."

I worry about leaving Mama, but she didn't specify when I needed to be back, not that she would, anyway. I wouldn't want her to worry, but she probably won't. She might just get hungry and angry. I've never really had rules, but just made up my own, and, strangely, as I think about it, they seem like the kind a set of strict or caring parents would expect from their kid. But I don't have either of those and neither does Brittany. Her mom left for some other guy, in some other trailer park, in some other town, and her dad's rarely around. I wonder if he's noticed his wife is gone and his daughter is nearly on her heels.

Then again, I have nothing better to do. "Um. Yeah. Why not?" I say.

I'm sure the people in the next state hear the whoop Brittany lets out as I steer toward the road.

After playing radio DJ all the way there, Brittany bounds out of the car toward the entrance. I waddle after her.

"I haven't been here in forever," she says, refreshing her gum and sticking the old piece on the side of the trash can outside the main door.

"Me neither," I say. "Actually, I've only been here once. With Hillary."

"And we are totally going to get you something to wear to her party," she says enthusiastically.

"Oh yeah. I can't go," I say.

Brittany stops midstride and studies me in the pause between snaps of her gum, asking, "Why not?"

Just like my inability to conjure a comeback on the spot, I'm also a terrible liar. I falter.

"Come on," says Brittany, "I'm sure so many people will be there that you'll just be among the entourage and go unnoticed. I mean—" She stops herself. "Listen, I know you don't like attention drawn to you because—" She stutters.

I exhale irritably.

"You know I didn't mean it like that," Brittany says. "It's just that—" She stops herself again.

"Listen, Brit, I thought you were supposed to be my friend. As in, beauty is beyond skin deep and all that. Like, you see me for who I am," I start to say, but then *I* stop. Because to tell the truth, I'm not really sure that beauty is beyond skin deep. I have yet to see that theory proven. "Never mind," I say. "I know what you meant. Let's go inside." If there are people that see the beauty within others, they sure as heck don't live around here.

Our first stop is a chain store that tries to be a hip boutique. I follow Brittany in and mindlessly browse the racks. Loud techno plays and the fluorescent light promises the store's employees migraine headaches as a bonus to their minimum-wage paychecks. I examine a dress with lovely beading down the back. I wonder if I might be able to replicate it with buttons instead of beads.

A saleswoman pops into my periphery. She has long purple nails and orangey skin from too much self-tanner.

"Can I help you?" she asks.

"Oh, me?" I say. "Just looking. Thanks."

"I don't think we carry your size, but you could try Sears—they have a plus section. Or Motherhood—they make really cute maternity clothes these days."

My jaw actually drops. The air leaves my lungs and a flush rises to my face. I can't speak. Maybe the dream of the dress made me forget who I am, because I wasn't expecting to hear those coarse words. Reality comes crashing back as I waddle over to Brittany, who's flirting with a sallow male employee.

"I'll wait for you outside," I say softly.

"Outside-outside or like just outside the door?" she asks.

I exhale, wondering if dragon smoke might actually pour from my nose.

"Right out there," I say, pointing toward the entrance of the store and the benches beyond.

As I exit, I feel eyes on me, but don't dare turn around to look. I tuck myself into a corner of a vacant bench and take a handful of M&M's from my bag. They crunch sweetly between my teeth. The sugar saturates that part of me that screams *ugly . . . fat . . . useless.* I exhale again and the tears that felt so close to flowing just moments ago are absorbed back into the deep well of sadness that each day grows fuller and fuller.

After Brittany emerges from the store with a large bag and the phone number of the guy she talked to, we go down the escalator and do a lap on the ground floor. Brittany complains about being cold and puts on a bulky sweatshirt. She stops at several more stores that don't carry clothes in my size. Each time, I wait on a bench and watch all the shoppers parade by. They chirp about deals and fashion and the new school year. Later, when we walk by the maternity shop, I wince.

Looking in store windows, I have to admit that none of the clothing appeals to me. It looks mass-produced. It's better than the baggy T-shirts, stretch jeans, and black everything I normally wear, but not as lovely as the clothing that I make. But I refuse to sew for myself. If I wore a flouncy cocktail dress, I would look like a clown in costume. Nope, if I'm not skinny, or at least less fat, I'm not wearing any of it. Nevertheless, my heart aches to feel the satin and lace against my skin and to look in the mirror and see pretty. I pop another handful of M&M's and wait for Brit.

Out in public, away from the well-worn grooves of embarrassment imprinted along the familiar roads of my town, I feel on display. I may as well be a freak show with the way dozens of eyes bore into me, silently wondering how a person can get this way. I don't want to look down, to acknowledge how much of me there is, but there's nowhere else to look, unless I want to meet their disapproving eyes. I think of Mama and wonder if she's OK. I check the time on my phone. The mall will close soon. I'm starving. Brittany acts like she's running on trucker speed and could stuff several more outfits under her giant cotton hoodie. I know shoplifting is wrong, but I pretend not to notice.

"Hey, there's a Taco Bell. Are you hungry?" I ask.

"Nah, I'll eat later. I don't want to spend any of my cash on food. It's not like I can wear food," Brittany says.

I can and do, I think, feeling my butt and belly wiggle with every step. And it's also not like she's spending all her cash.

"One more store and then we can leave. If you want to grab something, though, we can just meet at the car in, like, a half hour."

I agree, tired of having her skinniness draw the attention of passersby, salespeople, and kiosk vendors to my fatness.

I'm just finishing my Gordita Supreme when my phone vibrates. I'm hoping it's not Mama. Brittany's name scrolls by with a text. I click it. *Getting lucky. I ran into Cash after his shift. The guy who gave me his number. We're going back to his place. See you Monday.*

I think of what to text back as worry nags at me. Is that safe? Going home with that stranger she just met at the first store she went into? Will the girl with the purple nails blab to Brittany about her fat friend? How will she get back? What if her dad gets pissed? All these thoughts clamor around in my mind until I remind myself that Brittany is sixteen and that's what girls our age do. They meet boys. They flirt. They trade numbers. They kiss . . . and do other things. I'm not one of them. And I'm not her mother.

R U sure? I reply.

A second later, she answers with a winking smiley face. A mall worker sweeps crumbs, lights dim, and the sounds of the stores closing tell me to get going.

When I pass through Keene, I remember Mama's request for McDonald's. I pull into the drive-through and order double, eating my portion in the privacy of the darkened car on the way home.

After delivering the burgers to Mama, I retreat to my room and lie in bed, restless. My stomach makes unpleasant gurgling noises as if to protest all the greasy food I just ate. I place my hands on it, wishing it would settle down. Then, feeling the mushy flesh beneath, I remove them in disgust. I just wish it would disappear. Sometimes I even wish that I would disappear. I hate my body. I click on my light and go to the closet. I take out a box of fabric and my materials.

I cut a length of a vibrant white, aqua, and black floral-printed piece of fabric. The sound of the scissors slicing through the crisp cotton excites me. I thread a needle and get out my pincushion, closing the Velcro around a wooden dowel on my footboard since I can't fit it around my wrist. I envision the classic party dress with a full skirt, shawl collar, and the pearls I'll use to adorn the outside of the hidden zipper running up the back. It fills me with a fizzy feeling of anticipation.

I'm lost in my project until Skunk loudly storms in after midnight. He clangs around in the kitchen, no doubt drunk or high and searching for munchies. Then the TV turns on. It won't be long until he passes out.

My room is stuffy, so I open the window. Crickets and frogs perform their nightly symphony. I let the cooling air fill my lungs like a bellows. As I exhale, I replay each time, earlier in the day, when I stuffed my belly until it felt like it would explode and then double my punishment with a reminder of the coarse words spoken by the salesgirl at the mall and the stares I received from shoppers. I shift uncomfortably.

I continue to sew until the scolding in my head quiets. With each turn of the needle, there is the hint of a whisper on the breeze, the promise that it won't always be like this.

Chapter Four

The first day of school brings with it the misery that I expect. All I can say is I had a good hair day. The rest sucks. Skunk rides in with me and insists I stop so he can get a Big Gulp. He ends up getting into an argument with the clerk, which makes us late.

It's bad enough that everyone stares at me to begin with, but walking into a full classroom on the first day and having to shimmy my way down the narrow aisle of desks to the only available one at the way back halts the teacher's lecture about expectations. Students move in their seats to conceal the sound of laughter as I bump and bustle my way to the back.

The teacher says, "Nice of you to join us. Ms. *Legawksee-*Gracias, I presume?" He butchers my last name.

When I sit down my shoe squeaks. Everyone thinks I farted. This time, the chuckles and titters are audible.

With that award-winning introduction, the end of the day, never mind the end of the week, can't come quickly enough.

Thursday night, Brittany texts me: *What are you doing tomorrow night? Wanna go to the mall again? Party?*

She ended up spending the night with the guy from the mall and claims she slept with him. Thankfully, her gushing about that overshadows her pestering me about Hillary's party, which has the whole school buzzing.

Can't. :), I answer.

It isn't a lie, not really, but I'm not about to drive all that way so she can pound beers and screw some spindly salesman who wears too much cologne. I have other things to do. I'm just not sure what they are yet.

On Friday morning, Mama delays me because she needs help in the bathroom. I rush to class and make it in just before the bell. I'm panting like a dog as I drop into my chair, and as usual, I feel like I have an audience. Afterward, Mr. Hammons, my homeroom teacher, pulls me aside.

"Mercy, this is your third year here. I expect you know when the day starts," he says, raising his salt-and-pepper eyebrows.

"I'm sorry," I say. "I'll be on time from now on." I want to explain that Skunk made me late and Mama, too, but something stops me. I'm not particularly smart, but my grades have always been decent. I don't want something as stupid as being late for no good reason to give a bad first impression; my appearance does enough damage.

The teachers pile on homework because of the long weekend for Labor Day. By lunchtime, my stomach is growling. A senior girl with her hair pulled stylishly into a bun edges away from me in line. I fill my plate with spaghetti and meatballs and garlic bread, and take the apple pie on offer for dessert along with a bowl of Jell-O topped with a dollop of whipped cream. I can practically taste the jiggly sweetness on my tongue.

As I scan the cafeteria for an empty table, someone bumps into me, shoving me into someone else and knocking me to my knees. The tray clatters to the floor. My lunch resembles a fourth-grade science experiment gone wrong and red tomato sauce slowly slides down my white T-shirt. I look like a gory crime victim.

On my hands and knees, worn boots stand close to my shaking fingers. *Please don't step on me.* I glance up at a pair of jeans; they're nearly threadbare around the knees. Then I look up some more and then some more. My eyes meet a tall boy with brown, close-cropped hair—but it's tousled on the top.

He bends over, apologizing. He's doesn't look familiar. He says, "I am so sorr—"

A round of laughter from the surrounding tables interrupts his apology as a chunk of meatball plunks from my chest to the linoleum.

He tries again. "Listen, I didn't see you. I didn't—" He looks around irritably. "Come on; let me help you get cleaned up." But *he* doesn't have tomato sauce on his white T-shirt.

My face flames hot like the summer sun. I need to get out of here. "No, don't worry about it," I mumble, running out of the cafeteria.

His dirty boots scuff behind me in the hall.

"Wait, I'm sorry," he calls after me.

I leave him there. The door to the girls' bathroom flaps shut behind me. I place both hands on the white sink and let it brace me as tears fall into the drain. I don't have anything else to wear, so after wiping off as much of the sauce as I can, I sneak outside to my car. Dark clouds form overhead, threatening rain, but the tears that continue to fall from my eyes feel like they are enough to dampen the entire earth.

Just as I enter the house, Mama shouts, "Sugar, is that you?"

"I'm here, Mama. What do you need?" I poke my head into her doorway. Little silver aluminum wrappers dot the dark blue carpet beside her bed like stars, hiding stains and cigarette burns instead of mysteries.

"What are you doing home at lunchtime? Hungry? I thought you got free lunch?" A grating cough issues from her chest.

"I just spilled some sauce on my shirt," I reply. "I came home to change."

"You're one little piggy. Inhaling your food again?" She makes a tsk-tsking sound edging toward another cough. "You shouldn't eat so much." I hear Brandon and Zeke's teasing from the other day, coupled with Skunk's stupidity. But it is nothing compared to the sting of Mama's comments. Her remarks aren't anything new. In fact, she was the one who first called me Sugar after she discovered me with a five-pound bag nestled between my chubby legs, eating it with a spoon, when I was three. She's picked on me ever since, serving up a confusing and conflicting message that I'm too fat, but also that I should eat more, not get too skinny. Before she was laid up, she fed me plenty. I'm angry and embarrassed, and that all-too-familiar feeling of wanting to flee sets wings beneath my feet, but there's nowhere for me to go.

I quickly change my shirt and drive back to school, hoping to get to class before the bell.

At the day's end, Brittany catches up with me in the parking lot.

"Do you think you could give me a ride to the mall? Please? Cash gets out at five. I'll give you money for gas. Please? You could come to the party, too, if you want. Please?" she says again.

At least she said please. She doesn't sound overly inviting, but whatever I'd hoped would suddenly appear and serve as a worthy excuse to avoid driving Brittany to the mall eludes me.

In a text, Cash directs Brittany to his place instead of the mall. At the sound of loud techno pumping from behind the door to a duplex, I edge back to my car, telling Brittany I'll see her later.

Late that night, with the house quiet, I continue to sew. Stitch by stitch, I step away from insulting words, laughter, and eyes suggesting, and even demanding, humiliation.

• • •

Laundry day. Long weekend. Nothing to do. These words fill my mind as if I have a vacancy sign plastered on my forehead that advertises *Bland and mundane thoughts wanted. Preferably to play on repeat. Complimentary complete and utter nothingness to draw long days out even longer, a free bonus.* The house is almost too quiet. I assume Skunk passed out on someone's sofa the night before. I'm glad of his absence as I pick my way through piles of laundry to wash.

When I enter Mama's room, the smell of rancid milk and cigarette smoke burns my nose. She asks me for a fresh pack from her shelf.

"You missed Fat Henry last night. Where were you off to, anyway?" she asks.

"I went to the mall with Brittany," I say.

Mama gives me a look that could melt paint. "What, pray tell, were *you* doing at the mall?"

"She has a friend who works there. She wanted to say hi," I explain.

"Yeah, right. That girl's a skank if I've ever seen one. Trailer rat," Mama declares, exchanging her angry expression for an imperial one. If she sat upon a throne and was capable of doing more than tossing out snide comments, the look would suit her. Instead, she sits in a tangle of sheets and looks positively pathetic. I pinch myself for having the mean thought, wondering what has come over me lately. *Poor Mama can't help it,* I silently correct myself.

While searching for a shirt she asked for in the bottom of her bureau, I find an apron I'd sewn. It was one of my first projects. Alternating red and green apples dance along the bottom of the hem, and the straps have little seeds on them. I run my fingers over the frilly bit of lace and the pocket on the top. I smile, remembering Boo's strong hands—her fingers were always busy—Mama being able to get around, and when confusion didn't run quite so deep.

After I give her a sponge bath, I'm relieved to breathe in the fresh air outside, even though I have a larger than normal basket of laundry. I'm thinking about lunch when a dirt bike cranks in the distance. I wonder if it's Dougie or whoever Skunk was raging on about using "his" trail.

"Go for it," I whisper. If it isn't one of Skunk's crew, I hope they have fun speeding along under the canopy of trees, lapping freedom as they soar along the trail. Even though Skunk thinks otherwise, the trails don't belong to him or his friends, for that matter. As far as I know, a farmer owns those couple hundred acres and probably has no idea kids are cutting paths through it with their two-strokes.

I take a break from hanging laundry and go inside to fix myself something to eat. I turn on the TV for a few minutes and before I realize it, I doze off.

Someone at the door wakes me up a couple hours later. Sleepily I answer. The mailman, Mr. Sheridan, holds a package out in front of him.

"Hiya, Mercy," he says. "How's it going? How's your mom? It's such a nice day. She should get out more. I haven't seen her lately. We're not long for these sunny days. Autumn and then winter will come in fast. I hear the storms this winter are going to be tough."

I nod politely, not able to get a word in edgewise. My answers don't matter anyway. Struggling to hold on to the box, I back away and finally close the door after he insists I promise to say hello to Mama.

The box is for Skunk from Bandit Bikes, probably some parts or something. I slide it into the kitchen so he'll see it. I check on Mama, who's also dozed off, and then return to the basket outside.

Everything is still damp but sun-warmed. I pick up a large pair of her briefs and pin one side on the line. I drop the clothespin and turn to pick it up when boots appear beneath a sheet that's blowing in the breeze. I gasp. The underwear whack me on the head just as the face of the boy who bumped into me at lunch the day before appears from behind the sheet like a ghost.

"Did I scare you? Sorry," he says quickly.

"You're sorry an awful lot, aren't you?" I say more sharply than I mean to. I remember his apologies from the day before. With surprising speed, the comment he made after I dropped my tray piques my interest. He didn't see me. How could he have not seen me? I'm enormous. Hope flickers, but maybe I'm becoming so insignificant that he just didn't notice me. There is a difference.

"Hey, you're the girl I collided with yesterday in the cafeteria," he says. Even with the thin white line of a scar that cuts the edge of his lower lip, the corners of his mouth lift with the radiance of a thousand suns.

"The one and only," I reply, genially this time, his smile melting my suspicions about him stopping over to see how well I wear mustard or chocolate ice cream.

He laughs lightly and the sunshine lights up his blue eyes, otherwise heavy under burdened brows. "I wasn't watching where I was going. I'm really sorry about that."

"Yeah, you mentioned that," I say. Nonetheless, a smile comes, unbidden, onto my lips.

"Sorry to bother you. Does Skunk live here?" He says *Skunk* as if he isn't sure if that is a name reserved for friends only.

I nod. "Yeah, my brother."

"He rides this trail a lot, right?"

"He'd tell you that it's *his* trail," I say.

He rolls his eyes almost imperceptibly. "It actually belongs to my grandfather, but that's beside the point. I lost my wallet out here yesterday. You don't know if he found it by any chance, do you?"

I shake my head. "I haven't seen him since—Thursday actually," I answer.

"I figured I'd ask before I walked along the trail looking for it," he says as his shoulders lower disappointedly.

"Hang on. I'll go inside and see if it's there anywhere," I say politely. But knowing Skunk, if the wallet held anything of value that would explain why he's been MIA. I scrounge around, unsuccessfully.

When I get back outside, the boy leans languidly against the deck rail, his legs stretched out in front of him, ankles crossed, and his hands in his pockets. He looks so completely comfortable in his skin. Free and like whatever burdens rock him, they don't make him fall, or fat. I shake my head, to toss the thought out or to indicate the absence of the wallet—I'm not sure which.

"Darn," he says.

I shrug and then return to the basket to continue to hang the clothing, trying to be as inconspicuous as possible with the giant granny panties blowing in the wind. Then I curse myself for bothering with this right now. Hillary, heck even Brittany, would have the sense to flirt with a boy like him.

"You're Sugar, right?" he asks, again uncertain if that's the appropriate name to use.

"Sure," I say. Sweating in the afternoon sun, as I hang up the last item, reminds me that I do, in fact, look like a hog. I flip the basket over, but then decide not to sit on it, in case I break through it like Goldilocks and the three bears. No matter what I do, I'm sure to embarrass myself yet again.

"Nice to officially meet you, Sugar. I'm Even," he says.

I'm not sure if he says *even* or *Evan*. He must get the question a lot because his cheek quirks into something like an apologetic smile.

"Even, with an *e*," he adds, and his smile disappears. "My mom died when I was born, but said she wanted the baby's name to be

Evan. My dad is nearly illiterate, so I'm Even. Or Evan. Whatever. That's probably more than you wanted to know." He speaks dismissively about his preference as if he's making the choice mine.

"Even. I like it," I say. "It kind of dances on my tongue." I am so appalled that I said that aloud I want to run inside or drown in a river . . . of chocolate, never to be seen again. But I'd have to pass him, and I'm sure my footfalls would remind him of a stampede of elephants. Could I have said anything more awkward?

He smiles at me again. His bright blue eyes are a delightful distraction. I'm not sure why he's still hanging around, but he leans on the deck like there's nothing better to do.

"I'm sorry about your mom," I say.

He doesn't answer, though I know he heard me by the tender expression he wears. His face says many things, including an invitation to speak, to ask questions, but I'm not sure I want to hear the answers yet.

"Well, I ought to find my wallet." He hesitates a beat. "Want to take a walk with me on the trail and help me find it?" He presses up to his feet and walks toward the back of the yard. I'm not quick enough to say yes or no. I don't want to ask why he'd want to take a walk with me or see me huffing and puffing as I try to do the simple act of putting one foot in front of the other.

"Come on," he says, stopping for me to catch up to his long-legged gait beneath a slender yet muscular build.

My thighs rub together. I'm painfully aware of every plump cell in my body. On flat ground, I realize he must be at least six feet tall.

"So, do you ride?" he asks, meaning dirt bikes as one whizzes in the distance.

"Me?" I ask, wondering if he's joking or making fun of me.

"Yeah. Your brother does, so I thought maybe you do, too."

"Never. I, um, don't think it would be safe," I say.

"Sure it is, just wear a helmet. Don't be an idiot like those other guys out there. But girls ride. It's fun," he says with a grin.

I don't say that it wouldn't be safe because I'd probably break the bike. Skunk is heavier and bigger than I am, but he reinforces his shocks or something to handle the extra weight. I'm surprised I know this, but nevertheless, I wouldn't dare.

We reach what was once a wooden split-rail fence on the far edge of the property. The wood is rotten in spots and the thick bramble weaves in and out of the logs, creating a secondary fence warding off anything bigger than a rabbit. I stop in my tracks, wondering how I will get over it or through it. As if realizing my conundrum, Even tests a spot, pushing it back and forth with his hands.

"It seems sturdy enough," he says.

I'm afraid to acknowledge the possibility that he means it's strong in general and not just to bear my weight, but his eyes are tender and harmless.

The last thing I want to do is break it. I look for an opening to either side.

"I'll help you over," he says.

I freeze.

He extends his hand. "Don't worry. I won't let you fall."

I can't return my eyes to their normal size—they bulge. He must be joking. "It's not that . . ." I start to explain, but then catch myself. If ever there were an elephant in the room, I'd be it. No one talks about how huge I am unless they're teasing me. But it isn't something easily ignored. My size limits me and that's obvious, but it's just the way I am.

"Don't worry," Even says. He extends his hand again.

I reach mine out. Our fingers touch. *Warmth. Electricity.* His hand is calloused and solid in my soft and mushy one. I tremble. I lower my head as if studying the obstacle in front of me. It's now or never. No point in delaying the inevitable. My hair cascades down like a waterfall, hiding my red, and increasingly sweaty, face. I lift one leg up, anticipating the sound of splitting wood above the background music of cicadas. Nothing. I find a foothold, and then like an extremely out of shape Olympic gymnast, I get my other leg over the fence as if it's a pommel horse. On the other side, I trip over the long grass but manage not to fall. Even glides over the fence like an actual gymnast, light and easy.

"I was out here yesterday evening. Let's see; if we go this way, we'll loop back around to where I started, and then we can backtrack this way," he says, pointing left on the trail.

"What does your wallet look like?" I ask.

"It's brown," he says, deadpan.

I let out a giggle. "Everything here is brown: the dirt, the underbrush, the dead leaves."

"I know," he says. His laughter halts him on the trail. He turns to me, like I've materialized out of thin air, like he's seeing me for the first time. Our eyes meet. *Oh dear Lord, this is unexpected.* He tucks a loose strand of hair, plastered on my sweaty face, behind my ear, saying, "Brown is beautiful, earthy—"

A bird whistles. Even finds his stride again.

Did he mean our surroundings or my hair? It takes me a moment to remember how to walk . . . and breathe.

"It was my gramps's wallet," he explains. "On one side there is an eagle burned into the leather, if that helps."

I scan the ground, hoping to find it quickly and get back home, if only to figure out what to do with the way I suddenly feel.

As we go deeper along the trail, nature works her magic. I relax, as I did down by the river. The sunlight peppers the leaves overhead, filtering down to the ground. The air is fresh, yet woodsy, and cooler, comfortable. Most remarkably, I'm in the company of a very attractive boy. Wow. If Brittany could see me now.

We continue on, keeping our eyes out for the wallet, but making conversation about anything and nothing at all. Dirt bikes, school, and then he hits on a subject I'd rather have left behind with the laundry.

"Are you going to Hillary's party?" he asks.

I wonder how he knew she invited me. Then I worry she put him up to this; if she's baiting me with a cute boy and friendly conversation only to later humiliate me.

"Oh, um. I don't think so. You?" I say casually, as if my inner monologue isn't a tangle of fear and doubt.

"I don't know," he says. "I'm cousins with Will; that's why we moved here and presumably why she invited me. His mom is my aunt, but our dads hate each other. It's easy to hate my dad. I don't want to be insulting and not go. But to tell you the truth, I don't really know many people here. Just my aunt and uncle, Will, my grandfather, but he's so cranky he won't talk to us."

Someone as good-looking as Even shouldn't have a problem making friends. "When did you move here?" I ask, not sure what to say about everything he relayed.

"We left the sea coast at the beginning of the summer. My dad couldn't make the mortgage anymore, so we're renting one of the apartments Will's dad owns over on Birch Road. I got a job at Vin's Garage on High Street. I've been working all summer. Nonstop. To stay out of the house mostly, but also to save money."

"I know the feeling," I blurt.

He smiles again and I return it but quickly find something to say. "So the New Hampshire sea coast?"

"Yep. It's so beautiful. I was sorry to leave."

"I bet. I've never seen the ocean," I say mildly, my eyes trained on the ground for the wallet.

"Seriously?" Even asks, aghast, pausing on the trail.

I stop, too, and shake my head.

"Let's go sometime," he says. "Before it gets cold. I've been looking for an excuse to go back. You'll love it. There's this great fish shack—they make the best combo plate. And their lemonade—oh man, and the waves. We can play in the waves." His eyes glisten with daring and adventure.

This sticks my attention like Milk Duds in my teeth. His child-like enthusiasm is contagious, but doubt continues to taunt me. Why would he want to go to the ocean with me? "First, I suppose you'll need your wallet," I say.

We continue to look, and just as we loop back, the roar of a dirt bike buzzes in the distance.

"Uh-oh." I didn't mean to say that aloud.

"Huh?" Even asks.

"Skunk," I mutter.

"Why uh-oh? He's your brother, right?"

"Yeah, but he isn't very nice. We better hurry," I say, panicking. If he sees me out here, I'll never hear the end of it; and worse, if I'm out here with a boy who presumably has been using "his" trail, I'll really get it.

"I need to find my wallet," Even says.

"I know, but I should really get back," I reply.

"Well, OK," he says, still scanning the ground, but we move more quickly. The bike gets closer.

All I want is to be on the other side of the fence before the rider sees me.

Moments later, the bike is ear-splittingly loud. I can't move fast enough. I'm too late. I hope it isn't Skunk. When the bike comes around the bend, Even and I stumble into the underbrush, tumbling into one another because it doesn't look like the rider intends to stop. The momentary flicker of excitement at our proximity fades. The neon stickers plastered to the rider's helmet tell me it's Skunk. He whizzes past then comes to a halt, putting one foot down and spinning his back tire behind him, sending a rooster tail of dirt flying into the air. His thick fingers wrench the helmet from his head.

"What the hell are you doing back here?" he asks.

I'm not sure if he's talking to me, Even, or both of us. I'm as quiet as stone.

"Just looking for my wallet. Sugar here is helping me," Even says.

Skunk's lips twitch toward a menacing smile.

I instantly know he has, or *had*, the wallet. "Have you seen it?" I ask, feeling emboldened by Even's confidence or maybe naïveté. Most people back away from Skunk, knowing if they say the wrong thing, he'll pound them. In this case, with Even being new to town, ignorance is bliss. Even looks like he can handle himself, though I don't want it to come to that.

"No, I haven't seen it. You had better get home, Sugar. Mama needs you."

An unfamiliar flash of anger rises inside me, followed by an embarrassed flush. If he knows Mama needs me that means he was just there. Why didn't he help her? I don't say any of this; so far, he's let us off easy.

Skunk kick-starts the bike. "By the way, what was your wallet doing back here?" he asks.

"It fell out when I was riding yesterday," Even says simply.

"Really? And what may I ask were you doing riding back *here*?" Skunk says this in a faux-polite voice that I register as animosity, but Even doesn't back down.

"Back here? Riding my dirt bike, just the same as you," he replies.

"But this is my trail. I made it. I maintain it," Skunk says, as his face reddens with rage. He gets off his bike and comes closer. "I'll suggest that you stay clear of it, understand?" He's nearly in Even's personal space.

The only thing more embarrassing than me falling and breaking that fence back there would be if Skunk lost his temper and got in a fight with Even, who is the only boy in my entire life that has been kind to me.

"Actually, Skunk, this is his grandfather's land, so really, Even has rights to it," I say. I wish I could take the words back. That was too bold.

Skunk's eyes incinerate me, but then he turns his attention to the tall and handsome boy by my side. "Even, is it? We'll see about that. And Sugar, I'll see you later," he says menacingly and then gets back on his bike, revs it, and speeds off.

"I'm sorry," I say to Even.

He shakes his head. "No worries."

"I'll get your wallet back," I add.

"Did he have it?" he asks.

I nod. Juxtaposed against Even's kindness, Skunk is a brute. I clear my throat so I don't say anything against my brother. I don't have a winning track record with anyone at school, so my family, as unpleasant as they may be, are really the only people I have.

Even helps me back over the fence. When we're standing in front of the clothesline, the wash is nearly dry.

"Want a hand?" he asks.

"Nah, you better go, in case Skunk gets back," I reply.

He hesitates, takes a long look at me, then nods. Reluctantly he starts to saunter off, then pauses and turns around. "Hey, if you find my wallet, I, uh, should give you my number," he says shyly and runs his hand through his tousled hair.

"Oh, sure," I say, reaching into my back pocket to retrieve my cell phone.

He tells me the numbers and I type them in.

"Can I have yours?" he asks.

I stutter the first three digits, incredulous that I am actually exchanging phone numbers with a boy.

Chapter Five

Once inside, I tend to Mama and then sneak into Skunk's room. I haven't stepped foot in here in a year or so. I shuffle through piles and stacks of video games, candy wrappers, comics, magazines, and CDs. It's a wonder he stays clothed with all the dirty laundry on the floor.

Tasteless and tattered posters of women cover the walls. I look to the cluttered floor. Using my first two fingers, I pinch up a half dozen towels and toss them in the hallway to wash later. I make my way to his dresser and root through girlie magazines, unfinished homework assignments, and more food debris. I still don't see a brown leather wallet. I slide open his top drawer. Under some unmatched socks, I find a thick piece of paper. I unfold it. Smiling at me is an old and wrinkled photo of our dad, sitting astride a motorcycle, his cinnamon-colored skin bright in the sunlight. I've only seen a few other pictures of him, long ago and nearly forgotten. I study it, trying to find myself in his image.

Someone clomps up the stairs. I slip the photo in my back pocket and quietly shut the drawer. Skunk looks up from the top step and directly at me. His expression could ignite TNT.

"Well, well, well," he says. "What do we have here? Trying to find your boyfriend's wallet?"

"He's not my boyfriend—"

"Right. Who would want to go out with you, fat slob? But what I want to know is why the hell you're in my room." He steps over the towels.

For once, I think fast.

"Just rounding up the laundry," I say, pointing to his feet. "But if you do have the wallet, I'll take it."

His eyes narrow as if he's debating whether to believe me or hit me.

I bite my lip. "Listen, if you give Even back his wallet, he'll probably let you continue to use his grandfather's land. If you don't—"

"And what are you going to do?" he asks. "Petition to have me kicked off it? I've been using that trail for years. How do I know it's really his grandfather's land? Where did *Evvvennnn* come from anyway?"

I don't like the way he says Even's name, as if he's insinuating that someone who would be friends with me is a loser.

Skunk fools with something in his pocket. I suddenly know beyond a doubt he has the wallet. The question is if he'll hand it over.

"If you just give it to me there won't be a problem. I'm guessing you spent all the money anyway. He just wants the wallet itself back," I say.

Skunk does his weird tongue-chewing thing while he's thinking. I can almost see him turning the options over in his mind, a place that's musty and dank, like the laundry.

"So are there any more towels in here?" I ask to hurry up this process.

"No."

"No, what? No towels or no wallet?" I say, surprising myself with my assertiveness. I take a step toward the door, which he still blocks.

"Neither," he says.

He shoulder-checks me into the doorframe and then pushes me out. The flimsy door rattles on its hinges after he slams it. I trip on the towels and dive toward the stairs, head first. My foot catches on the edge of the wall. I'm halfway down the stairs, splayed and instantly feeling bruised. My shoulders shake as I let out a cry.

"Sugar? Is that you?" Mama calls. "What the heck are you kids doing?"

I roll to my side and reach for the banister to pull myself up. I slide down a couple more stairs in the process; my fat cushions me, but hardly. "I'm fine, Mama," I lie and make my way to the kitchen, blinking away tears.

Shaking, I find a sleeve of crackers and some squirtable cheese in a can. I polish it off, stuffing the crumbly crackers into my mouth. I choke on tears and crumbs. I rip into a package of chocolate-and-vanilla sandwich cookies for dessert. I like to save the best for last. First, I scrape all the cream off the chocolate cookies with my teeth, then, just as I am about to eat the stack of cookies themselves, Even's smile brushes into my mind. I imagine us, in the woods, surrounded by nothing but trees and hope.

I wonder if I'm actually hungry now.

I'm not, not really.

The little tower of chocolate cookies begs me to eat it, so that I can feel the soft give in my mouth as I bite down. Then there's the bittersweet flavor of regret that when I eat them, they'll be gone, and I'll still be left wanting more.

I think of my difficulty with the fence, and how if I just had a different body I would be able to move more easily. But that's impossible. I'm stuck being fat. Always have been. Always will. Maybe it isn't so bad. Maybe I can learn to like myself, however

I look. But that thought topples out of my head and lands on the words *too difficult*. Then I hear Mama's voice in my head whispering words like "ugly" and "stupid" and "fat." I let the idea go. I take the top cookie off the tower. Then another and another. Halfway through, the shower glugs on upstairs. Skunk will be busy for a while. With each step up, the bumps and bruises remind me of my fall.

I quietly enter Skunk's room. His pants are on the floor, wet with sweat. I root through the pockets. Eureka! My fingers touch the smooth leather, and I run them over the indentation of the eagle.

Skunk is notorious for long showers, but I don't want to push my luck. Knowing my brother, I'll probably end up all the way at the bottom of the stairs this time. Although, given the state of his bedroom, he probably won't go back to those pants for at least a couple of days.

I go into my room, change into a clean shirt, brush my hair, and grab my bag. I check on Mama and tell her I'm going to Hillary's birthday party, which is a lie, but something she'd like to hear.

I sink into the seat of the Honda, my heart pounding. I dial Even's number. The mechanical ring echoes in my ear and goes to voicemail. Just as I'm about to leave a message, the car door wrenches open. I squeak.

Skunk stands there in his boxers, looking ready to murder. "Give it back!" he thunders.

"You give it back," I say.

This has him for a second, but then he reaches into the car and swipes for my bag. I fumble for the key. As I try to fit it into the ignition, his fist meets the soft flesh of my cheek and upper lip. I cry out. Tears instantly blind me, but I don't need my eyes to start the car. I paw for the keys again and start it up.

We're both too big to allow him to get across me to the passenger side, where the wallet hides in my bag. As he scoots around the front of the car, I take the opportunity to put it in reverse. My door slams with the motion, though I can barely see for the tears in my eyes and blood soaking my mouth and chin. I leave him in the dust, shouting and looking like a blubbery walrus wearing underwear.

I peel down the road, completely unsure of where to go. Blood oozes from my lip. I have to clean up. I drive to the gas station, hoping the bathroom around the side of the building will be unlocked.

I jiggle the knob, but it sticks. The adrenaline rush from obtaining the wallet fizzled when Skunk attacked. I'm weak and uncertain, my footsteps awkward and out of time.

The bell to the gas-station door jingles, announcing my arrival. The clerk, the one Skunk fought with on the first day of school, looks up at me, unconcerned. Maybe my face doesn't look as bad as it feels. A throbbing pulses in my lip.

"Bathroom key?" I ask.

He looks me up and down with what might be disgust. "Out of order," he says.

"Please," I say. He shakes his head, not even looking at me.

I don't argue. I grab a few napkins. I return to the car and angle the rearview mirror to look at myself. The blood has stopped, but my splotchy face looks terrible. Nonetheless, I want to give Even his wallet back. Better he has it than me if Skunk tries to get it back from me again later. Tenderly, I lick the blood from the corner of my mouth and lip, wipe my chin, swab on some lip gloss, and dial Even's number. I clear my throat. At the sound of the first mechanical ring, I want to hang up, but it's too late—my number will appear on his caller ID. I've lost my momentum. It rings a half dozen times and then goes to voicemail. "Hi, this is Even. Please leave a message."

The way he says his name sends an unfamiliar feeling winding through me. There's a tingling in my stomach that is different from hunger or self-loathing.

"Hi, Even, this is Sugar." I say my name as if it belongs to a stranger. It feels like it doesn't belong to the version of me I want Even to know. "I, um, I've got it. Your wallet. If you want to meet, I can give it back to you. Call me."

After I hang up, the words echo in my head, playing on repeat. I analyze each one as the sun sets behind the banks of gas pumps. Did I say the right thing? Did I play it cool? Did I say "um" too many times?

A car pulls up beside mine. I glance over to see upperclassmen from school inside. A kid wearing a trucker hat who I recognize gets out and then meets a guy I remember graduating with Fat Henry. They loiter by the bathroom doors and then exchange money. The older of the two ambles into the store. The kid from school gets back in the car, and the music already straining the car's speakers gets louder.

I hope they don't notice me. Moments later, the guy returns and pounds on the trunk. It pops and he lowers a case of Pabst in. I overhear the words "party" and "Oak Hill Ave," and instantly know they are going to Hillary's party, which reminds me that Even is probably there.

I tilt my head against the headrest as they pull away. I debate whether to go there and bring the wallet to Even. If Skunk retaliates, I'll simply no longer have it. If he wants to deal with Even, he can. Though I doubt he'll bother with Even because of the trail. Then there's my ghastly lip. Hillary wouldn't have invited Skunk, so I'm safe there. Relatively. Not safe from embarrassment for umpteen reasons, starting with my giant ass and ending with the bloody gash. But the wallet . . . Even.

I have another look at my lip in the twilight. It isn't so bad. Or maybe I'm just convincing myself because each time I think about Even something sparks inside me. I start toward Hillary's, hoping I'm not walking directly into disaster.

When I turn onto Oak Hill Avenue, cars line both sides of the street. I hesitate. The entire upperclassman student body appears to be at Hillary's house. What am I doing? I drive slowly, hoping I'll just see Even, give him the wallet, and be on my way. When I reach the end of the street, one parking spot remains before the road turns into woods. I take a steadying breath and pull in.

I check my lip one more time. It's now or never.

When I reach the front walk, music, loud conversation, and laughter mash together in a way that makes me feel alone, even when so close to so many people. The last time I was here, Mama dropped me off to swim, but it was before I realized that a person's size and how they look in a bathing suit determine whether they're friend material or not. Something burns inside me and it doesn't have to do with Even. A splash, followed by laughter and hooting, tells me someone did a cannonball into the pool. I'm just about to ring the doorbell when I realize I'd save myself some hassle just by going around to the backyard.

I slowly open the wooden gate. As soon as I am through, it's open season. I need to look around, but don't want to make eye contact with anyone.

I avoid the splashing in the pool and bump shoulders with Allie, Hillary's best friend. She looks at me as if I'm a slug she'd like to squish and moves on. I'm just glad it wasn't Hillary. I count on whatever Allie drinks out of the red cup in her hand to wipe away her memory of my presence at the party.

A boy in loose swim shorts chases two girls in bikinis. They squeal in delight, jumping into the pool. Dots of water appear on my T-shirt, punctuating the fact that I'm out of place. I have to get out of here. Fast.

There's no sign of Even outside, so I go in the back door of the house. They've remodeled the kitchen since I was last here. Everything looks clean and uncluttered, despite the snacks set out. The sleek organization at Hillary's always made me feel comfortable. But also deficient and jealous at the clean scent of flowers and lemon, not stale with cigarette smoke and overcooked canned ravioli.

I move into the living room and pick out Even talking with Will. Thankfully, Hillary is absent. As I approach, Will notices me. His face puckers. I tap Even on the shoulder. He turns around, offering a warm smile.

"Hey, you came," he says cheerfully.

"Did you get my message?" I ask.

He shakes his head.

I notice Will looks stuck between boredom and curiosity as to why I would have left his cousin a message.

"Got your wallet," I say, reaching into my bag and passing it to him. "Skunk isn't sorry it's a little lighter than when you dropped it."

Even's eyes linger on my lips.

I flush and then remember the cut.

"I can see that," he says seriously. "Let's take a walk. Hey, I'll see you later, Will." Without another word or room for argument from me, he turns. Taking my elbow delicately in his hand, he guides me toward the front door. I feel eyes on us, including Allie's and those of a few of the other girls with high ponytails and the kind of confidence that draws envy, guiltily, out of me.

Even closes the door behind him.

We sit on the slate front step.

"What happened?" he asks.

I take a deep breath and let my shoulders fall. "What didn't happen? The good news is I got your wallet back," I answer.

"Yeah, but you didn't have to, you know, go through that much trouble. I mean . . . He didn't hit you, did he?" Even speaks with a mixture of horror and anger in his voice, maybe something else, too, but I can't place it.

“It’s certainly not the first time and probably not the last,” I say, again shocked at my candor. “I didn’t mean that. Skunk’s all right. You know, he’s my brother and all. Just, he has anger issues.”

“Yeah, I’m familiar with those,” he says. Then, “Not me. Never mind.” Even looks down at his boots.

“How’s the party?” I ask.

Even shrugs. “What you’d expect, I suppose. How about we go take care of that lip? Where are you parked?”

For a minute, something lights up within me. He wants to take care of my lip? Seventeen and never been kissed. Then I scold myself. He means my bloody and swollen lip. Duh.

“Yeah. Sure. Thanks. I tried the convenience store, but the clerk wouldn’t let me use the bathroom,” I say. As soon as the words are out, I realize I sound pathetic, but Even follows me down the slate path to the street nonetheless.

Chapter Six

When we get to my car, I ask Even how he got to Hillary's party.

"Walked. No better way to learn a new area, unless you're on a motorcycle."

I think of the photo of my dad, still hidden in my pocket.

"Do you have one?" I ask.

"Yes and no," he says.

I tilt my head with confusion. Under the dome light of the car, the shadows highlight his cheekbones and his knees bump the dash. After he buckles up, I have the silly thought that we could drive anywhere, but I realize I probably don't have enough gas.

"I'm rebuilding one," he says, raising his eyebrows conspiratorially. "Let's go; I'll show you."

Even directs me toward Birch Road, even though I know where it is because I've traveled the roads in this small town my entire life. He shows me where to park and seems relieved mine is the only vehicle in the driveway. He leads me up a set of outdoor stairs to the second-floor apartment and gives the door a good push to get it open.

"Have a seat. I'll grab a washcloth," he says.

I sit on a stool in the sparse, distinctly bachelor-inhabited kitchen. There are a few pots and pans, still on the stove burners, some open cans sticking out of the trash, and a sink full of dishes. When Even returns, he notices the mess.

"Damn. OK, let's get you cleaned up, and then I better get this cleaned up," he says, gesturing to the disorder. "After that, I'll show you what I've been working on."

Even carefully dabs at my lip, removing the dried blood. When the dangling washcloth lightly touches my collarbone, I let out a giggle. "Sorry, ticklish," I say by way of excuse. I'm also amused that this boy, who by all rights should be the new hottie in town, with girls chasing after him, is with me, in his kitchen, cleaning my lip.

"All better," he says after he spreads some antibiotic ointment on it, which will blend with the lip gloss I quickly apply when he turns to the sink. "Do you mind keeping me company while I do the dishes and take out the trash?"

"Not at all. Did you leave in a rush?"

"No," he says, exhaling loudly. "My dad—"

I slide off the stool, scrape the food stuck on the dirty pots and pans into the trash, and bring them to him.

"Thank you, but you don't have to help," he says. "Take a seat."

"I don't mind," I say, happy to be useful. Even if he was just being polite, I feel appreciated for once. We're quiet for a minute as Even washes and rinses. I dry.

"Tell me, why on earth is your brother called Skunk?" he asks. "And please tell me it somehow explains why he's so mean."

I chuckle. "When he was a kid—let's see, I wasn't in kindergarten yet, so he must have been about six or seven—he got sprayed by, you guessed it, a skunk," I explain. "He hated showering, and so he just went to bed, stinking to high heaven. Mama had a job at the time, from three to eleven at night, and she smokes. And so, dead tired and in a cloud of nicotine, she didn't smell him when she got home. I'd tried to stay up and tell her what happened, but I must have dozed off. I couldn't wake her up the next morning—she sleeps like a log—and so Ernesto, aka Skunk, went to school smelling like one. You can imagine the fun the kids on the bus and in his class had with that. Eventually, the school nurse sent him home and Mama had to give him a bath in some nasty concoction, peroxide and tomato juice or something. He's never lived it down, and I think it just plain turned him mean." I pause, wondering how careful I should be with my words.

Even glances at my lip as if that explains how mean he can be.

"He wasn't very nice before that to begin with. I remember he took my bike once—you know, the girlie kind with pom-pom tassels and a pink seat. He tried riding it like a mountain bike down the ravine by the river. It's still there, broken and rusting away," I say, sighing, remembering how happy I was to get that bike, a hand-me-down from Hillary, and how crushed I was when Skunk destroyed it. "So what about your family, aside from your mom?" I ask carefully, yet eager to change the subject.

"Nothing to say, really. Just my dad and me. My aunt and uncle, Will . . ." Even pulls the trash bag out of the can and motions for me to follow him. We go back down the stairs. After he deposits the trash in a larger bin, I follow him to a shed behind a detached garage.

Even turns on a single bare bulb hanging from the ceiling. A snowmobile fills the corner along with some yard equipment. In the center of the space, Even pulls a tarp off what looks like a hunk of metal.

"Ta-da!" he exclaims, and he can tell I don't fully appreciate the fine mechanics of a disassembled motorcycle. "I'm just waiting for a few more parts, and then she'll be ready to roll. It's a Harley. Trust me; it's going to be one fine ride."

I turn to him and smile, unable to help myself. "I'm sure it will be. Where are you going once it's ready?" I ask.

Even doesn't answer right away. He gazes at me, and for a second I worry he looks through me, but no, it's almost as if he's looking into me, perhaps wondering if he should risk the answer.

He stutters as he starts to speak again. "Everywhere. Anywhere." He takes a breath. "You have some smile, Sugar," he says sweetly. "And your hair . . ." He reaches out, his fingers trembling slightly as he glides them through to the ends. The hint of a rosy glow rises to his cheeks.

My blush matches his and I hide behind my hair. "I had braces for, like, four years. We had dental insurance when I got them and then lost it, so it took a while to save up to have them removed. My older brother, Fat Henry, offered to pull them out for me, but no thank you. The good part is my teeth are so perfectly straight I've never had to wear a retainer." I bumble with my words and have no idea why I am telling him these stupid details. The only other good thing about braces was I lost a few pounds from not being able to eat so many sticky treats, but I don't dare reveal that. I gained it all back and then some, but wish he could have seen me then. There is a moment of silence, and then we hear a loud truck rumble in.

"Shit. My dad." He hustles out of the shed, but then just as he's about to turn the corner, he stops and I run into him. "Sorry." He turns around and faces me.

"Why are we always bumping into each other?" I ask, absently.

"I don't mind bumping into you, but let's not bump into my dad. I know this is weird, but he's probably half in the bag, and it'd be better if you didn't meet him right now," Even says in a whisper.

"But my car—did he pull in behind it, blocking me in?" I ask.

"Probably, but if you wait here, I'll go up, grab the key to the truck, and move it." He hesitates as if he wants to add something, then says, "I'll be right back."

I linger in the shadows by the garage. Doubt plagues me. I fear that Even is embarrassed to introduce me to his dad, like the stereotypical fat-lady-and-skinny-farmer couple I see shopping at

Walmart. My jaw drops open. We're not a couple. Why did I even think that?

I remember his comment about my smile. No one, not a single person in my entire life, has ever paid me a compliment. I'm at once excited and humbled. Did he really like my smile? I search my mind for a reason he would need to be nice to me. It's unlikely he wants to get into Skunk's good graces. Maybe he likes Brittany. But she's so eager, especially lately with the body-baring clothes, boys don't really have a problem approaching her. Before I travel too much farther down the rabbit hole of self-loathing and doubt, footsteps approach from the wooden stairs.

Even appears and puts his finger to his lips. Again, I worry about why he feels the need to sneak around.

"I'm glad we got to hang out tonight," he says. "And thanks for my wallet. I owe you. If I get the bike fixed soon, I'll take you out to the coast. Promise." With that, he gets in the truck and backs up, giving me room to do the same.

I drive home elated, like I'm riding a magic carpet. I imagine this is the way normal girls feel when they have a crush and it's mutual. But no, wait, that's moving too fast. Way too fast. Even is maybe just becoming a friend. An actual friend. Nothing more.

Avoiding mockery at Hillary's party, hanging out with Even, and returning home to find Skunk out of the house and Mama asleep is like winning the lottery. I float off to sleep, recalling Even's gentle touch while he cleaned my lip, his concern and laughter, and his comment about my smile and hair.

The following morning I go to church and thank God, with everything I have, inside and out, that the previous night turned out to be OK. Maybe even more than OK. I pray my grandparents are at peace and that Mama gets better. Healthier. I have the fleeting thought for myself, but like Mama says, I was born fat and will forever be fat. That's just the way it is. I pray for my father, too, wherever he is, and that he'll someday find his way back to us, if that's what he wants.

Afterward, I head over to Od Town and pick up our groceries for the week. Disappointingly, the Twinkies are gone, but those little bags of cookies, the fancy ones stacked neatly in little cupcake wrappers, are five for a dollar. They are out of date, but I doubt they're stale; the regular grocery store just can't sell them anymore. I buy ten packages, five for me and five for Mama. If Skunk wants any, he'll have to get them himself.

When I get home, I surprise Mama with my purchase. She coughs for a good spell before opening the bag.

"Do you want me to call the doctor about that?" I ask.

She insists it's nothing.

Later, I bring her oven-cooked french fries and a TV dinner that was also on sale at Od Town. She seems content, so I excuse myself to get some of my homework done. I'm polishing off the second bag of cookies while conjugating Spanish verbs when Skunk comes in, as loud as ever.

He hollers for Mama, as if she's going to miraculously get up onto her feet and greet him. It's quiet for a few minutes, but I stay cloistered in my room, hoping he's had enough time to cool off after yesterday's confrontation.

Around dinnertime, I sneak downstairs to get something to eat. The familiar sounds of explosions issue from Skunk's video game. I try to be as quiet as a mouse, but drop a metal bowl on the floor. For a moment, the game is quiet. Seconds later, Skunk walks into the kitchen.

"Hello, dear sister. How are you this evening? Making dinner, I see?" he asks in his syrupy, faux-polite voice, which is almost more venomous than his angry tone.

"Yup," I reply.

"Shall I set the table? Iron the napkins? Bring out the fine china? Polish the silver?"

I'm about to roll my eyes, but think better of it, not wanting to let him get a rise out of me. "Nah. You don't have to trouble yourself, but thanks anyway," I say lightly.

"If there's anything I can do to help you, just let me know, 'K?" he asks.

Facing away from him, I roll my eyes beneath my bangs and continue to stir the macaroni I have boiling on the stove.

He shoves me and my belly hits the pot.

"Ow," I cry out.

"Oops. Butter fingers. Sorry, Sis. No, I don't have any Butterfingers, if that's what you're thinking. Don't get excited, fatty," he says.

I should have known better than to turn my back on him. I grab a cloth and run it under cold water. Then I lift my shirt and expose my stomach, letting the cold soothe the burn. I see how he's playing it. He's not done seeking vengeance. I'll have to be watchful.

By the time I finish cooking, he's gone. I settle on the couch and eat my mac and cheese followed by the other cookies, including my favorite, the soft-baked ones with the chocolate chunks. This reminds me of the little island off the coast of Massachusetts where Hillary went one summer. She returned with seashells and the story of her first kiss. All I can think about are Even's lips and how he said we'll go to the coast.

The following day we have off from school because of the Labor Day holiday. I loaf around the house, alternating television with homework and fixing Mama snacks. A show called *Hoarders* sucks me in. I get teary toward the end when the lady confesses she can't stop collecting things, especially those weird plastic troll dolls with pointy hair. I flip off the TV and look up at the porcelain-doll collection, with their smooth, perfectly symmetrical faces and delicate fingers. After a moment, I remember how when I was a little girl I felt like they stared at me, their glassy eyes teasing that Mama loved them better than me.

I realize this space looks like prime fodder for that show. There's so much clutter. Piles, stacks, and heaps of junk cover every surface and fill every corner. When we moved in, Mama didn't bother discarding or storing Boo and Granddad's belongings. It served as a foundation for all of our stuff. Before Mama was stuck in bed, she loved going to the dollar store. I look at the meaningless tchotchkes and suddenly feel tight and breathless with claustrophobia.

With effort, I slide the back door open and let fresh air in. I sit on a deck chair and look up to the stars, wondering if there's one for me up there, if somehow, something far, far away will make this get better. The burn on my belly stings. I feel hungry, but for the first time ever, not for something sweet or savory. Not for something salty or creamy. I'm not sure what I want, but I don't think it's something to eat.

On Tuesday, I prepare to leave the house fifteen minutes early to avoid Skunk's routine of rolling out of bed and hitching a ride to school with me, inevitably making me late. I also just want to be on time for once. Even if I can't dress like I belong, I quickly double-check my hair, smoothing my bangs and combing my fingers through my long, silky locks before sweeping it over my shoulder and rushing out the door.

When I get out to the Honda, it looks lopsided. I tilt my head, studying it. I scurry to the other side. Both front tires are flat. I run my hand along one of them; a deep gouge slices through the rubber.

I look around dumbly as if whoever did it will be hiding in a bush or something. I glance toward the end of the road and see the taillights of the bus rumbling by. I slump. Just my luck. I have no one to call to bring me to school. I sling my backpack over my shoulder and start to walk. The seams of my jeans rub angrily together, chafing my inner thighs. I happen to know it's nearly three miles to the school. I will be late. I promised Mr. Hammons to be on time. I do something I haven't done since fourth-grade PE, before I claimed to have injuries each week or got surly with the instructor.

I put one foot in front of the other and run. Kinda. More like lumber. But it's not walking either. Faster. The breeze sweeps my hair from my neck. My breath wants to catch somewhere between my throat and chest, but I push it down, filling myself up like a balloon. Maybe I'll float away. I pass Natty Gimbal's. She's put a potted mum on the porch, and a scarecrow on a stick leers at me. I laugh in its face as I press forward, trying to outpace humiliation and the ticking clock. I'm sure I look like a fool, worthy of a fat-girl joke. Maybe I don't care.

I miss homeroom, but make it to first period on time, although completely out of breath. My skin is moist with sweat, and my face is as red as the traffic light I spotted Hillary drive through.

Between classes, I go to the water fountain and gulp the trickle of water that comes out of the gummy spigot, feeling refreshed and having forgotten how good plain old water tastes.

In Spanish, Hillary glares at me. I ignore her until Señora Whitaker arranges us in groups for conversation. Hillary and her friends whisper, looking in my direction as they stifle laughter. I have the urge to roll my eyes at them. But the bell rings before I can make up my mind.

At lunch, I carefully carry my tray toward the back of the cafeteria. Before I take a bite of pizza, Even appears.

"Hey, wanna join me on the picnic table outside?" he asks.

I look around, but no one appears to be gawking or waiting for the punch line.

"Sure," I say when it appears safe. I follow him into the fresh air. I feel myself standing a little taller as I walk behind him, and somehow my stomach and butt don't feel quite like the usual giant locomotive and caboose on the chubby train.

"How was the rest of your weekend?" he asks when we sit down.

"Homework, grocery shopping—oh, and Skunk, I think, slashed my tires," I answer.

"He wouldn't do that, would he?" Even asks.

"Remember my bike?" I say. I want to mention my lip but avoid it. "He would. I mean, it's just a guess, but he also—" I stop myself, knowing that Even doesn't want to hear about how Skunk pushed me and scalded my belly. I don't need to draw any more attention to it.

Even waits for me to finish, but I shake my head and look down at my tray.

"If I can get your car to the shop, I can change the tires. I'll meet you after school and have a look. Sound good?" he says.

"You don't have to do that."

"No, but why not? You need your car, right? And, plus, then we can hang out for a while. Cool?" Even asks.

I'm brightly aware that this is what normal sounds like.

I nod and eat about half of my lunch. I leave the extra cup of Jell-O, not feeling the need to join the clean-plate club today.

I wait for Even in front of the school, stricken with the thought that maybe he rides a different motorcycle to school than the one he's repairing. His offer to take me to the ocean on his soon-to-be new bike was sweet, but nothing is funnier than a fat chick on the back of a motorcycle. I cringe, anticipating the rumble of a bike, but it doesn't come.

Even scuffs toward me with his backpack slung over one shoulder. Since he grew up by the sea, his skin retains a warm color from the sun; it's not pasty and doughy like mine.

"How'd you get here this morning anyway?" he asks.

"I kinda ran. Walked," I answer.

"Then let's go," he says.

We make it to the end of the bus loop when I remember I forgot my history book.

"Fudge," I say.

Even's eyes get wide. I fear that he might think I want fudge. I explain about my book and then add, "As a rule, I don't say the *F* word. When I run out of alternatives or when I really need to use it, then maybe it'll cross my lips, but not until then."

"So 'fudge' for now?" he asks.

"Or 'fark,' 'feck,' 'ferk,' 'flak' . . ."

Even laughs.

I smile.

"There it is again. I like to see that," he says.

"What?" I ask.

"Your smile."

When we reach my house, I thank God for answering my prayers that Skunk *not* be there. Even has a quick look at my car, shakes his head, and then leans against the hood. I feel like I should offer that he come inside and have a glass of lemonade, but the thought makes me cringe.

"What are you doing this afternoon? Homework? A job? Rescuing remote villages from war and famine?" he asks.

Two weeks ago, his comment would have colored my cheeks pink, but Even's words don't cause embarrassment to worm inside my head. Instead, I shrug. "I've been working on a dress. I thought I might add some—" I interrupt myself. I've never told anyone about my sewing, not since Mama chuckled and in her most venomous voice said, "Sugar, don't kid yourself; ain't none of that ever gonna look good on you."

"You sew?" Even asks, apparently genuinely interested.

"Yeah," I say, feeling out of breath but excited like this not-secret was burning for me to share it. I don't hide my sewing, but I don't advertise it either.

I lead Even away from the house. I don't care where we're going, but my passion for sewing, *my thing*, threads me along, away from Mama's ears.

A memory, like a warm quilt, teases more of my not-secret hobby from my lips, and I say, "My grandmother, Boo—she's passed away now—taught me how to take scraps and string and make something beautiful. I started simple: a heart on a potholder, a cloth bookmark, and beanbags. Then moved on to clothes for my dolls, then other projects like Christmas-tree decorations, bags and purses . . . For a while, I got carried away. Seriously, I sewed everything: pillowcases, hair accessories, a teepee—except Skunk ripped it. I made my mother an apron . . ." I wonder if it means anything that she kept it.

I take a deep breath, letting the memories of Boo and me together, sitting in her sunny sewing room, warm me. She'd swear in Polish, under her breath, every time she accidently knotted a stitch. She'd pat my hand, telling me I was a natural, letting me pick my favorite threads from her sewing box. In those moments, I wasn't Sugar or fat or afraid of anything.

"Then Boo was gone and—" I want to say that so much as looking at a needle made me weep, but that was brief and the truth was stronger: I returned to sewing clothes, but full-size. I found vintage fabrics and patterns in the sewing room, and kept Boo's box for myself. But for me, the clothes just aren't big enough. Making a dress that big would almost be like making this version of me permanent. I exhale and say, "—and I couldn't *not* sew." Unable to help myself, I smile.

"Maybe you can make me something."

I can't think of anything that would make him look better.

We reach Even's street.

"Like what?" I ask, not sure if he's just indulging me.

Even stops, scratches his head, and then turns around and says, "An invisibility cloak, to start."

I glance back; a pickup truck looms in the driveway.

He and I aren't that different, appearances aside. We're both stuck, with nowhere to go and no way to get there.

Chapter Seven

It takes nearly a month to get the tires in for the Honda. Even tells me it's because he's getting them for free, but I secretly think he likes waiting for me on the corner halfway between my house and his apartment before school, walking together, and repeating it in the afternoon. Or maybe that's just me.

I glance at the clock. I'm running late. I check my teeth and, sure enough, they appear whiter. It was hard, but I'm glad I ditched the soda for the last few weeks. One morning, much like today, while I got ready for school, the sun's light in the bathroom shone so it made it appear my teeth were discoloring. I recalled a science experiment in grade school with different beverages and their staining ability. I reasoned that if Even likes my smile—heck, if I like my smile—I can't have rotten teeth. I picked up some whitening toothpaste at the drugstore and ditched the soda. I also started flossing. My old dentist would be proud. I tried to get Mama to use the paste because I noticed her teeth looked yellow, too. She said it was too spicy for her and spit it out, missing the cup, and showering me in the process.

After fussing with my hair a minute too long, I decide my waterfall braid is good enough, and I fish around my dresser drawer for my pair of pants with the flared bottoms but can't find them. After dervishing my room, I discover they're in the laundry. The sour smell of dirty clothes scolds me for not getting it all done over the weekend because Even and I had hung out.

I grab a different pair. When I bend over to hastily stuff all my books in my backpack, my pants slide down. I tug them up and then realize I need a belt. *I need a belt.*

My mouth falls open. I don't dare look down, but run my finger along the waistline, and sure enough, there's room to spare. I don't have a belt, so I try for a third pair of pants, ones I've never worn because they were too small, that being a relative word. Sure enough, they're perfect.

As I stride to our meeting spot, standing a little taller, the leaves on the trees, just beginning to turn from a muted green to the colors of autumn, rustle. Even's in the distance, waiting. His outline is like a wood etching, solid and rooted, but something tells me he could just as easily fly away. I'm smiling already. I have no idea what he sees in me, aside from so much of me, but he's sweeter than sugar. I stop in my tracks, disarmed by the thought.

He takes a step toward me and shouts, "Did you forget something?"

I hurry toward him. I think back over the recent weeks and realize my craving for sugar, my consumption of food for that matter, hasn't been made with as fierce a desperation to feel full of . . . I'm not sure of what I wanted to feel full of, not exactly. All I know is that I feel perfectly satisfied right now. There might very well be a skip in my step.

"No, nothing," I say when I catch up. "How's progress on the bike?" This has become my routine question at the beginning, middle, and end of each week.

He smiles broadly and his blue eyes twinkle. He usually fills me in on technical things, and I listen intently because he describes it all with such passion.

"Next weekend, you and I are going to the ocean," he declares.

I haven't officially agreed to this yet, but don't want to dampen his spirits. This trip has motivated him to work on the bike as often as possible, clearly something he loves to do, and I don't want to rob him of that by saying no. My feet will remain on the ground.

"Wow. You're making quick work of it," I say, pushing away my thoughts and the disappointment sharing them will bring. The conversation turns to a project I've been working on for English, a band he had me listen to, and then our favorite seasons, holidays, and the holiday we'd invent if we could. Me—a day to be happy just 'cause. Everyone, everywhere, smiling, laughing, and being kind all day. He riffs off this with complimentary smiley-face T-shirts for all participants. Even says he'd vote for a day of peace, which I realize is so similar to mine we could combine them, but I don't say any more because I probably already sound like a dork.

"You look nice today, your hair especially," he says.

Before I can say thank you, he disappears into the pack of students rushing to class.

The week breezes by with the only hiccup being Mama's increasingly raspy cough. I hear her at night, hacking, but when I ask her about it, there's nothing for me to do. She refuses help. I meet Even on Friday morning as usual, but I'm tired from listening to and worrying about Mama all night.

"Ready for the big ride tomorrow?" Even asks.

I stammer. "Well, I don't know. Laundry day. I have to help Mama out. And Skunk, he hasn't been to school in over a month. I think he's going to fail or drop out. I don't know if it's a good idea," I say.

"Sugar, those all sound like reasons to get the hell outta here," Even says.

He's right, of course. I haven't left town since I dropped Brittany off at the mall. Since then, apparently, she took up with some guy who moved into a trailer in her park, and I haven't seen much of her. Even looks like he wants to say more, but the first bell rings, and we both hurry inside.

The day slogs by. I need to pinch myself to stay awake during a long, droning history lecture. Finally, I wait on the low brick wall under a maple tree to meet Even after school at two thirty to walk home. When he approaches me, he looks serious.

"What's up?" I ask.

He exhales.

Allie and Hillary bustle by, shooting dirty looks in my direction.

"My dad never made it home last night. Not a huge surprise; sometimes he passes out in his truck before he comes home, you know, to sleep it off, but I found out from Aaron Irons, Officer Irons's son, that he was arrested. Drunk driving."

"Futz," I say, and think about my dad, wondering why he never made it home, period. But there's no use in thinking about that; he's gone. I turn my attention back to Even.

"Yeah. This isn't the first time. I have to get him out." Even looks exasperated. "But, first, I want to show you something. Actually, one thing now, and if I can convince you, something else tomorrow."

Instead of walking to my house, we walk down Birch Road to Even's apartment. It's quiet as he stashes his backpack in his room and fills up a glass of water for each of us. This is only the second time I've been inside; usually we hang out in the shed so he can tinker with his bike while I sit on the snowmobile and we chat. I've never invited him into my house, mostly because of Skunk, but also because of how unacceptable it is: dirty and cluttered no matter how much I clean. Lately, I've been keeping to my room as much as possible.

"It seems peaceful in here today," I say absently, noting the empty sink and the sunlight casting checkers on the linoleum.

"Yeah," Even agrees. "A rarity."

I've gotten the sense that Even and his dad don't get along, but he never talks about it. All I know is Nash Anderson works at the box factory like Fat Henry, but unlike my brother, Nash gets wasted after his shift.

"Let's go out to the shed," Even says.

He's tossed a giant oilcloth over the hulking form of the bike. He hesitates before he unveils the motorcycle, like he's also going to see it for the first time. The cover whooshes when he lifts it. Dust rises into the air like confetti.

All I see is perfection. Polished chrome beckons me like a magpie to shiny treasure. The gas tank is glossy black. The contours and details are all kinds of sleek, James Dean cool.

"The Switchback is new again," Even says, referring to the vintage Harley model.

I only know what this means, and about one hundred other useless-to-me motorcycle facts, because he loves them so much. I imagine he had a poster tacked to his bedroom wall when he was a kid with a photograph of a bike just like this.

Pride, backed by the promise of freedom, glistens in Even's eyes.

"It's amazing," I say, running my hand along the smooth seat.

He gazes from the bike to me, and it's like he's found the thing that makes him whole: taking a beat-up, abandoned old bike and giving it a new purpose, much like what I do with my needle and thread.

Met with so much possibility, my distorted reflection in the tailpipe makes me forget what's underneath the baggy clothes I wear.

"Listen, I have a feeling you don't want to ride on this because of—" he begins, but I don't let him finish.

Tears well in my eyes, but I don't waver from meeting his. For my entire life I've wanted the truth, and not in the form of cruel ridicule, whether spoken by Mama, my brother, kids from school, or perfect strangers. I want to hear the truth about who I am, boldly, indiscriminately. Not under the apologetic guise of *She's just big-boned* or *It's just baby fat*. I am fat, and I know it. *Own it,* a voice in my head whispers. There's no way to hide it or the scrutiny I face every day from the public and, worse, from myself, but there's no point in pretending it's not there.

"Because of my size," I blurt.

Even takes a step toward me. A toolbox lies on the floor between us. He pushes it aside with his foot. It grates on the dirty floor.

Tears stream down my face. I don't care if he sees me exposed. I can't hide behind the obvious fact that I am overweight and have an honest friendship at the same time. It's crushing me.

Even extends his arms. Finally, all those tears welling up breach, as if his embrace is the floodgate. He envelops me. I continue to cry, and his sweatshirt becomes damp. I stand wrapped in his arms for what feels like ages. I let him hold me and pour myself out. He's patient, firm. Even doesn't waver in his ability to support me as I count a tear for each time someone's called me fat.

Dark thoughts crash through my mind. I see Mama, when she was still able to get around, feeding me fried chicken and mashed potatoes topped with half a stick of butter along with gravy and mayo. I downed it with a liter of soda. She insisted I eat, saying, "You've got to grow. I don't want no string bean for a daughter." Then she let me eat an entire tray of brownies. I ate until I felt like I was going to throw up. All the while, she watched, working through her own plate. I see myself over the years, mindlessly eating, filling my belly until it ached. I feel at once disgusted with myself and yet relieved that I've allowed these thoughts to surface as I'm held in the safety of someone else's arms.

After a time Even asks, "What is it?"

I shake my head and say, "Never mind."

His forehead wrinkles with concern.

My face must look puffier than usual, so I put it back against his chest. His heart beats against my cheek. He strokes my hair, his fingers occasionally grazing the back of my neck.

"I know it must be hard for you, Sugar," he says softly. "I hear kids talking, but you know what? You're better than that. You're—"

That shadow within me that reminds me how worthless I am reckons Even can't come up with anything nice to say. Then I catch his clear blue eyes and feel his warmth, alive, courageous, so close to me. Real.

"You're my friend, Sugar. You have the biggest heart and the best laugh. And your smile. It melts me," he says.

My breath catches in my chest. All I can do is cry. I don't want to, but it's as if the tears lubricate the kinks in the rusty chain that just barely holds me to this life. Even's words grease it, and I suddenly feel lighter, like some slack has been let out, and even though that shadow doesn't want to believe what I heard, my heart does, and, for a fraction of a minute, I'm free.

"Listen, you've seen bikers. Big dudes with huge mustaches, flashing their plumber's cracks?" he asks.

I squeak out a snot-filled laugh.

"Compared to them you're a mouse and they're—oh, I dunno, big ugly ogres. If they can ride, so can you. I'd be happy to have you on the back of my Harley," Even says, smiling at me. This time his words pierce the web of lies inside of me, created by years' worth of insults that have gelled into ugly truths.

"OK. I'll do it," I say.

His smile is magnificent. It looks like Christmas morning.

"I'll pick you up at seven," he says.

I think on this. "Maybe it would be better if we meet. Just in case of Skunk," I say.

"Yeah, I get the sense he doesn't like me."

"It might just be a good idea," I say quietly.

"Now, I've got to figure out how to get my dad out of the clink," Even says.

I grimace and turn to leave. "Oh hey, wasn't there something else you wanted to show me?"

"Tomorrow," he says and smiles again.

When I get back to my house, Skunk's in the kitchen. After putting four Hot Pockets in the microwave, he directs a tube of Pringles toward his mouth, pours, and then with his mouth full says, "Mama's ripped. You better go see her."

Bubble burst. If cloud nine existed, I just fell from it. I squeeze down the hall and knock on her door.

She coughs before answering.

I cautiously enter.

"Where the hell have you been?" she asks. "I told you to come home right after school. I need you to pick something up for me. I saw this stuff on TV; it will help me lose weight. Some kinda vitamin." A cough interrupts her. "I wasn't always so fat. At least *I* could get into a skirt. You've seen the pictures, Sugar. After having you kids, this extra padding decided to stick around. Too bad your papa didn't." She scowls something fierce. "But I'm gonna wear a skirt again, you watch."

I'm pleased she wants to lose weight, but worry about her taking another pill. Lydia Monroe took some kind of diet pill in freshman year and ended up having to go to the ER because her heart got messed up.

"Well?" she says.

I can't say no to Mama.

"Yeah, sure," I say. "What's it called?"

She gives me the details.

"The only problem is my car is being fixed," I say.

"*My* car. What happened to it?" she asks.

"Flat tire."

"That shouldn't take long to get fixed."

I think about how it's taken quite a long time, but don't care because it's free. More importantly, I've been able to spend so much time with Even. I don't tell Mama this.

"Henry should be by in a little while to bring me my smokes. Tell him to bring you to the store. Or walk, girl. Goodness knows you could also stand to lose some weight," she says disdainfully.

From under my bangs, I look at Mama, splayed on the bed, wheezing. No, I'm not like her, I tell myself, then the dreaded voice in my head tells me I will be someday. I turn to leave and she asks me to bring her something to eat.

Skunk left one package of Hot Pockets, so I nuke them for myself. Meanwhile, I warm Mama up a box of Hamburger Helper and bring in her favorite Doritos flavor, Cool Ranch.

"Bring some sour cream and Pepsi," she hollers.

She has me running back and forth, shouting orders. I don't hear when Fat Henry comes in. When I bring her a refill, he stands by the door in her room, having deposited the cigarettes on the shelf.

She immediately lights one up, followed by a round of coughing. "Fat Henry, you bring Sugar to the store. I need her to get something for me. And stop at Mickey D's. Bring me back my usual," Mama orders.

Fat Henry looks less fat than the last time I saw him. Also, he's wearing a new pair of shoes. He playfully pushes me. With a rare smile, he says, "Well then, come on."

I haven't spent much time with him since he left home, and back then, I wouldn't have wanted to—he was just about as ill-tempered as Skunk. Tonight, the way he's acting tells me he's softening a little. Maybe his girlfriend's influencing him.

We pass the church on our way to the store; it glows softly in the light, like a beacon. We're both quiet with reverence until it's out of sight. Then he makes friendly small talk. "So tell me about school. Mr. Hammons is your homeroom teacher, right? Is he as dull as ever?"

"Pretty much, but it's Mrs. Nelson who's the worst. I think she remembers you and Skunk. He didn't make a good impression," I say, remembering the dead mouse he left under her chair. "She takes it out on me."

"Sorry about that," he says. "I saw the mail in the kitchen. I see he hasn't been going. Truant."

"I made sure he saw the letter, but nothing I say gets him to listen. I think he hangs out in someone's garage all day working on his dirt bike." This makes me think of Even and his motorcycle. "How's Stacy?" I ask him about his girlfriend, whom I've only met once. I'm beginning to think we have the same reason for not bringing friends, girl, boy, or otherwise, around the house.

"She's great," he says. "She just finished her third year in college. She really likes it. She's studying to be a nurse and minoring in nutrition and Spanish. And she's got me eating a little better."

"I can tell. You look good."

"Thanks. I feel good. How about Mama? How's she doing?" he asks, though he already knows the answer.

"Same as ever. 'Ornerier than a rattlesnake,'" I say, quoting Granddad.

Fat Henry lets out a laugh. "That's good. She wouldn't be Mama unless she was mean."

This comment strikes me like a venomous bite. Mama *is* mean. Really mean.

"Stacy keeps telling me to stop bringing her cigarettes. She's got that cough," Fat Henry says.

"I know. I ask her about it, but she claims she's fine. It worries me, though."

We pull into the drugstore parking lot. The blue letters of the sign flicker, as if they're unsure if they want to be on or off in the dusky evening. I find the vitamins that promise to suppress appetite and help lose weight. I read the label. Maybe I should take them, too.

We stop at McDonald's and Fat Henry buys us both bacon-and-ranch salads. For Mama, he gets a couple Big Macs and fries. "You know, she probably shouldn't be eating this," he says, taking the bag, already stained with grease, from the drive-through window before parking in a spot so we can eat.

"Yeah, but she'd pitch a fit if you didn't bring it to her," I say.

"True," he says.

She'd probably throw whatever was within reach, but more than likely, she'd wait to strike until well after I'd forgotten about the tantrum and my defenses were down. She's cunning like that. She never forgets if I talk back to her or don't do something right. I have the scars to prove it.

Once back at the house, Fat Henry drops me off without coming inside.

"See ya, Sis," he says with surprising affection.

The smile playing at the corners of my mouth disappears as I close the front door behind me.

"Suuuuuuuuuugar," I hear from down the hall. Then coughing. I go to Mama's room. "Skunk says Henry left some donuts. Bring me a couple," she says.

Unsure why the request required her to yell like that, I look around and find the box, half caved in, on the sofa in the living room. Fat Henry said he took a few mornings at Dunkin' Donuts after he switched from the day shift to the night shift at the box factory. He said since he was up all night anyway, he may as well keep on working. Based on the way he looked when he talked about Stacy, I think he's saving to buy her an engagement ring. A half-dozen donuts remain. As requested, I bring Mama a couple along with the greasy fast-food bag.

"That's a good girl," she says flatly. "Now, I need some more to drink to wash down this cough."

I don't think soda will do the trick, but bring it to her anyway.

As I exit she says, "You seem different lately. Happy? Don't get too used to it. Life's a bitch and then you die." Then, more softly, she adds, "I thought it was all rainbows and cupcakes. But you get tangled up with a man and have a few kids, people stop looking or they look so long it's like their eyeballs are frozen. When you get old, if you don't keep up, the world leaves you behind and makes you bitter. There's no mistake; it's that bitch called life that's made me mean, Sugar. And maybe a few people who said they were friends, but turned their backs. You'd do well to watch out."

Her acidic words follow me through the hall, into the kitchen, burning into my vision and scorching my skin. I see the cupboards are nearly empty, courtesy of Skunk. I settle down on the sofa with the remaining donuts. I flip on the TV and finish off the box, licking the cinnamon sugar from my fingers.

Sometime later, I wake to slamming, swearing, and very bright light. Skunk stumbles into the living room. The malty smell of beer and sweat bites my nose.

"Move," he says.

Sleepily, I push over to the side of the couch, ready to go up to bed anyway since I have to get up early in the morning. I look at the clock above the television. It reads one a.m.

Skunk flops down and his hand hits my foot. "I said to fuckin' move."

I scramble to my feet.

He glares at me. "What's the matter with you? Lazy-ass, worthless, fat piece of shit. Where are the rest of the donuts?"

I clear the cobwebs from my throat. "Mama and I ate them," I answer.

He slurs something unintelligible and then makes to get up, but thick, invisible glue holds him down. His head tilts from side to side like a daisy in the wind. For a moment, I feel bad for him. Then he swings his arm behind the couch to swipe at me. I jump back, but fall over an old swivel chair piled with books and outdated magazines. It moves and I careen backward, a heap of abandoned sports equipment poking painfully into my back. I cry out.

"Serves you right, fatso," he says.

I struggle to my feet and then go upstairs. Once in the bathroom, a dark stain on my shirt tells me that something, probably the old pair of ice skates, cut my side. I stare at my naked upper body. Fat rolls down my middle in the broken mirror. I don't bother angling so I look thinner, even though I have lost a few pounds. I consider going downstairs and sneaking some of those pills I got for Mama, but while we ate in the McDonald's parking lot, I read the warnings on the box. I think of Lydia Monroe. If I took diet pills and the EMTs had to rush me to the hospital, I'd never live it down. And worse, would they be able to lift me? *Not that it matters,* I think bleakly.

I go to my room and collapse on the bed. I hope that tomorrow, a day spent with Even, will be brighter than the hopelessness I feel during the seemingly interminable hours I spend each day in the presence of Mama and Skunk.

Chapter Eight

I'm downstairs by six thirty, showered and dressed. Skunk's passed out on the couch. I debate whether to tell Mama where I'm going, but figure it's better she doesn't know. She snores loudly when I bring her a tray of food and set it beside her bed before I slip out the front door. For once, Skunk will have to look after her. I tread lightly down the sidewalk in the hush of the early morning.

As I near our designated meeting place, a motorcycle purrs in the distance. It grows louder and then Even, astride the Harley, comes into view. My eyes work their way up his body. His smile, as bright as the one from the day before, spreads on his lips. He isn't wearing a helmet; it isn't the law in New Hampshire. Our state slogan is "Live free or die." Apparently that extends to protective bike gear, too. An image of the motorcycle not being able to support me, then Even and me spilling to the ground, our heads mashing into the pavement, flashes through my mind. I must look terrified when Even's close enough to read my expression.

"You all right, Shoog?" he asks.

He's never called me anything but Sugar before. A smile replaces whatever look I wore.

"No need to be nervous. This thing is solid. It's supposed to be a beautiful day. Let's ride," he says.

Getting on the bike is by no means a graceful act. I have to hike up the leg of my jeans, the material puckering and pinching my thigh, in order to get my foot up and over to the other side. When on the seat, I wrap my arms securely around Even. I feel something akin to perfection. I wait to question it, dismiss it, but the loud bike drives out all thought.

He accelerates down the road. As we pass the church, I say a silent prayer, unsure if I should ask for us to be safe or for no one to laugh at me, but then reprimand my selfishness and ask for something bigger, like world peace or—but before I can decide, we're whipping past familiar houses, fields, and then the woods. It's enough just to wave goodbye.

He stops on the shoulder just before we get on the highway.

"How are you doing back there?" he asks.

"Never better," I say, leaning my cheek against his back as he tears off toward the highway. The air blows through my hair and my eyes water, but I don't care. I feel like a bird with the wind in my wings. No, like an eagle. Free. The sun has come all the way up, its rays beaming through the clouds. My chest and belly are against Even's back, and I feel a different kind of warmth than I've ever known. I feel full of life.

About halfway there, he pulls off to a rest stop. "I need a coffee," he says. "You?"

"Yeah, sure. I could go for a coffee." I stay with the bike and he returns with two coffees and a donut to split. Guilt from the night before nudges me.

"Nah. I'm good," I say.

"You sure?" he asks.

I nod. Like soda, my former vehicle for caffeine in the morning, a donut would bring further attention to me and my chunky butt. I'd rather not go there this early in the day. We sit on the top of a picnic table and Even, who I notice has a small cut and a tiny purple bruise under his eye, now that he took off his sunglasses, tells me he got his dad out of jail.

"What happened to your eye?" I ask.

He looks at me a long moment and then shakes his head. "It's nothing," he says softly. "Let's go."

We get back on the road. By midmorning, the air smells different. Salty and cooler.

"Nearly there," Even hollers over the roar of the bike and the wind. The wind tickles his tousled hair.

We move through light traffic along a street populated by fast-food joints, restaurants, quick lubes, and gas stations. Even smoothly turns down a suburban street. He points to a ranch-style house with a pair of sycamores in the front. Mums and pumpkins decorate the front entryway.

"That's where I grew up," he says. "Looks like someone else lives there now."

The only reason we haven't lost our house is that my grandparents paid off the mortgage long before I was born. But the state of it may soon mean it's condemned. Then where would we go? I think about Mama, in her bed, and hope she's all right without me there. Surely, by now, Skunk must have woken up and tended to her.

We cruise down another street, and another, and then come to an intersection. Directly across the middle, I see it. The ocean spreads wide and blue, the exact color of Even's eyes. I gasp.

He turns his head to reveal the corner of a smile. "What do you think?" he asks.

The sea is almost too much to take in. Bumps form on the horizon in long corduroy-like lines, each one getting nearer until it crests then drops in a skirt of white foam. And they only get bigger, and louder, the closer we get. The salty air clings to my skin; it won't wash off for a while.

"It's amazing," I say. "And so big. Vast. I can't see where it ends." There aren't enough words in my head to say how it makes me feel, so I linger there, bathing in the enormity. It makes me feel small and yet like all things are possible.

"Straight on until you hit Europe," Even says. "Or so I've been told."

The tide is out, revealing polished rocks and long strands of seaweed. We trek through the sand. Wind whips at my hair and I feel wild with potential. I shiver.

"Chilly?" Even asks.

I nod.

"It's always cooler by the sea, the breeze," he says. "I think it's refreshing. It's like the air itself is alive." He puts an arm around my shoulder and pulls me close. Insta-warmth. We continue to the water's edge. When a wave comes in, I put my hand in the foam. It's freezing. Even takes a seat in the sand. After watching the waves rolling in and tickling my feet, I join him.

He continues to observe the waves, so I do the same. Even sighs and then reaches for my hand and gives it a squeeze. I flush pink.

"I told you I had something else to show you," he says. He weighs a small blue book in his hands. "This. These are my life plans."

I give him a curious look.

"When my mom was pregnant with me, she kept a journal." He lets the pages slip open to show a woman's cursive writing looping along the slim blue lines. He thumbs the inner cover, where the name *Tansy* is written in the same script.

"She wrote about her hopes and dreams. And the future. I guess that, sometimes, pregnant women do that. They get all introspective. She wrote about herself, but also what she hoped for us." Even swallows before continuing, "When she was born, she had a twin, but that baby died. Growing up here, on the Atlantic, she dreamed of visiting its twin, the Pacific Ocean, and maybe rediscovering that missing part of herself. She wrote about how she wanted us—her sons, I was a twin, too—to go there together someday." Even looks out to the water, gathering himself. I get the sense he's never shared this with anyone.

"When she went into labor, the other baby, my twin, died. And so did she. She had some complications, and when the doctor announced they'd lost the other baby, I think she gave up." Even's voice sounds thin, but then when he continues it steadily regains its usual strength. "But I won't. I'm going to get out there to the Pacific. I have her ashes." Then Even's voice cracks.

We watch the waves a moment, the sun dancing off the Atlantic.

"I'm so sorry. That's sad, but beautiful, too. You'll get there." While I speak, the fissures in his composure disappear.

"I was so mad when we had to move inland, when I had to leave here. Even though she and I never met, to me, this ocean was, no, *is* my mom. And the Pacific is like, all that we both lost, even my dad. I lost him when we lost her. I know it was hard, but people who knew him said the grief changed him. He didn't try, not even for me. I'm hoping in some strange way by making it out there, I'll be able to put myself back together. Or something."

I know just what he means, but am so moved and surprised by how deeply I relate, I let the ocean speak for me as it crests, crashes, and then tinkles on the pebbles and shells as the water washes back out. I think about my father and Mama. I think about how all my life it's felt like something is missing or broken inside me, too.

All is quiet except for the rush of the waves. I feel awake because of the breeze and bright sunlight, but tired, as if the water's ebb and flow hums to me like a lullaby.

"I think that's a good plan," I say simply.

"It's the only one I've got." Then he smiles. "Here, let me show you." Even flips past his mother's writing and I see his own, angular, in black ink.

"My first stop, New York City. I've always wanted to go there. Be a tourist for a day, y'know? Ever been?"

I shake my head. "Nope. I've been to Vermont and Massachusetts, once. That's the extent of my world travel." Even laughs lightheartedly.

"That about sums it up for me, too," Even says. "So New York and then Washington, D.C.—pay homage to our country's forefathers, wave hello to the president, and then zip on down to the Carolinas. I've heard the beaches there are beautiful. Then I'm going to drive through the Smoky Mountains and on into Graceland." Even has tidily written directions, mileage, gas estimates, and his pit stops or points of interest, along with a couple of campsites, on each of the pages corresponding to the destinations.

"You've really thought this through," I say.

"I've been dreaming about this for as long as I can remember. Since I learned my mom's story, I've felt like part of me is missing, like I'm being called home. A home before this home or something. Maybe just a place away"—he clears his throat—"safe from Nash's rage. Then, when we moved, I said, The hell with it, I'm going. So where was I, Graceland?" he says with unshakable conviction.

"And what exactly is Graceland?" I ask, imagining some kind of theme park version of heaven or at least some kind of place of worship. Safe.

Even turns the page to a photograph of Elvis Presley glued onto the paper and says, "Graceland is the home to the one and only king of rock and roll."

"I see."

"It was his estate. He was my mom's favorite singer. I guess her mom's favorite, too. Legend has it that my grandma met him after a concert or something. Then I'm going to head south to the Big

Easy. New Orleans. Here, look," he says, flipping to the back of the book and pulling out an accordion-style map glued onto a page near the back. He traces his finger from a star in New Hampshire next to the words *You are not here,* then down all the way to the Gulf Coast. "After that, I'm going to visit my aunt in Texas. She's got a sense of humor as big as the whole state. Next stop, New Mexico. I want to see the pueblos. And, finally, on into California, where I plan to drive straight to the ocean. I'll go through LA, but I'd really like to drive all the way up the coast. Big Sur seems like the perfect place—"

I know he means to part with his mom's ashes. "That sounds like an epic road trip," I say.

He nods.

"When do you set sail?"

Even laughs. "Right after I receive my diploma, I'm outta town."

For a moment, I feel stung. What about us? Our friendship? Then I see that this is his dream, something he's planned for longer than we've known each other and that has probably buoyed him through long winters, long nights, and the move inland.

"Well, I'll miss you," I say. But I don't think he hears me because just then a flock of seagulls screeches overhead, drowning out even the waves.

"My dad calls those flying rats," Even says.

"What about your dad? What does he think?" I ask.

"Who cares?" He shakes the words out of his mouth. "I don't really mean that, but he doesn't care. He's wanted me gone since the day he brought me home without his wife. My grandparents took turns taking care of me when I was really little. He's never given two shits."

"Sorry, Even," I say, because, truly, I know how it feels. I reach into my back pocket and pull out the wrinkled and folded old photograph of my dad.

"This is my dad. I've never known him either. He's somewhere out there, I think," I say, looking toward the ocean. The world's a bigger place than Johnson Regional High School, Od Town, and the bitterness within the walls of my house.

"You and I, we go together just like peanut butter and jelly, huh?" Even says, shifting the mood to a lighter one. "How about we get some lunch?"

We walk back to the promenade. After Even checks on his bike, he leads me to the fish-and-chips place with a perfect view of the ocean he'd raved about.

"The food is almost as good as the scenery," he says when we sit at a picnic table.

Even buys me lunch. For once, aside from eating in the cafeteria with him, I chew and savor, instead of gobble and glug my food. Eating with him is a different experience than normal mealtimes. Not that I really have normal mealtimes. Sometimes it seems like I eat around the clock, but with Even something else replaces that endless hunger, a kind of fullness I can't define. Warmth, maybe. Companionship. Perhaps it isn't so much what is present as it is what's missing: guilt, shame, ridicule, Mama alternatingly urging me to stuff my face and telling me how fat and worthless I am. I take a deep breath. I dare not say it aloud, lest I jinx myself, but I feel something bordering on *good*.

We walk up and down the sidewalk. Looking into store windows, I see beachwear that will never fit me, and notice many shops have closed for the season. A couple passes by on the sidewalk, foolishly in love, fawning over each other, arm-in-arm. I pause midstep, seeing a warped version of my future self, walking next to Even, garnering double takes and whispers coupled with quiet laughter when they think that tiresome question: *Why is it that tall, skinny guys often end up with obese women?* I don't want to be that woman, the subject of ridicule, but I nearly am—*minus the couple part,* I think, embarrassed.

Even wrests me from these shadowed thoughts. “Come on,” he says, leading me back out toward the beach.

“There are never too many this time of year,” he says, looking down at the ground.

“Huh? Too many what?”

“Hang on. I’ll find one.”

I’m about to ask what, when he dashes over to a spot in the sand where the incoming waves washed a large hash of debris in, including yards of seaweed. I step closer while he roots through rocks and shells.

“Hmmm,” he says. “Let’s go a little further.”

We near a breakwater, but before we get too much closer he says, “Aha!”

The sun hovers above the trees at our backs, toward the west, as if it isn’t ready, just yet, to settle in for the night. Even takes a seat in the sand again and pulls me down to his side. I still haven’t gotten used to his touch. Each time I feel his warm hand on mine, with mechanic’s grease under his nails, I get a thrill I never thought I’d have. The kind of feeling made for TV or reserved for girls like Hillary.

“See this?” Even holds out a shell smoothed into the shape of a heart by the tumbling sea. “It’s for you. A shell like this one, beautiful to begin with, can get cracked and slivered, and then time, the tides, maybe even the wind, tumble and toss it, and it becomes something new, a perfect version of itself.”

He tucks the shell into my hand. I can’t ignore the fizzy feeling when our fingers touch. His grin, I can tell, is just for me.

“You’ve got it. From that smile, to your careful listening, to your courage.” He smirks and gathers my hair, whipping in the wind, out of my face, letting his fingers loop it by my shoulder. “You’re a beautiful person, Shoog. Don’t let anyone, not even the people you think you’re supposed to trust, tell you different.”

I grasp at his words, hoping to memorize them so that, like a ship, they'll carry me to safer shores. He places the shell in my hand, and I know I will never forget. At least not entirely.

We remain there for a while longer, the setting sun casting sparkles on the peaks of the waves and everywhere in between. Suddenly a bittersweet feeling of joy, and a sense that it's fleeting, winds its way into the moment. Mama's coarse words, "Life's a bitch and then you die," echo in my head once again. I don't want to believe she's right.

"What do you think happens after you die?" I ask, out of the blue, surprising myself.

"I don't know. I think your body dies, but I'm sure my mother is still with me," says Even. "Always."

"Heaven?" I ask.

"Maybe."

"Angels?"

"Sure," he says, winking at me and pulling me toward him. We hug, shoulder-to-shoulder. "But that doesn't matter right now, because we are very much alive." He gets up to his feet and pulls me along behind him, whooping loudly, daring the incoming water to splash him. I chase after him and our laughter carries on in the wind.

Chapter Nine

On Sunday, Mama launches into a tirade, going on about me being gone the day before. I'm sure the whole neighborhood can hear. Mama lets me really have it when I deliver a fresh bag of chips after I return from church, where I sat quietly next to Fat Henry before my weekly trip to Od Town. I accidentally get close enough for her to grab me by the hair, and she hollers directly into my ear.

"Don't you dare ever leave me again, you hear me, you little bitch?" she says, and when she lets go, she shoves me across the room. I fall into a shelf that once housed curios and family photos, and is now a hodgepodge of junk and empty bottles, packs of cigarettes, and forgotten books. The side of my head that hit the shelf throbs and the side that didn't sears where she pulled my hair.

"I'm sorry, Mama," I mutter.

"You better be. I hear you've been running around with some boy. There ain't no one that likes you, Sugar. You're too ugly, too fat, and too stupid. I had better not find out about you going anywhere with him again. You hear?"

I heard her, but my friendship with Even is too precious to let go of. She can't even get up and out of bed; she's not taking away the one good thing in my life. She can't. I tumble out of Mama's room and into the hall. I reach into my pocket for the heart-shaped shell, running my fingers and thumb over its smooth surface.

Skunk pounds down the stairs, wearing what Granddad would have called a "shit-eating grin."

"I heard Mama let you have it," he says, laughing. "I know you've been with that Elven kid. Or whatever that twit's name is. I don't know why he's hanging around with you. Probably wants to get you knocked up so he can have an Eleven Junior. Dirty fuck."

A series of retorts rise to my lips, but I stop myself. Skunk looks at me self-satisfied as if he's won a fight; but it's one I'm not interested in having.

I retreat to my room and sew and sew and sew. I'm lost in a sea of blue cotton, a fine weave with eyelet holes that challenge me to get the stitches straight. I form a gathered front for a skirt that lets down like a mermaid's tail. The back, the best part, is open in the center in an oval, but with pointed ends, letting just a sliver of skin show. A band stretches across the belly and joins just above the seat. It's remarkable and carries me back to the afternoon by the seaside.

• • •

Even returns the Honda with new tires, including a complete tune-up, and just in time for the chilly weather, but now I prefer to walk to school. This also helps me avoid spending any extra time with Skunk, who, after facing the possibility of not graduating, starts going to school in the morning but disappears from the building about midday. Mama doesn't seem to care, or maybe she just isn't aware. He doesn't have his license, so I don't have to worry about him taking and wrecking the Honda, at least I hope not.

Even and I meet as usual. On mornings when it's frigid, he offers to pick me up on his motorcycle, but with Mama's threat in mind, I tell him that I'll just walk and he joins me. It's a few days before Halloween and jack-o'-lanterns, with mouths agape, decorate front stoops as if they're breathing frost onto the ground. When we're in front of the school, Will and Hillary approach, but Even doesn't notice them.

"Halloween plans?" Even asks me.

"Nada," I say.

"I hear there's a pumpkin festival. I've never been, but the guys at the shop say it's cool," he says casually.

"I haven't been since I was little. That might be fun," I say. "I guess we're too old to trick-or-treat." As soon as I say these words, I realize Will and Hillary are right beside me. It's like I've got a neon sign over my head that says *Fatty* with a blinking arrow pointing at my head. Usually on Halloween night, I stay in, under the guise of having to hand out candy. Instead, I eat most of it and watch movies. They can't know that, but it must be what they're thinking given their matching smirks.

"Oh, but I'm sure Sugar still eats plenty of candy," Hillary says to Even and Will. "I remember when we were in second grade; I caught her in the kitchen stuffing my Halloween candy in her mouth. She said she had to go to the bathroom, but instead she snuck into the kitchen and ate my favorites, Sour Patch Kids. I'll never forget. I was so upset." I turn as red as the imaginary neon sign.

"Yeah, well, that was a long time ago," Even says.

"Sticking up for your g—" Hillary starts to say, but Will interrupts her.

"We're having a party at my parents' lake house before they close it up for the winter," he says. "If you wanna come, *you're* welcome to—costumes optional."

"Yeah, Even, if *you* want to come we'd love for *you* to be there and Allie, too," says Hillary. "She'd like to see you."

For one dreadful moment I'm afraid he is going to say yes because he's so quiet.

"I'm actually hanging out with Sugar," he says.

I don't dare look at either of them.

"I better get in," I say. "Mr. Hammons will—" but I don't finish because the stream of students entering the school sweeps me into its midst. I don't want to get on the wrong side of Hillary or Allie or any of them. Why can't she just leave me alone? Then I think she did leave me alone when she realized she was friends with the fat girl. She seems to take issue with the fact that I'm not so obviously alone anymore. Or maybe Allie just has a crush on Even and Hillary is trying to play matchmaker.

Even and I decide to go to the pumpkin festival in costume. We opt for motorcycle-riding pirates, the scourge of the asphalt seas. I promise to come up with a couple of great costumes. Saving my homework for Sunday, I spend all of Friday night and Saturday cutting, stitching, and distressing fabric so we look like authentic pirates for later that night.

I root through some boxes in the attic and find an eye patch and an old belt that looks like it came straight off a boat in the seventeen hundreds. I'm so absorbed in the project that I don't hear Mama calling me. I hear her coughing, though, long and hard like she can't catch her breath. I race down the stairs.

"You OK, Mama?" I say. Her face is splotchy and purplish.

"What took you so long?" she demands.

"Sorry," I mutter.

She calms down, though her chest still heaves. Something rattles in her lungs, but she insists on a cigarette and that I bring her something to eat.

When I return she says, "Don't get any ideas, Sugar. You ain't goin' out this Halloween. You gonna give out candy. Just like always."

Last year, without any prospects of going anywhere, I wouldn't have protested.

"Actually, I was invited to go up to the pumpkin festival," I say. "I'm going as a pirate."

"Honey, there's no such thing as a fat pirate. You think they stuff their faces full of what? Stale bread and salt water?"

I decide not to answer. I don't know what to do. A killjoy, that's what she is. Maybe she's just jealous since she can't do anything.

"I'm sorry," I say.

"Huh?"

I realize I apologized for my mean thoughts, aloud. "Oh, uh. Nothing. I don't know why I said that."

"Airhead. Why don't you bring me a bag of candy and put on that clown wig, get ready for visitors?" she says.

I'm not sure how she knew I might have the idea to leave the confines of our troubled home; maybe Skunk, but I haven't seen him since the day before. I contemplate climbing out the window, but I'll be eighteen soon, and she can't dictate whether I go to a pumpkin festival. It's not like I'm going out to a raging party or getting drunk, which is exactly what Skunk has been up to. I bring her the candy, but not before sneaking a Tootsie Roll out of the fun mix and putting on the clown wig.

"Happy Halloween," I say with hard-won enthusiasm.

She pops a caramel in her mouth and grunts. I take this as a dismissal.

I return to my room with a frozen pizza I'd heated and an enormous bowl of fudge-ripple ice cream. I love when it melts and gets creamy. While I put the finishing touches on the costumes, I try to figure out how to get out of the house. It's not as if she can stop me, but when she discovers I've left, she'll have my head. I decide to call in reinforcements.

"Brittany," I say when she answers.

"I haven't talked to you in ages," she replies.

"No, just in Spanish and English Lit, almost every day," I say, but I suppose I haven't called or texted in a while.

"What's up?"

"What are you doing tonight?" I ask gingerly.

"There's a party. Mason and I are going," she says, referring to her boyfriend, whose crusty teeth and buggy eyes make me pretty sure he does meth. "You?"

"Mama is being a—" I want to say jerk, but instead opt for "difficult . . . and, well, I have plans. I'm wondering if you could provide me with an alibi."

"You have plans? What do you mean?"

I dive right into the out-of-character scheme I've hatched. "I forgot we have that huge project due for English, and we're partners so we have to work on it tonight," I say. "Tomorrow, you're too busy, and if we don't get it in on time we'll fail."

Brittany laughs through her nose at my far-fetched fib.

"I see. OK," she says. "What do you want me to do?"

I've never had the sense that Brittany has to lie often, but that's mostly because she doesn't have anyone to answer to, since her dad doesn't really care what she does. Although, when she does lie, she doesn't appear to experience the sweating, red cheeks, and nervous hands that plague me, and this makes her fibs less like fibs.

"Call me back in two minutes. I'm going to go to Mama's room and you'll ring," I say. "Exclaim that we just have to get this done and that I have to come over. You can't get another fail and neither can I. Just be your most convincing. 'K?" I know Mama doesn't like Brittany, but that's mostly on the principle that Mama doesn't like anybody, plus Brittany is all I've got to make this work.

Two minutes later I'm back in Mama's room with a bowl of the fudge-ripple ice cream, claiming I saved the rest for her so Skunk wouldn't eat it all.

"That's a girl," she says. "You know what your mama likes."

My phone rings in my pocket. I look at the caller ID.

"Brittany," I answer.

She launches into an Academy Award–worthy speech about how vital it is we get our English project done. I'm just close enough that Mama can hear Brittany's best stage voice.

"I'll check. Hang on." I explain to Mama about the English project, which isn't necessary, since she heard everything. She looks sleepy and distracted by the ice cream and a show that just started. She seems to buy it.

"Fine. But don't you be out late," she warns.

I zip upstairs, shove the costumes in my backpack, and dash out to the car. I drive to Birch Road and park on the street. I worry for a second that Skunk might see the Honda parked here, but he has no reason to be in this part of town. I take a deep breath and head up the wooden stairs to the second-floor apartment. Meeting up with Even, except before and after school, has yet to settle into a comfortable practice. Fiery nerves fill me each time we see each other, doubled tonight since we're going out together and because I hope he likes the costumes.

I knock.

A lined and bearded face appears behind the pane of glass in the door. Nash, Even's dad, shouts to Even and then opens the door. He turns toward the living room without saying hello. I close the door, but stand as close as possible to the exit.

Even appears and proffers an apologetic smile. "Not exactly mister personality," he whispers.

"I'm used to it," I say.

I pull the pair of costumes from my backpack, tucking mine under my arm, and then I hold his up.

"This rocks. Wow. Where did you find them?"

"I made them, actually."

"Seriously?" he asks.

I nod.

"You seemed so enthusiastic about getting dressed up, but I thought you'd head to, like, one of those pop-up Halloween shops at the mall or something," he says. "Wow. These look so real, like straight off a movie set."

I'm wearing clothes that I can put my costume over so I'll stay warm. Even excuses himself to his bedroom to change and I use the bathroom for privacy. I'm quickly dressed, and I put some makeup on so I look like I have scurvy, but don't emerge from the bathroom until I hear Even pass by with his clompy boots. I want to avoid Nash.

"You look fantastic, in a piratey kind of way," he tells me.

"Arrgggh," I reply in my best pirate voice.

We cruise to the pumpkin fest and, unlike most visitors in their SUVs and minivans, we have no problem finding a parking spot. There are hordes of people and even more pumpkins, stacked on scaffolding as high as the eye can see. They're all lit up and they look magical and spooky.

Even and I people-watch as costumed revelers parade through the town. The pumpkins are a remarkable sight. We sing the praises of our favorites; mine is a flying pig and Even's a detailed motorcycle, also a hog. He laughs at my observation of the similarities. After a time we duck into a café and order sandwiches with enormous homemade dill pickles on the side.

"Will texted, begging me to go to the party. I promised him I would, later. You know, when we've seen enough jack-o'-lanterns to last a few years. Whaddya think?" he asks.

I think a thousand flaming pumpkins crush me and set my cheeks on fire. I thought Even was on team Sugar. Not team mean girls and their boyfriends.

"If you think your mom would flip or if you don't want to go, I'll just drop you off at your car," he says.

"Yeah. I should probably get back anyway. Church in the morning and all that." I'm quiet the rest of the night. I wonder if he'll hook up with Allie.

When I get behind the wheel of the Honda, I don't want to go home. I don't want to see Mama, Skunk, or candy for that matter. I just want to be with Even. But the brutal truth is he and I, whatever we've been doing for the past couple months, has been too good to be true. He'll see Allie tonight and her slender body and big boobs. She'll giggle at all his jokes, they'll end up in some empty room together making out, and I'll be the laughingstock of Johnson Regional High School. Oh, wait, I already am.

I wind through the streets, behind the wheel of the Honda, watching as ghosts and cowgirls, princesses and Luke Skywalkers go door-to-door, asking for sweets. I take the long way back to my house.

I quickly take off my costume and rub the makeup off my face. Mama's passed out; I probably didn't have to come up with such an elaborate ruse to begin with. I feel guilty about lying.

I close my door and fall backward onto my bed, the springs groaning under my weight. I click on my phone and look at a picture I took of Even and me, dressed up, cheek-to-cheek, the glow of pumpkins illuminating us. I click to a few photos before, a very similar one taken at the beach minus the costumes, and this time the ocean provides the backdrop. There's one more, just Even, astride his bike. I bring it to my chest and drift to sleep.

Later, my cell phone, still on my chest, vibrates. The light from the phone is painfully bright. I read a text from Even: *Lame party. Home now. Had fun, matey. See you- Mon?* I smile. The time is 10:02. He couldn't have gotten to the party, made out with Allie, and already made it back to his apartment in such a short span of time.

"Can't come soon enough," I say quietly.

Chapter Ten

Halloween initiated the season of eating, leaving me feeling unusually unsettled. Although we don't own a scale—Skunk broke it weighing "moon rocks" he tried to sell on eBay—I'm sure I've lost a little more weight. Minus soda, with all the walking, along with time spent with Even, curbing my appetite, I feel lighter. However, with Thanksgiving just around the corner, followed by Christmas, New Year's, and eventually the Super Bowl, which I usually just watch for the food, I'm sure to gain it all back. I hurry to get ready for school, skirting panic, trying on three shirts before I settle on a plaid button-down with dark jeans.

I scuttle to meet Even. The morning is unseasonably warm for mid-November, but it has been ever since the freak snowstorm earlier in the month, which shut everything down for a couple days with heaps of snow and ice, and then this warmer air was ushered in from the south.

Even is not in his usual spot. I hope he's just running late. He's always waiting here for me. There is no sign of him at quarter past, and I have to hustle to get to school on time in order to avoid Mr. Hammons's wrath. The advent of the holidays seems to have him on edge, too. I missed an assignment last week, a complete mistake on my part, making me eager to get back in his favor.

Halfway through the day, there's still no sign of Even. I text during lunch. Just before I'm about to enter English Lit, my phone vibrates, and the message reads: *I'm OK. Taking a personal day.*

A personal day? I thought those were necessary for office professionals who do the thankless job of three people, have a tyrant for a boss, and a crappy home life. Well, maybe some of that does apply to Even.

After school, I hurry home and heat up the oven. I haven't baked since before Halloween. Volts of excited anticipation shoot through me as I think about vanilla versus chocolate, crispy versus chewy, and gooey versus smooth. My mouth waters as I look at recipes for sugar cookies, oatmeal raisin, magic cookie bars, and peanut butter. I decide on the classic, chocolate chip.

I mix the dry ingredients. In a separate bowl, I blend sugar and butter. I dip my finger in for a lick. I close my eyes as the gritty sugar electrifies my tongue. Then, I crack two eggs and mix some more. I follow this with vanilla, then combine the wet and dry. Lastly, I add chocolate chips—the perfect treat for someone who needs a personal day.

After they've cooled and I've eaten about a half dozen, licking the melted chocolate off my fingers, I root through a cabinet. I find a storage container with Easter eggs—the only one with a lid. I fill it with cookies.

I bring a small plate of cookies and milk to Mama.

After she extinguishes her cigarette and coughs, she takes a bite. "Next time add more salt," she barks.

They tasted fine to me, but Mama is hard to please. I slouch to the car. When I get in, I lament the fact that it was me, not her, who baked the cookies. That it is me, not her, who cleans the house; that it is me, not her, who takes care of everything, leaving no one to take care of me. Tears bite my eyes, but I wipe them away. I take a shuddering breath, hoping Even is home and doesn't mind me popping by unannounced. I could really use some Even right now.

Thankfully, Nash's truck isn't in the driveway. The motorcycle is parked in the shed with the door propped open.

"Even?" I call.

Metal clangs, like a wrench hitting something, and then I hear scuffling. Moments later, his head appears from behind the bike in the shed, but disappears quickly.

"Hey," he says, from under the motorcycle.

"Hi. I, um, brought you something," I say. I wait tentatively at the entrance to the shed, feeling something other than welcome.

"Oh, uh, thanks. Yeah, I had to get a few things fixed on this thing. Now that I've ridden it a bunch, I see where the bugs and quirks are. Anything happen today?"

The Harley still shields him and his voice strains, but I'm not sure if that's because he's concentrating, if he's in an awkward position lying down there, or if it's something else altogether.

The thing that I've always liked—no, loved—about Even is he offers his full attention. There's none of the talking over the television like with Mama or the constant self-reflection of Brittany. Never mind Skunk. Lately, I've begun to think if I never speak to him again, I'll live a full and contented life. As for everyone else, I've noticed they don't like to look at me full-on, in the eyes, or really get very close, in proximity or emotionally, for that matter. This isn't the case with Even. I get the sense he isn't afraid to see me for who I am.

"I baked some chocolate-chip cookies for your personal day. They always cheer me up. I thought maybe—" I don't finish. It's quiet outside except for the low sound of a car going by. The nearly bare trees sway faintly as their finger-like branches reach toward the gray-and-white clouds.

"Oh, I also got your homework. I hope that's OK. I mean I know you probably don't want your homework on a personal day and all, but I just thought it would be helpful . . ." I trail off, thrown by how Even is hidden behind his bike. I clear my throat and say, "Well, I guess that's all. Have a good evening." I place the container of cookies on top of a toolbox in the corner and turn to leave.

Even's legs scrape against the dirty floor of the shed as he gets to his feet. I continue on my path toward the Honda, feeling downcast until I hear my name.

"Sugar. Wait." Even stands partially shielded by a tall but scrawny hedge. Beneath the shadow cast by the brim of a baseball hat that I've never seen him wear, a bruise balloons around his eye.

Not thinking, I hurry toward him. "What happened?"

Even shakes his head. "Please don't ask." He swallows. "Would you mind sitting with me a little while? You're good company, Shoog."

We return to the shed. He takes his place behind the bike. I sit down on the back of the snowmobile in the corner. I try to think of things to say, but the sight of the bruise blew every thought out of my head like wind across desert sand.

"Nothing big at school today. There were announcements for homecoming this weekend. I'd been wondering when they'd reschedule it since the freak snowstorm we had a few weeks ago halted everything, including that. Oh yeah, Allie and Hillary, in true form, asked me, 'Where's the picnic?' apparently making fun of my choice of shirt for the day," I say, looking down at the red, brown, white, and orange pattern. "I mean, maybe if it was red-and-white checks, but—" I'd taken to letting Even know just how mean the girl who has a crush on him can be. I'd heard, only because Allie wanted me to and not from Even himself, that she'd texted him a sexy photo of herself in a bikini taken over the summer. I've seen Allie in a bikini. Any guy would be crazy not to be turned on, but her personality dampens any chance she'd have with Even, who appears to value attitude over looks. At least I hope so.

I try to catch sight of more than an elbow or a foot, but Even continues to work, remaining concealed.

"Any plans for Thanksgiving?" I ask.

He's quiet, but a movement between the spokes of the back wheel may have been a shrug. If he enjoys my company, I assume he wants me to talk, but maybe he doesn't want to respond. "I'm actually not really sure what we're doing this year. My brother, Fat Henry—or Henry now, I guess, since he lost, like, fifty pounds—is going to spend it with his girlfriend Stacy's family. Skunk hasn't been around much, though if there's an abundance of free food, I'm sure he'll make an appearance, and, as for Mama, well—" I hesitate. I didn't plan to tell Even about her now or ever, but it seems the truth wants to slide out of me. I clear my throat. It could be a slippery slope.

"Usually we go to my aunt and uncle's house," I say. "I have loads of cousins, and we all meet there for the meal. Well, before that, it would be at the house where I live now, but that was when my grandparents were still alive. But, this year. I don't know. You see, Mama, she can't move around anymore. She was real heavy to begin with, but then it just got out of hand. I think her body, her joints, or whatever holds you together, couldn't take the weight anymore. One day, she stepped wrong and hurt her knee. After surgery, instead of going to physical therapy, she took to her bed and has been there ever since. She can't move. She eats, smokes, and drinks soda, sometimes beer, but only Skunk will take it to her. She takes a lot of pills, and I have to clean up after her. It's—I dunno, it's like she's eating herself into an early grave."

There's nothing else to say after that. Even is quiet. I close my eyes. The tears I held back as I confessed it all to him fall, leaving bottle-cap-shaped splatters on the dirty floor. Strong arms wrap around me. As I slow to a sniffle, he loosens his grip before pulling away and looking at me.

"I guess I'm not the only one with secrets," he says softly.

It's almost dark, and the dim bulb above us in the shed makes his eye look ghastly. As requested, I don't ask.

"We could both use a ride," he says, with a grin this time. "I think I've fixed the problem with the running lights. Let's go." I grab my jacket out of the Honda and get on the back. I've only ridden with him twice since Halloween, but he fits the bike like a glove. I feel safe with him.

He rides out of town and opens up the throttle on a long stretch of rarely traveled road that leads to a trailhead for hikers. We reach a spot with a view out over the valley. He stops and cuts the engine. We watch as the last sliver of sunlight vanishes in a crush of orange in the distance. We're both the kind of quiet I feel at church.

We turn back toward town. The tension that Even carried in his muscles relaxes as I grip him around the shoulders. I tilt my head back. The wind breezes my hair behind me. A star emerges like a light turning on in the sky. I make a wish.

Even cruises past his house and goes farther on. I'm not sure where he's going. *Maybe dinner at the diner,* I think, as my usual mealtime has come and gone. I hope Mama is OK. Sometimes I wonder if we could hire a nurse so I wouldn't worry about her while I'm out. Then again, I can't imagine anyone tolerating her.

Even pulls into the parking lot of Johnson Regional High School and brakes in the far lot, under a bank of bright lights. The beat of the marching band practicing on the football field replaces the rumble of the engine. It's so bright that if I hadn't seen the sun set, I'd think it still shone.

Even gets off the bike, but then sits sidesaddle. Our knees touch and he takes my hands. I try not to think about his eye and the bruises, but don't know where else to look. I secretly hope whoever did this to him looks worse.

"Sugar, I'm not usually one to make suggestions about a person's life or talk ill about their family, but we've known each other for a few months now. Sometimes it feels like I've known you forever. I hope I do."

His comment settles over us like stardust.

"What I want to say, and I'm afraid this will be difficult to hear, but what I've gathered about your situation with your mama is that it isn't right. You aren't her mother. She's yours. Despite the hope that families always help each other when times are tough, what you said about an early grave, well, that tells me she's given up. And if she doesn't care about herself, she can't care too much about you. That's not to say she doesn't love you, in her way, but she needs help. Like, professional help. Nurses, doctors, probably a shrink. She's taking advantage of you and preventing you from living your life. She's imposing her problems, whatever they are, onto you. I can see, day to day, there are burdens weighing you down. Your mama needs to get healthy and she isn't going to do it with you helping her do everything."

I want to jump off the bike and run away, but the way he's sitting and the way we're balancing on over a thousand pounds of metal keep me there. And maybe the weight of the truth of what he's said has me frozen. But I don't want to hear it. I can't look at him.

"I hope I haven't offended you. If so, I didn't mean to do that."

I'm quiet, trying to order my thoughts. "It's just that Mama doesn't have anyone else. She needs me to look after her and our house. Who's going to do it if I don't? I can't just let her rot there," I say with exasperation.

"No, but then what? Are you next? Is she going to eat herself to death, and then, in your grief, you'll do the same? Is that house just going to fall in on the two of you, swallow you up? Or maybe it will be Skunk, drunk one night, out of his head? What's it going to be, Sugar?" He's practically yelling. He's gone too far.

Before I can stop them, more tears come. "No. I just don't know what else to do," I say, finally finding my voice.

Even takes a measured breath and softens. "You've just got so much potential hidden inside there, Shoog. You're seriously one of the coolest people I've ever known. I'd hate to see this one-star town, your mother and her problems, and the bullies at this shithole rob you of any of that," he says, pointing at the school.

There is so much truth in what he says that the river of tears continues and threatens to carry me away, but Even holds me fast and bears with me through the deluge. He doesn't tell me to stop crying; he lets it flow. When I'm quiet, he speaks again.

"I don't know much about your relationship with your mother, but I do know abuse when I see it."

I look at his eye, a purple-and-black blemish with his father's name written all over it.

He sighs. "As I've gotten older, it's gotten better. He knows I'll probably hit back now, but last night, he came in drunker than I've seen him since we moved here. How he drove home without being arrested again or killing himself or someone else, I have no idea. He caught me by surprise and took a swing, blaming me for taking his wife away from him." Even doesn't cry.

"He used to beat me pretty badly until he'd be reduced to a pathetic, whimpering fuck, begging for Tansy, my mom, to come back. But, Sugar, there is another kind of abuse. The kind we learn about in those dreadful but well-meaning assemblies at school: bullying. It's still violent, emotional, but I think for you, maybe—" He hesitates and takes another breath. "Well, your mom bullies you, and I don't know if she ever hit you or anything, but I think—" Again he pauses as if afraid to say the words. "I think the emotional abuse has taken the form of physical abuse with the way you"—I know what he's going to say before he says it—"eat."

My mouth tastes like stale bread. I feel nauseous. My body vibrates with shame and anger. How dare he? Anger takes flight inside me. "I didn't ask you to deconstruct my life, Even Anderson. I thought whatever we had going on here was a friendship. Friends don't say things like that to each other." Our position on the bike traps my legs. "Please help me off. I want to go home."

"No, friends are honest with each other. I'm sorry. Listen, I'll bring you—" He pauses. "I'll bring you back to your car."

"No, I'd rather walk. I want to be alone."

Slowly and carefully, he gets off the bike.

I do the same, stomping off through the empty parking lot. The bike starts. I want to look over my shoulder and glare at him, hoping I get some kind of space-age superpower and shoot laser beams out of my eyes. After I'm a dozen parking spaces away, I feel the bike's rumble on the pavement below my reluctant footfalls. It gets closer. I want him, but I also want to shout, "Just go away." I want those cookies I baked earlier and a lot of them. I want to hide under my pillow. I want to scream at the top of my lungs. I want to be held. I want to curse at Mama and I want her to hug me. Or maybe I want Even to.

Then Even is by my side, astride the Harley.

"I know you want to be alone, but please just listen to one more thing I have to say."

I look right into his eyes, not politely avoiding the evidence of abuse that he, too, wears. My brown eyes hold steady on his blue ones. The depths I see there make me realize he said all of those things because he understands. Still, the darkness inside counters, *He shouldn't have said any of it.* It's not as if I don't know; I'd just rather not endure the pain of hearing it out loud.

He opens his mouth to say something, but then closes it. I don't even care if it was an apology.

I simmer, standing there. Mama's words, about watching out for the bitches in life, ring in my ears over the echo of the bike and Even's plea, both now quiet. She said something about if I'm not careful, life will turn me bitter. But, suddenly, I realize she has it wrong, at least about me. If I don't take the risk to be myself and let someone like Even see that person, no matter how scary it might be, then I *will* turn mean and angry and stuck in a bed.

I toss my head toward the sky, quilted with stars. God and everyone else up there listens, I'm sure of that. Now it's my turn. I wonder what I did to deserve such genuine kindness in the form of Even's honesty. Worse, what did I do to deserve everything that came before Even? But it doesn't matter now because the irrepressible smile playing at the corners of my mouth tells me everything I need to know. It's gratitude. Relief. Joy. There's comfort in his understanding, even though I don't necessarily want to acknowledge the ugliness of it. Maybe someone has been conspiring to answer my prayers.

"I like it when you do that," he says, returning my growing grin. "I think I know of something that might make your smile even bigger."

Chapter Eleven

Even turns off the bike and nudges the kickstand with the toe of his boot. He gets off the motorcycle and puts his hands on either side of my arms. His eyes rest softly on mine. Time stops. "Shoog, I think it's time you learned how to ride. Become your own driver in this thing called life."

I'm floored. I thought this was my big moment for us to kiss beneath the moonlight. Or parking-lot lights, but, whatever, it's romantic enough. I so hotly anticipated this moment being my first kiss that I never in a million years thought he'd say that. He mistakes my expression of disappointment for fear but then quickly catches up.

"Don't be afraid. You can ride a regular bike, right?" he asks, not knowing that at all, but only knowing that at one point, I had a bike. I rode it, though it was short-lived, since Skunk busted it. I must look stricken.

"OK, not like riding a bike at all, but it is. I guess I'm not explaining it right. Let's see, the first thing to do would be just to sit on it and feel comfortable in the saddle. Ah, I know. Have you ever ridden a horse?"

"Even, I cannot ride your motorcycle. Firstly, it's your baby. If I broke it or something—"

"I thought we were past that? You can't break the thing. Trust me."

"What if I crash?" I ask. "What if I can't make it go? What if small animals and children have to flee for their lives because I can't stop?"

"What if you're a biker babe and this is your calling? Opportunity knocks. It's your turn to answer." He laughs lightheartedly.

"Even, I just don't think it's a good idea." I want to let him off easy, but I have no plans to ride his Harley.

"There's nothing like it. It's freedom, Shoog. You could use some of that."

"I've felt it while riding on the back."

Even shakes his head.

"Not the same way you would if you were the one with your hands on the bars, directing where you want to go, choosing where to stop." His analogy for life flows from his tongue and into my ears easily, almost like a familiar song.

"Yeah, but, what if—"

"No more what *ifs*. Let's talk about what is."

"But don't I need a license?"

"Not right here. Not for me to teach you. It's fine. Say you wanted to get your own bike, come on the road with me this summer, then, yes, you'll need a license." His face lights up as if he's made the big reveal.

"You want me to come with you this summer?" I ask.

"I can't think of anyone else I'd rather be with."

Surprise at this statement makes my knees tremble. My neck beads with sweat.

"I think getting out of this town would be the best thing for you. It eats people alive or from the inside out or fill in the blank with your favorite life-sucking expression."

I'd never thought about leaving. What about Mama? The house? Skunk? Every reason not to move a toe overwhelms me.

"Anyway. It's something to think about. But you have to start somewhere. Right?" He gestures to the seat and holds the bike steady for me.

I sit in the seat without thinking about why. I have to shut out the chaos in my head and be solely in my body. All some-odd hundreds of pounds of it. Even before it broke, I'd stopped checking the tormenting scale. But every fat cell, every hunk of cellulite jiggles. My awareness of it reminds me of my guilt as I straddle Even's bike.

"Breathe," Even says. "Don't worry. I won't let go until you're sure of yourself."

"I don't think that will happen."

I dare to look at his face; his expression is gentle, so sweetly gentle. "Put your hands here, a firm grip, but easy. No white knuckles," he says, pointing to the handlebars. "Yup, just like that. Now, one foot stays on the ground, the other right there on the—"

I instinctively put my foot up in the right place.

"Yup, that's the pedal, just like a bike, but it isn't going to get you moving. Now, deep breath. You're OK."

I am OK. I'm going to do this because *maybe*, a very quiet voice inside says, *my life depends on it*. Even continues to instruct me, step by step. Now the bike is running. My flab rumbles. I hate my flab. I hate my body. I hate this. It's too hard. *I can't do this,* says the tickertape in my head. *Shut up,* I silently shout back.

"Take a breath. You're almost there. Ah, hang on." He reaches into the compartment behind where I usually sit. "Here. Wear this. Just in case."

"Not the biggest vote of confidence," I say, squishing the helmet down over my head. Moments later, he tells me how to accelerate and brake. The helmet makes his voice sound as if I'm on Mars. I may as well be, for how strange this evening has become. Some part of me must have registered his words because I'm moving. A thrill shoots through my stomach. The wind moves briskly across my face. I make my way to the entrance to the parking lot and turn around in a wide arc. All the while, Even jogs along near me.

I let out a whoop as I come to a stop.

"You just did that," he says.

"I just did that," I repeat. "I can't believe it." I'm in awe.

"Believe it. Believe you can do it. I do." He's quiet a moment while the bike continues to rumble. "Want to try again?" he asks, nearly as excited as I am.

I nod.

We loop around the parking lot until Even says, "Let's not run out of gas. We still have to get back to my house."

When we pull into the driveway to Even's apartment, he stiffens at the sight of his father's truck.

When he's steered the bike into the shed, I pass him the container of cookies from earlier. Still filled with the power of riding the motorcycle, words spill out of my mouth without me thinking them through. "You could come to my house. It's not much. I mean, it's actually pretty nasty, but you're welcome to if you, um, don't want to go upstairs."

"Thanks, Shoog. I better head up anyway. Night." He turns, his head hanging.

I walk to my car but stand, listening intently for any shouts or sounds of struggle—as if I could do anything, but still, I wait. Nothing. The light in his room clicks on. With my own sense of heaviness, I return to my house.

Over the next few days, I sneak out of the house after I'm sure Mama has fallen asleep. I meet Even, after his shift at the garage, in the parking lot at school. He continues his riding lessons. I learn how to work all the controls and how to increase speed, shift, and come to a stop without skidding or jerking, at least not too much. Even is a patient teacher. With each mile I put beneath the tires, I imagine myself a little bit farther out of town. The image of a new life takes shape, one I never in a million lifetimes thought could exist for me.

I picture a cottage by some far-flung sea, maybe in the next galaxy. Even rumbles home after a day at work, and I sew, making custom clothing for a boutique in town. We share a hot meal. I picture us laughing and smiling. If I squint hard in my mind's eye, I can almost see myself, well, not quite so fat. But maybe that doesn't even matter.

It's Wednesday night. The next day is Thanksgiving. The block of time between now and someday is too long.

"So all you have to do is get your license," Even says, drawing me out of my thoughts.

"And a bike."

"Well, that, too. We have plenty of time. Graduation isn't until June." Even breaks into a smile, and even in the near-darkness it glows, radiating warmth and honesty. I fight against a sinking feeling of what life will be like next year, after he graduates, and I'm a senior minus an Even.

"Tomorrow?" I ask not about riding, but about his plans.

"I'm going to Will's. Just hoping my father keeps a lid on it."

"Have a good Thanksgiving," I say.

"You, too."

Mama doesn't have too many visitors, so the relatives arranged to have the holiday at our house, so she can see them—not her idea or mine. This means I'm mostly in charge of the whole shindig. My aunt will bring a few dishes and my cousin, who was once thin and beautiful, but is now fat like me after having three kids, said she'll bring the desserts. I'm worried because the house is in rough shape. In other words, it's a mess.

Skunk has wreaked havoc by night, and not having been around to pick up after him, I have a lot to do in the next fifteen or so hours. Still high from the bike ride, I brew a pot of coffee to give myself the stamina to stay awake as late as possible to clean and then wake up at dawn to start cooking. Mama took a sleeping pill, and I'm thankful I don't have to listen to her bark orders from the other room, which she did all afternoon before I left to meet Even.

I start in the kitchen with the dishes, the counters, the floors, and purposefully throw away two giant trash bags filled with junk. All the cleaning works up my appetite. I dig into a box of low-fat devil's food cookies. They're a little stale, courtesy of Od Town, but they fortify me as I move into the dining room. I know everyone will spend the most time in the living room, watching the football game, but I imagine a proper Thanksgiving with everyone gathered around the dining-room table, or at least that is what I've seen on TV and remember from when Boo was still alive. She was always one for tradition.

I fill another garbage bag with old newspapers, magazines, a broken video-game console, several long-dead houseplants, a bag of cat food—I don't remember ever having a cat—and countless other bits of trash. Skunk comes in through the front door, slams it hard, and grumbles.

Cabinet doors open and close, there's rustling, and then he plods into the living room and throws himself on the couch, his belly acting as a shelf for a ream of crackers and a mug of soda. To his side is a box of blueberry Pop-Tarts. It's two a.m. and he reeks of booze.

"What the fuck are you doing, lazy shit?" he says, his glossy eyes barely focusing on me.

"I should ask you the same thing," I answer.

He turns to the TV and mindlessly stuffs his face, then washes it down with a mouthful of neon-green Mountain Dew.

I watch him for a minute, disgusted.

"What the hell are you looking at?" he asks, slurring. Without letting me answer, he repeats, "I said, what are you looking at?" He leans to the floor and then throws his boot at my head. I duck, and it narrowly misses me, but dents the wall behind me and leaves a brown streak from the muddy sole.

"Now look at what you've done," I say.

"Now look at what you've done," he mimics.

"Don't wake Mama."

"Shut the f-u-c-k up," he says, spelling out the swear word. He returns his attention to the TV.

My next chore was going to be the living room, but I'll wait until the morning. Instead, I wipe the stain off the wall, which needed a fresh coat of paint about ten years ago. Then I bravely head to the downstairs bathroom to make it at least presentable.

I crawl into bed at three thirty and pass out.

The next morning I wake, for some warped reason, feeling cheerful about the tasks ahead. Mostly, I want this Thanksgiving to be pleasant and memorable, because this year I have something to be thankful for: Even.

Throughout the morning, as I check off items on my list, I think about what Even might be doing and hope he's steering clear of his dad. I can't help but think of my own scratches and scrapes at the hands of Mama and Skunk. It hurts inside worse than it hurts on the surface, but still, his eye looked painful.

The turkey is in the oven, the green-bean casserole is ready to go in, Mama's favorite marshmallow-and-Jell-O ambrosia is chilling, and I'm about to pour the instant mashed potatoes into the pot when Skunk enters the kitchen. He bumps into me, and the dried-potato flakes fly everywhere.

"Freakin'-a, why'd you have to do that?" I say.

"You were in the way."

"In the way of what?" I ask.

"You're in everyone's way. You's like a booger that I can't thump off."

Mama hollers at us.

"You get any beer?" Skunk asks.

I shake my head and say, "Of course not." I exit to check on Mama.

Moments later, back in the kitchen, I clean up the flaky potato mess, hoping to find another box of mashed potatoes, when the oven starts smoking.

I'm in a lather because I know everyone is going to arrive within an hour and I still haven't showered. I discover the smoke is just from some juice that dripped on the heating element in the oven. I'd been hoping to make these cute little turkeys out of cookies, peanut butter cups, and candy corn like I saw on the TV, but now I'm worried I won't have time. The shower gurgles on upstairs.

"Effin' Skunk," I say under my breath. Unwittingly, he's given me the opportunity to get everything finished, but I will have to take a cold shower since he'll have used up all the hot water.

After I'm dressed, the living room is still a mess. I consider just begging Skunk to clean it, but he puts his feet up on the coffee table and turns on the pregame show.

It's noon. Our guests should be here any second. I scrounge up some snacks to put out, but the kitchen is a disaster. I'm frazzled and not sure where to start. Instead, I check the turkey and then Mama, but still no guests.

I check my phone and see Even left me a message: *Happy T-Day. Happy. Happy. Happy.*

I detect sarcasm. An awful thought crosses my mind. I worry that Hillary will be at Will's house for the holiday and fear she might bring Allie if she finds out Even is going to be there. My spirits plummet further.

After I've cleaned the kitchen, made the turkey cookies, and gotten out mismatched dishes, there's finally a knock on the door. Aunt Sandy and Uncle Bruce come in, letting in a gusty draft, with their three kids. Cousin Amanda follows shortly after. Her kids aren't with her. She explains they're with their dad this year. Cousin Jerry arrives with his girlfriend, who doesn't speak English well. He explains she's a refugee from some country he can't pronounce properly.

Skunk doesn't say hi to anyone, just grunts. I direct everyone to visit Mama down the hall. The three kids, ranging in ages from four to nine, all have runny noses and sneeze on the green-bean casserole.

Amanda takes several trips back out to her car, returning with a total of six pies. She says, "Why have three when you can have six? I have pumpkin, apple, blueberry, pecan, banana cream, and my favorite, the cherpumple."

"The cher-what?" Despite my love of all things sweet, including pie, I haven't heard of this particular dessert.

"Oh it's delicious," Amanda says. "It's a cherry pie, a pumpkin pie, and an apple pie all baked inside cake. You'll see."

I'm not sure whether to be enticed or grossed out.

"The cherry pie is baked inside a white cake, the apple pie is baked inside a spice cake, and the pumpkin pie is baked inside a vanilla cake. You understand?" Amanda asks.

Oh, do I ever.

"Then I put them all together, spread it with chocolate frosting, and see these up on top? They're little tiny turkey sprinkles. Cute, huh?"

I swallow back a mouthful of saliva. It sounds heavenly.

"You be sure to save some room in that little belly of yours for a big ol' slice," she says cheerfully, either blind or kind to the fact that my belly isn't so little, but then, hers isn't either.

Before I know it, everyone has dug into the main meal, including Skunk, who's rude to everyone, including Jerry. But he keeps a close eye on his girlfriend, who wears a low-cut top that invites thoughts about what could possibly be holding everything up.

I bring Mama a plate, and then return to her room with my own.

"How'd you like the ambrosia, Mama?" I ask from my perch on the end of her bed. She tries to angle to get a view of the TV as she takes a bite of the yams Aunt Sandy brought.

"Hmm?"

"I'm just wondering if you like the ambrosia."

"Oh, it's OK. I would have added some of them colored marshmallows."

"They didn't have any at Food Town," I say, feeling disappointed. I want to add that the white ones and the rainbow ones taste the same.

"Sugar, fetch me the salt. I can't taste any of this," she says, letting her plate fall onto the bed. Because of the conversations I've had with Even, this stings more than usual. Then I think of how awful it must be to be stuck in bed, unable to cook for herself or do much else, and I'm sobered.

I go in the kitchen and find Skunk eating directly out of the pot of mashed potatoes, having poured the entire boat of gravy on top.

"What are you doing?" I ask.

"Shut up," he says loudly enough for everyone to hear.

"Mama loves those. And maybe someone else wants seconds," I protest.

"Maybe I did, too." He takes a swig from the can of Pabst that Uncle Bruce brought over and then spits it in my face. Beer mixed with bits of potato covers me from head to chest.

"How'd you like that?" he asks. He squirts the turkey baster at me and liquid drips down my arm.

I can't make myself move.

"Go on, now. Surely you've had enough," he says through a mouthful of food.

I have had enough of his violent and immature attempt at a food fight. But before I can step away, he throws the carving knife at me. I dodge with a yelp, hoping that his aim is off. The blade sticks into the plastered wall. This draws no one from the other room.

Shaking with anger and nerves, I bring Mama the salt. She lit up a cigarette; the smoke hangs dismally in the air.

"It's about time," she says, sprinkling it liberally on her food.

I hurry upstairs, take a quick detour to my room, and grab a bag of York Peppermint Patties I'd stashed along with an entire grocery bag full of candy after picking them up on markdown after Halloween. This time, I take a warm rinse in the shower. In the privacy behind the curtain, I wonder what Even is doing while I eat the chocolate mint wafers one after another. The chocolate comforts me. The mint cools my simmering fury.

When I get back downstairs, Amanda is eager to present her cherpumple. With great fanfare, she unveils it and begins to slice, explaining what it contains.

"Cher*plump*le is more like it," Jerry says, looking at all us women, except his slender but well-endowed girlfriend. However, he takes a sizeable piece anyway, and as we chew, for once, everyone is quiet.

Amanda and I bring Mama a piece. "Nice to see you didn't forget me," she says with a nasty edge to her voice. Next to the side of her bed are three empty cans of Pabst. Skunk must have brought them to her.

As if on cue, Uncle Bruce shouts, "Where the heck did all the beer go?"

"I brought you a special dessert platter. You see, there is—" Amanda says as she begins to list off the pies, but Mama interrupts.

"I can see what they are, Amanda, and I can see you've eaten your share. You're as big as a house. Now tell me what in God's name this is?" She points to the cherpumple.

Amanda explains with a grin on her face, hoping this will please Mama.

"Sounds weird," she says, but then eats the whole thing anyway. As she starts on the blueberry slice Amanda also brought, she nods off.

"She's been tired and cranky lately; being in bed will do that," I say to Amanda by way of excusing her behavior, though words against Mama beg to leap off my tongue.

As we exit Amanda mutters, "I never knew my cousin to have a nice bone in her body, but, yeah, it'd really stink to be stuck in bed like that."

Over the next hour, everyone filters out, without as much as a thank you, except Amanda, who is a well-meaning slice of sunshine. They've left me with a moderate mess and a drunken Skunk. He stumbles out of the house—hopefully to wherever it is he goes that isn't here.

I plop down in a chair in the dining room, where I view part of the kitchen and a good part of the living room. The remains of the cherpumple sit next to me, a deliciously rich, luxuriously layered sugar-bomb of a companion. I grab a clean plastic fork, dig in, and finish it off.

I doze and wake to hear what I think is a chainsaw, but is just the combination of Mama snoring and Skunk starting up his dirt bike. It sounds unusually close to the house.

A draft raises goose bumps on my arms. The sliding glass door is ajar. Skunk backs the dirt bike into the living room and revs it. He takes a good look at me over his shoulder and then rockets through the living room, like a runway, onto the deck, and off a ramp that he's put out there.

"Skunk, you can't use the house for jumps," I shout. But he can't hear me, and I'm pretty sure he doesn't care. I don't know what to do. This is one of his worst ideas, all the more so because he's probably still very drunk or perhaps even more drunk.

I'm in the kitchen, where it's slightly warmer, trying to think of what to do. I text Even, telling him what's happening.

He replies: *Pretty toasted myself, otherwise I'd come. Call police.*

I consider this. What if I call the police? What is the worst that could happen? He could be arrested. Though I could never press charges. I could call anonymously. Hmm . . . how does that work with caller ID? Even said he'd come, but he's toasted? Drunk? Hopefully he hasn't been making out with Allie. Why does this stuff have to happen to me?

Furniture grates across the floor. I assume Skunk's trying to get a longer start. I begin to dial the police. But he's my brother, I counter. Then I remember the knife he threw at me. I'm at once terribly worried and afraid that if I did get him in trouble, he might threaten me with worse than a poorly aimed knife. Which fear is greater? I struggle to think clearly over the revving of the bike.

I pause at the foot of the stairs, then take the rest of the ambrosia with me and go to bed.

Chapter Twelve

In the aftermath of Thanksgiving, I'm sinking in disorder. Skunk abandoned his living-room-cum-dirt-bike jump after he dumped it and sprained his wrist. Unfortunately, he claims he can't remember, though I don't believe him. Thankfully, from her bed, Mama can't see the scratches he put in the floor and the trashing he gave the living room. During the long weekend after Thanksgiving, I do my best to put things right before meeting up with Even Sunday evening.

I tell him about my Thanksgiving, leaving out the peppermint patties, cherpumple, and ambrosia. He fills me in about his far more reserved and respectable afternoon at Will's house.

"Hillary was there," Even says, rolling his eyes.

"Did she bring Allie?"

Even bristles.

"Yeah. She showed up in the evening."

"When you were toasted?" I do air quotes when I say the last word.

"I wasn't doing wheelies and blowing donuts in the living room," he says defensively.

"No, I know. I just wondered—" But I don't finish. Even seems unusually agitated.

"Nothing. She tried—never mind."

I want to know everything. I want details. This apparently also means I want to torture myself. Even and I are friends. Just friends. I turn away, not wanting him to see my rosy cheeks because I have the growing desire to be more than friends.

"Listen, let's get you on the bike and forget Thanksgiving," Even says.

"Yeah, let's."

We go to the parking lot of the school, but it's mobbed because of band rehearsal. I direct Even to the church parking lot, hoping God forgives me if our purposes are unholy.

I get my leg up and over the saddle and look up at the glowing steeple. I feel the tug on my pants as they strain against my thighs. The only thing that might have the chance of diminishing the crushing rejection I feel is something sweet. Short of that, a ride on this motorcycle will have to do. I bow my head and cross my heart. My thoughts briefly flit to my dad and the image of him astride his bike, and I can't help but wonder about God's sense of humor.

When I'm about twenty yards away from where I set off, two things collide in my mind: Even is not jogging by my side as he normally does, offering commentary and tips as I progress. More importantly, I'm cruising along, on my own, verging on the edge of freedom. I continue, not stopping to see if he's going to catch up because I might lose track of this feeling.

Oh my God, oh my God, oh my God, I think. I'm doing it. My breath comes in short bursts. I can't stop the bike. Not because I physically can't, but because I don't want to. If I stop, I won't be able to see where I can go. The growl of the engine drowns out any potential for distraction as an invisible compass moves me forward.

I loop around, but am not ready to see Even as I process what is even larger than I am. Riding the motorcycle is open-sail, bird-on-the-wing, wind-in-my-hair, full-bodied liberation. I pass the empty parking places lining the back of the church and continue out onto the road. I don't have my license yet. I take it slow. I also don't imagine one of the few cops in town will pull me over.

I hardly notice the familiar landmarks breezing by me as I whoop loudly, pumping my fist in the air. I don't blink, so as not to let this moment pass me by.

I pass by a bar near the box factory when tires skid on the gritty pavement. Reality crashes back to me. A Ford took the turn ahead much too fast and slammed into the telephone pole on the other side of the road. When I get closer, I slow and try to get a look in the cab. It's Nash's truck. I pull out my phone and try to do my best to pilot the motorcycle as I dial. I feel like I'm losing control of the bike and don't want it to be a double accident, so I steer to the side of the road. I call 911 and then take off as quickly as I dare, hoping Even is still in the parking lot.

Even leans against my car with his hands in his pockets. It doesn't escape me how relaxed, cool, and attractive he looks in the shower of the dim light, but this isn't the time to think about that.

"Even, hurry. Hop on. Your dad."

He doesn't ask any questions. I assume he understands what's happened, given his father's history.

When we get there, a cruiser blocks the road and blue light bounces around in the darkness, disorienting me.

The officer tries to hold Even back, but he explains it's his father. I maneuver the Harley to the side of the road and get off, remembering I'm not supposed to be riding it. I hope that this escapes the cop's notice.

Sirens wail in the distance. I stand off to the side, praying. Eventually Even appears out of the fray of emergency workers. He looks grim.

"Is he OK?" I ask.

Even shrugs stiffly. "He's been worse. Why people like him are allowed to drive or drink for that matter is beyond me." He speaks with a hint of disgust in his voice, but I catch a glimpse of his eyes before he gets on the bike. They're moist.

"I'm going to bring you back to your car," he says.

"I would have just called you and told you to meet me here in my car, but the keys were in my pocket. I'm sorry I took off. I just needed to clear my head," I explain. It sounds lame in light of what just happened.

"No worries. Good thing you did; he may still be laying there," Even says. With that, he guns the engine and we're off. I can tell he wants to go faster, if only to escape his thoughts, but holds back. When we get to my car, I ask him if he's going to the hospital. He nods.

"Can I come with you?" Silence, just a slight incline of his head.

I follow in the Honda.

In the glaring light of the emergency room, I smooth my windblown hair and try to be strong for Even. I think the last time I was here was when Skunk dared me to jump from the trampoline into a big pit of old couch cushions and I fractured my collarbone. Then a more recent memory replaces that one. I recall Mama, her body spilling from the stretcher after she hurt her knee. I shudder.

"You OK?" Even asks.

"I should be asking you the same question," I reply.

A nurse calls him into the triage station, and I wait. I'm nervous and itchy and low from finding Nash. I desperately crave a Snickers bar from the vending machine down the hall.

Why?

Because it tastes good.

Why else?

Because I'm hungry.

No, I'm not.

Why, really?

Because this is incredibly difficult.

Because being here reminds me of pain.

Because inside I hurt for myself, for Mama, and for Even.

Because if I have something sweet I won't feel the ache quite as sharply.

Bingo.

As plainly as if it's written on a doctor's chart in front of me, I suddenly see that when I feel bad, sad, mad—whenever I feel *anything*, I turn to food. I recount the most recent times I did this. Earlier today, I binged on some warm cinnamon buns topped with ice cream when I felt anger mixed with disgust at the enormous mess I had to clean up after Mama went to the bathroom. And yesterday morning when I went to get ready, I saw that Skunk, likely in a drunken state, must have missed the toilet completely and peed in the cabinet all over the towels: the ones that I wash, dry, fold, and put away. That time, I turned to a box of frozen waffles doused in almost an entire jug of Aunt Jemima syrup.

Each time I was upset, I fled to the kitchen in search of food. I think back over the previous days and the cherpumple. I tremble with interest, confusion, and desperation as the truth about my relationship with food surfaces.

Even reappears, shunting me back to the brightly lit hall, my hand resting on the vending machine. I pull it away as if the plexiglass window was in flames.

"He'll be OK. Broken arm. Some stitches. He'll be here overnight. Let's go."

I know Even isn't a coldhearted person, but I also know how much anger he has for his father after eighteen years of pain and resentment. I walk, unsteadily, out of the hospital. Even out of the glare of the ER, I'm still shaken by how vulnerable and fragile I am. How we're *all* so vulnerable to food, drunk driving, and life. In the parking lot, I ask Even if he's going to be all right.

"Me? Of course." He dips his head. "I'm gonna go dream about my route west. And you. I'll see you bright and early."

As I wind my way home, Even's last words pop into my mind. "I'm going to dream about my route west. And you . . ." Did he mean "And *you*?" As in, what am *I* going to do? Or as in "And me, I'll see you bright and early"? Or did he mean he's going to dream about me? I can hear his voice in my head, but can't be sure of where he placed the pause, emphasis, or the upturn of the word into a question.

By the time I am back home it all blurs together, but I can't stop thinking about him. I've never had a crush on a boy, not really. In grade school there was James McCarthy, but he drooled over a girl named Sasha and then got pimply when we hit eighth grade. I've fixated on various heartthrobs on television, and very briefly, freshman year I was interested in a kid who played trumpet in the marching band, but when I realized how fat I was, I let the idea of him go. It wasn't worth it because it would never happen. However, the thing about all of those boys is that my relationship with them lived in a fantasy in my head. I'd never spoken to any of them, and I doubt they knew I existed; certainly the TV stars didn't.

But here I am, friends with Even. We've hugged. He's said sweet and kind things to me. He listens so well, plus he's arguably the dreamiest guy at Johnson Regional High School, but doesn't know it nor has he fought for it by playing football or doing some other studly activity to gain the attention and adoration of all the girls.

Then there's Allie. She's certainly taken notice of him. What did he say about her on Thanksgiving? *Never mind.* And he was drunk. I sink into my pillow and fret. What if they—but I don't allow myself to go there. I'm Even's friend. That should be enough.

As I drift to sleep, Skunk comes into the house as loud as ever. Something thuds and then he stumps up the stairs, slower than usual. He groans at the top. When his door creaks open, it sounds like he puts down something heavy. His door closes, and then I'm asleep.

Chapter Thirteen

Finals prep has the school in a tizzy. As if anyone there, students or teachers, really cares. At the start of each year, I take bets on who's going to make it to graduation—a handful drop out, some get pregnant, and others move. What rattles everyone is the fact that we're forced to take these tests and our grades depend on the outcome.

The students at Johnson Regional are a rebellious lot. It's because there's a general disinterest in higher education, and we're New Hampshire bred and live by the motto "Live free or die." We bristle at the thought of required exams. Required anything. Also, we're all so bored with our lives that when something comes along that's different from the usual, we battle against it, just to be contrary. Instead, we could go with it and make something of ourselves.

For these reasons, I'm not surprised when someone pulls the fire alarm during second period, essentially ending school for the day.

The fire and safety department has to inspect the entire school unless someone fesses up. No one does. I shiver in the cold, and snowflakes flurry down, meeting the dead grass for the first time since the big storm back in November. I hope for snow on Christmas; it's the only gift I want. Mr. Hammons scolds some guy for hugging his sophomore girlfriend to keep her warm, so I don't make an effort to find Even, since we can't leave our homeroom cluster.

After a time, we get the OK to go into the cafeteria and gym while they examine the rest of the school. There's no sign of Even. This is worse than study hall, lunch, or even just sitting at a desk doodling while the teacher drones on about the Civil War. I take a seat at an empty table in the cafeteria, thankful I had the sense to grab my backpack as the alarm blared. I pull out a book and start to read, hoping to make practical use of this time, when girlish giggling grabs my attention. It's not the kind of laughter that belongs to a good-natured group of people joking, but the kind that tells me I might be the butt of the joke.

I exhale, forcing myself not to give whomever it is the pleasure of turning around and acknowledging them. The giggles continue. I reread the same sentence over and over as I bristle with curiosity. I don't want to give them the satisfaction.

Something hits the back of my head. It doesn't hurt, but I rub the spot anyway. I sneak a peek under the table. A paper airplane lies upside down on the floor. I step on it and slide it to where I can reach. There's no telling what it might say, if anything. Better to be safe.

Five minutes pass. I've managed to turn the page, and again, something hits the back of my head. Then another. I have three airplanes under my shoe. Amidst the laughter, someone snorts like a pig. Brandon, no doubt. I turn around, ready to give him the finger, when Hillary, Allie, Will, Alexis, and a few others sitting on or around the table behind me all go straight-faced, pretending to be occupied with their hair, nails, or whatever.

My face flushes. Couldn't Even have at least told his cousin to leave me alone? I turn around. They laugh. My eyes fill with tears, blurring the words in my book as I try to ignore their juvenile game.

Suddenly, a shadow darkens the pages in my book. Floral-scented shampoo and a straightened sheet of hair breezes by my shoulder. Allie's voice hisses in my ear, "Listen, fat-ass, I really like Even, and on Thanksgiving I got the feeling he liked me, but you are becoming a problem. It seems your neediness is taking up too much of his time. Either that or he can't get around your enormous body and flee to safety. But I'm telling you to back off. Got it?"

She's gone. I bury my head in the book, letting my own hair form a privacy partition as I cry. Tears dot the table and the crisp pages of the paperback. I try not to let myself shudder, knowing they're probably all watching me.

The principal calls for our attention and says, "It's safe to return to your classes now, everyone. Whoever pulled the alarm had better not do it again. Please walk in the halls. That's all."

It isn't much of a reprimand, but it also isn't safe to return to my class. I have Spanish this period, with Allie and Hillary. I bend over for my backpack and pick up the airplanes. Dark lines of ink bleed through the thin white paper. I open one to see a sketch of me from behind, just as I sat moments before at the cafeteria table. Whoever drew it depicted me as taking up the whole thing, fat rolls dripping down my sides, my butt crack showing, and right in the center, a curly pig's tail. Ears are drawn at the top of my head, too.

I crumple all three airplanes and toss them in the trash on my way out. Instead of going to Spanish, as I was dutifully intending, I exit and shuffle home. Never mind Even. Never mind Allie. Never mind the rest of them. I want to be alone. Well, almost.

I quietly creep into the house, hoping Mama doesn't hear me. I riffle through the kitchen cabinets and find an outdated box of

Ho Hos and some Funyuns, and I take a full two-liter bottle of Orange Crush up to my room. Never mind Skunk.

I flop on my bed and inhale the snacks. I will do anything to drown out the sound of their laughter echoing in my head, to get the smell of Allie's shampoo out of my nose and the sight of the cartoon of pig-me, burned into my mind, *out, out, out*. I let the act of eating, the surge of sugar and salt, carry me away from my body. I don't care. Never mind me.

Skunk must have left school after the fire alarm, too, if he even went. I hear him moving around the house followed by a skittering, a stream of curses, and then Mama shouting. That lifts me out of my stupor. I clod downstairs. Skunk looks at me in surprise.

"Why the hell aren't you at school?"

"I didn't feel good." It isn't entirely a lie. Also, now I actually really don't feel good. My stomach punishes me after I topped off my binge with half the soda. "Why aren't you at school?" I ask.

He ignores my question. "Keep your germy hands away from me, then."

With pleasure. "Why's Mama hollerin'?"

"She thinks she saw a mouse," Skunk says.

I furrow my brow. "She *thinks* she did or she did? Big diff."

"Whatever. She's on so many pills she probably imagined it."

I roll my eyes. Mama isn't afraid of much, in fact just one thing, rodents. I begged for a hamster when I was in second grade. Not a chance. Once a mouse got in the house, which is really no surprise, since it's in such disrepair, and she stood on a chair in the middle of the kitchen for a full four hours until Fat Henry got home and trapped it. It's a wonder the chair didn't break.

I edge into Mama's room. She is as white as a sheet.

"What's going on, Mama?"

She points across the room. She's shaking so much the large swath of flesh on the underside of her arm vibrates. She continues to point at a heap of blankets, towels, and clothing on the floor. It does look like it would make a nice nest.

"*M-m-m-mouse,*" she says, her voice echoing the shaking of her body.

"Did Skunk say he is going to trap it?"

She shakes her head no.

I let out an annoyed sound. I don't especially like mice either, but can't have her freaking out like this. It's not good for her already elevated blood pressure. I poke around the room, but don't see any sign of a mouse. I continue pulling things apart for about a half hour when something falls above me on the second floor, and then I hear more scurrying. Skunk comes thundering down the stairs. I go to see what the fuss is all about, and he dashes out the door. I go back to Mama's room. By now, she's smoked half a pack of cigarettes to calm her nerves.

"Listen, Mama, Skunk went to get some traps." This is what I'm hoping anyway. "I don't think it's in here, so I'm going to look around the rest of the house. 'K?"

Mama nods vaguely, lost in her afternoon soaps. She'll probably nap soon and forget this ordeal.

I peruse the rest of the house, but don't see a mouse anywhere. Grabbing a container of honey-roasted party nuts, I go back to my room. Aside from the nuts, all I can think about is what's in my closet: a needle, thread, and virgin fabric.

I settle on my bed, imagining what I'd like to create, when I notice a message on my cell phone from Even: *Where are you?*

I don't want to answer. The scene in the cafeteria crashes into my mind. What did Allie mean about Thanksgiving? What wasn't Even telling me or what was he telling her? Am I a needy nuisance? Is he hanging out with me out of pity? I don't want to believe it, but he *could* seamlessly blend in with the cool crowd with his good looks, charm, and the fact that he rides a motorcycle. I wonder why he does hang out with fat, worthless, and stupid me?

I pour a handful of nuts into my mouth and chew them until they're smooth like peanut butter. I clutch my phone, wondering if I should text him back what I'm thinking. Nah, if he's playing some stupid game with me and reporting to Allie, Hillary, Will, and the rest of them, I'm not going to go along with it.

Darkness comes early in December, but by then I've stitched a skirt in crepe de chine in the lightest of yellow sunshine. It's calf-length with an underlay of toning yellow to make the sequins, which I'm laying out to form a sunburst pattern starting at the hip, pop like beams of light.

My phone vibrates again with a message from Even: *I'm sorry I missed you after school. Crazy day. Is everything OK?*

"No everything isn't OK," I say aloud, poking myself with the needle. I mutter one of Boo's Polish curses, and think, *In case you haven't noticed, I'm big, fat, and ugly.* At Johnson Regional High and the Legowski-Gracia household, that is the currency for jokes, laughter, and mockery. I poke myself again and try to get a thimble on my stubby finger. That's when I see it. A white mouse dashes across the floor of my room and under my dresser. I squeak.

I'm not necessarily afraid of mice but don't like the idea of one in my room. I scurry downstairs calling for Skunk. He's not here. I root through the jumbled basement, searching for a mousetrap. I triumphantly march up the stairs with two; they are rusty, but they will do the trick.

I tear off a couple chunks of Velveeta cheese and set the first trap. Mama watches *Wheel of Fortune* and shouts at the TV. When she sees me, she hollers, "What took you so long?"

"Sorry."

I put the trap on the opposite side of her bed where she can't see it.

"Anyone winning big?" I ask, hoping to smooth things over.

"They're all so stupid. They use this one all the time. Event. Two n's in the fourth word. 'Slipped on a banana peel.' See?" She says as a letter lights up. If Mama had a purpose in life, it would have been to go on *Wheel of Fortune*. She'd make it to the bonus round and get the million-dollar wedge. We'd be rich. I watch the rest of the episode with her and get the answers moments before she says them aloud. Maybe all the years of watching it with her have paid off, but for what? She doesn't even notice when I leave the room.

Even texts me one more time: *See you in the morning? G'night.*

The next day, in a daze from staying up so late sewing, I walk to meet Even. When I see him waiting for me with a big smile, the previous day rushes back to me. I grimace, not wanting to give him the satisfaction of him thinking everything is fine.

"What's up?" he asks, concerned.

"Nothing." I stomp past him and continue toward school.

"Did something happen?" he calls, catching up to me.

I stop, whip around, and raise my voice.

"Yes, something happened. Allie happened. You tell me."

His expression is blank with a knot of concern between his eyes. I don't want to believe that he's in on some stupid bet. I don't want to believe he and Allie are seeing each other. I want to believe in the Even I know. I want to believe in us.

His smile chips at my frosty exterior. I lower my hackles. The school comes into view in the distance as we trek on.

"Listen, yesterday—" I begin, but a honking car interrupts me.

A black Toyota Corolla pulls up. Hillary's behind the wheel and Allie's in the passenger seat. Allie rolls down the window. Her jacket is open and she leans on the edge of the door, her cleavage spilling out of her shirt and into the cold.

"Hey, handsome. Remember these?" she says, laughing. "Want a ride?" she asks in a sexy voice.

"Uh. Nah. I'm good. Thanks," Even says. He looks like he just ate a lemon, whole, along with a dill pickle.

Allie looks annoyed. "Fine. Remember what I said, fat girl," she calls as Hillary pulls away.

His jaw tightens. "Eff you," Even shouts. He looks at me, anger flashing in his eyes. The chill air and his words freeze my tears. "What did she say?"

"To me? The fat girl? What didn't she say?"

"No really. I want to know. That isn't right. What a bitch," Even says, spitting mad.

"I'll tell you if you tell me what happened on Thanksgiving," I say, bargaining.

He looks confused, and then his eyes grow wide. He starts to laugh.

I fear this is the moment. The girls are going to circle back and he's going to tell me, in front of them, that our friendship was just a hoax.

"Sugar," he says, putting his arm around my shoulder, "she flashed me her boobs."

I turn my head, my mouth agape. Our faces are so close I see a few freckles, left over from summer, and the scar on his lip.

"I'm an eighteen-year-old dude. I'd be lying if I said they weren't, well you know, but—" he shakes his head. "She's just needy. She kinda makes my skin crawl and *blech*, so much perfume. She smells like a department store. I had the hunch she was a total idiot, but she just proved it. No chance. Not at all."

Every fiber of my being relaxes and heat pools in my fingers and toes again.

"Just ignore her. I mean, I'm sorry she's a douche to you, but people suck. We know that. Whether they're our relatives or jerks at school. We'll find our tribe. Someday."

As we approach the entrance to Johnson Regional High, Even takes his arm from my shoulder to open the door, then pulls me close again. I have one of those Edward and Bella moments when they parade through the parking lot, having just come out as a couple. Though I know I'm no beauty.

Nothing, and I mean nothing, bursts my bubble until I get home. Skunk's passed out on the living-room couch, greasy wrappers littering the floor and the credits of some stupid movie running on the TV screen. I go upstairs to get started on my homework, grabbing crackers, veggie dip, and a tall glass of water, determined to get back on track since I'd been eating so much junk. About halfway up, something smells foul. I wrinkle my nose, sniffing the dip. It's fine.

At the top of the stairs, Skunk's left his door wide open. This is unusual because he's kept it locked since the wallet incident. I peer in to see if he's conducting some nasty science experiment or if there's a basket of socks that need washing. I discover the source of the smell.

I drop the glass of water, and it smashes to the ground, sending liquid-covered shards of glass onto my sneakers. I scream. If Mama is afraid of rodents, it is nothing compared to my fear of snakes.

I scramble down the stairs.

"Skunk, you wake up this instant. Wake up, wake up, wake up. Now!" I scream in a panic. I rush to the kitchen and lock myself in the pantry. Then I realize it is under Skunk's room. I run to Mama's room. Groggily, she wakes up.

"Skunk. He has a snake. In his room." Mama is well aware of my intense fear of snakes. The mousetrap on the floor in the corner helps me figure out where the mice came from. He was trying to feed the thing and the mice escaped. I panic. What if the snake escapes? Skunk isn't too bright or careful.

"Mama, snakes eat mice. That's why there have been mice in the house."

She looks at me from behind a puff of smoke. I don't know if she heard me or maybe she doesn't care.

"Skunkkkkk," she yells in the way that only Mama can.

Moments later, he's in the doorway, standing at attention.

"What?"

"Come here, boy. Sugar here tells me you done got a snake up in your room."

He takes a step in, and I dash out the door. She has fire in her eyes. If she had a Taser, which I wouldn't doubt, she'd use it. I run up the stairs and hover in the doorway of Skunk's room. I take aim with my cell phone and snap a photo of the scaly, writhing thing. Its body coils in the filthy tank. I barrel back down the stairs and into Mama's room.

"Look, see?" I show Mama the photo amidst Skunk's hemming and hawing.

Mama lets out a noise between a hiss and a growl. "You get that rat-eating thing out of this house now."

I'd like to think Mama understands my fear of snakes and urges Skunk to get rid of it for my benefit, but I know her well enough to be sure that it's the mice that terrify her, probably because there's no chair for her to stand on anymore.

"What do you want me to do with it? I can't just let it go."

"I don't care. Send it back where it came from," she says with venom.

"I can't. It's just a python. Look, it ain't gonna get bigger than five feet."

Mama gives him a look. "And just how many mice does a five-foot python eat?" she spits at him.

"I got it from some kid to give to my girlfriend, but she didn't want it. Her name's Petunia."

At this, Mama bursts into hysterics followed by the tickle of a cough.

I stifle my laughter.

"Who is Petunia, the snake or your girlfriend?" She lets out a loud whoop of a laugh, but stops herself before she has a coughing fit. "You? You have a girlfriend. I'll never cease to be amazed. What kind of floozy did you get to take up with you?"

"Well, actually we broke up. But—" Skunk starts to say, but Mama cuts him off.

"Is that where you've been? Is that why you've been missing school? I got a call, you know. I told them, no, not my son. I've got good kids. Raised 'em up right. They're good students, and they go to school. No truancy in this house. Now you done make me look like a liar." Mama starts to cough, and the fit doesn't stop for what seems like minutes.

When she catches her breath, she says, "Skunk, I may be stuck in this bed, but if I find out that thing is still here in the morning, I will hang you out. You understand? That's a promise."

The three of us—Fat Henry, Skunk, and I—have seen the inside of Mama's hand enough times to know she means business. Finally, I'm relieved.

Chapter Fourteen

Christmas lights and slush decorate town. I still hold on to hope for a fresh white blanket of snow on Christmas morning. Like Thanksgiving, I'm not sure what this year will bring. Maybe everyone will come back to our house, but I doubt it. We weren't the most gracious of hosts.

Skunk got rid of the snake, but holds me responsible and is nastier than ever. I meet Even after school the day before the last day leading up to Christmas break.

"Plans?" he asks.

"Nothing. You?"

"Same. My dad's arm is still healing, and he's zonked out on pills. I think he's smoking pot, too. Kill the pain, y'know?"

"It's just his arm. I've broken my arm. It's bad, but not like—I mean—" I'm suddenly afraid I'm saying the wrong thing, but then I realize Even's probably talking about another kind of pain. Grief, nearly two decades' worth, that he and his father have suffered in their own ways.

I'm quiet as we walk through the streets before we each go to our houses. The backs of my pants are damp almost up to my calf.

However, this pair is getting looser, evidence that sticking with walking, staying away from soda, and eating a little more sensibly is helping. The day after next, I'm going to Keene to pick up a couple of Christmas gifts, including one for myself, a new scale. Then I have an idea.

"Want to go to Keene and go Christmas shopping with me?" I ask.

"I'd love to, but I can't. I have a couple extra shifts at the shop; guys with families requested them off, and I snapped them up. Still gotta save for the trip. Not long now. Just slog through this winter, then spring, and graduation. That reminds me, when is your eighteenth? We've got to get your motorcycle license."

Even knows I repeated first grade, making me the oldest and fattest girl in eleventh, but somehow, we've never discussed birthdays. Skunk repeated two grades, so I don't feel bad about it. As for Fat Henry, he breezed through, but caused a fair number of gray hairs on the teachers' heads.

"New Year's Day," I say. "The big one-eight."

"No way, New Year's Day? That has to be good luck or something. Cool. We'll have to celebrate. Hmm . . . I already have a Christmas present in mind for you, but now your birthday, too. The pressure is on." He smiles like this is a good thing, and I reward him with one of my own. His grows bigger, he winks, and then he heads down Birch Road.

When I get home, I text Brittany and ask her if she wants to come Christmas shopping with me. I suppose we've both been preoccupied with boys this year, so we haven't spent as much time together as we used to, but it's as if she and Mason are glued together at the hip. I've noticed she's been absent from school a bit the last few weeks but haven't thought much of it. She texts back a few lazy minutes later, and we make plans for the next day.

I crack open my history book to study for my final the following day, my last one. I drift off to sleep and Allie, with snakes for hair, curses me while Brittany runs around me in circles. She becomes a wisp of a blur. Then there's Even, trapped on a mountain, presumably cast there by evil Allie/Medusa. I call for him, he calls back, and I wake up in a sweat, gasping for breath.

At the end of the next day, my brain is fried from exams and too little sleep. A long break from school is welcome, but when I get home, Skunk quickly reminds me why spending the day at Johnson Regional High School is preferable to spending it at our house.

When I open the door, a rank smell, along with a haze of smoke, makes my eyes water. I go in the kitchen and find a perfectly round, burnt piece of meat in a skillet on the stove.

"Skunk?"

I turn off the burner and turn on the vent fan, but it groans, sputters, and refuses to whir.

"Skunk!" I call again.

I go into Mama's room, but she's asleep. The fact that she slept through the alarm and smoke worries me. I go up to Skunk's room, but find the bathroom door is shut. I rap on it, and he tells me where to go.

"What the heck are you burning downstairs?"

A mean laugh echoes through the wood.

"What do you think?"

I actually have no idea, but it smells gross. The door to the bathroom opens. A rivaling disgusting smell wafts out as he exits.

"We're having snake meat. Grilled Petunia for Christmas dinner." He laughs in a sinister way that doesn't convince me he didn't actually kill the thing. I don't like snakes, but I didn't want it dead, especially not to eat. I'm disgusted. I won't be spending Christmas here if that's the case.

I go to the kitchen to clean up and get myself a snack. There is no sign of a dead snake in the fridge or freezer, but it could be in the deep freezer down cellar. I know Skunk is an a-hole, but I don't think of him as that cruel, so I sneak down there for a look. As I'm in charge of acquiring most of the food, I'm well-acquainted with what we have, and there aren't any suspicious meats wrapped up. I hope to the good Lord that he isn't stupid enough to keep it in his room. Dead or alive, I don't want a snake in this house.

When I get back upstairs, I watch through the window as Fat Henry gets out of his car. He comes up the walk. I open the door before he does. He greets me with a smile from ear to ear.

"Looks like you've lost some weight. You haven't been taking those pills you got for Mama, have you? I saw an exposé. Those things are dangerous. I told Mama, but she don't listen to me. She isn't taking them, is she?"

"Nah. I don't think so. I make sure she takes all her pills before I go to school in the morning, and she hasn't asked for them since about a week after I got them. She said they made her gassy." I notice he doesn't have his usual box of donuts.

"I came by to say hi and see what y'all are doing for Christmas. I'm going to Stacy's grandma's. She's ninety, so this may be the last one. Y'know?"

I deflate. After the last few times I saw him, mostly at church, I'd hoped he'd be joining us, since he's maybe the only tolerable person in my family—a new honor. I shrug my shoulders.

"No plans that I know of. Church, of course. I'm just hoping for snow. Maybe watch a movie."

"You always have loved snow on Christmas. Remember that year we all got sleds? That was fun, huh?"

"Until I broke my arm. Remember Skunk ran me over trying to get ahead of me on the jump?"

"Oh yeah. Sorry. I forgot."

"Everyone usually does," I mutter.

"Speaking of Skunk, where is he?"

I fill him in on the latest of Skunk's escapades, including the questionable burnt meat.

"He's probably upstairs. You should interrogate him," I joke.

Fat Henry, who really can't be called "fat" anymore—I guess I just call him that out of habit—pokes at the questionable contents in the skillet.

"Don't you worry; that's just bologna. He let it burn. I reckon he was playing a joke on you. Or he just forgot about it. I'm going to see Mama. How's her cough?"

"Bad, but the same. I really think she should go to the doctor, but I don't know how to get her there. It's too bad they don't do house calls like they did in the olden days."

Fat Henry inclines his head toward me and speaks in a hush. "Sugar, you're doing well in school, and it looks like you've been taking better care of yourself. Don't you worry about Mama. I'll make sure to come by twice a week from now on. You just be a teenager. When I was your age, I was out causing trouble, but I was having fun."

It's easy for him to say, harder for me to do. Nonetheless, I'm impressed by how nice he's become. I make a mental note to thank Stacy next time I see her, knowing it's probably all due to her influence. He gives me a hug, possibly for the first time ever, and then vanishes down the dim hallway.

I go to pick Brittany up the next day, and since she's not waiting outside as I'd hoped, I pull open the flimsy screen door and knock on the regular one. I rub my hands together, shivering. Two days until Christmas. Snow, snow, snow. Please. I bounce on my toes and cross my fingers.

A few moments later, Brittany shouts, "Hang on. I'm coming." Her smeared lipstick tells me she and Mason were making out. "I'll be back in a while," she calls to no one I can see. "He's back there. Anyway, let's go," she says to me. She's wearing her oversize, don't-mind-me-I'm-just-shoplifting hoodie.

I'd noticed Brittany's badly broken-out skin last time I saw her, but it looks like she's done something to clear it up a little and she seems to have gained back a few scant pounds. In public, I often feel like the disparity in our sizes calls attention to us. I'm tall and big, she's short and tiny, but it is good to see her again. I guess.

"How are things with Mason?" I ask.

"Oh, you know, he's wicked good in bed. He can't get enough of me. We do it, like, three or four times a day. Since he dropped out of school he gets bored all day, watches porn while I'm at classes, and then can't keep his hands off me."

"TMI. I thought you said he has a job."

"Oh, he does. But still, without having to go to school, there's, like, so much time in the day. Seriously. Sometimes we'll be up for like two in a row, and there's, like, so much time, y'know? Mase and I are like together twenty-four/seven. Sometimes he starts to get annoying, but he knows how to keep me happy, so it's no big deal."

After she tells me this, I'm sure they're both on meth, and that accounts for the staying up, missing school, bad skin, and everything else. A couple years ago, a group came to Johnson Regional and held an assembly on methamphetamine awareness. I think it had the opposite of the intended effect and drove half the student body to try the stuff, Mason being one of them.

"So, are you still hanging around with that Even kid?" Brittany asks. I don't like how she says his name. I'd wanted to tell her about the motorcycle and the trip, but I decide to keep it to myself.

We pull into the Walmart parking lot. "Yeah. We still hang out. So, who are you shopping for?" I ask to change the subject.

"Hmmm. Daddy. He's been really cool about me seeing Mase. He don't care whether I stay at our house or his. So I want to get him something nice. And Mase, of course. Oh, and my cousin and her daughter. Her boyfriend just left her, and so we was thinking she might come to stay with us, so I should get them something."

We walk into the brightly lit store. I'm hoping for Christmas carols or something similarly festive, but clanging shopping carts jostle me as people fight for the last few. I don't have much to get, so I bypass them and grab a basket.

Brittany and I cruise through the store, stopping in the electronics section. I get Skunk a video game. Mama is going to be hard, but I find Fat Henry and Stacy a cinnamon-scented candle. At the last moment, I decide not to get myself a new scale. I don't care that Brittany sees me waffling in the aisle. Before, this would be the kind of thing I'd want to keep from her, but knowing that I've already lost a few pounds has given me confidence. I decide I don't need to know the number, and leave the box on the shelf. Maybe I've stopped caring about what she thinks about me because clearly she's lost track of what she thinks of herself.

A gift for Even stumps me.

As we circle back toward the registers, Brittany says, "Hang on; I've got to see about something." She ducks down an aisle in the health-and-beauty department. I mindlessly follow. I see a funny little humidifier in the shape of a UFO and think that might help Mama with her cough. I saw something about it on Dr. Oz. Suddenly, I know just what to get Even. I'm about to tell Brittany that I'm going back to the photo department when I find her around the corner looking at pregnancy tests.

"Are you—?"

She looks at me with her eyebrows raised.

"Four or five times a day, it's bound to happen," she says lazily.

"But don't you use—"

"Protection? Nah. Who needs that? I'm on the pill. Well, when I remember."

For a long time, I've been fixed with the baseline idea that I'm not that smart. Heck, Mama's told me that I'm as dumb as a box of rocks since I could remember, but now I realize that I don't win the prize for stupidity. Brittany does.

"But having a baby is—"

"I know. But listen, Mase and I love each other. He's the one. He's got a job, makes good money. We'll be fine. Come on, you'll be Auntie Sugar. Doesn't that have a nice ring to it?"

While she consults rectangular boxes that will likely forecast an uncertain future, I go to the photo department. I try not to think about how she's probably not going to pay for her items.

I'm quiet for the rest of the evening. Brittany claims she isn't hungry even after I offer to buy her Burger King since she and I decided not to exchange gifts this year. I can't even tempt her with fries, her favorite. I don't argue that if she's pregnant she ought to lay off the drugs, with the hope that she's mistaken and there won't be a Mason Junior in her future.

When I get home, I pull Even's gift out of the paper envelope. I look at a photo collage of him and me, at the beach, on Halloween, and a couple others I'd taken with my phone. In the most recent one, my face looks slimmer and my eyes brighter. Maybe he's right, I do have a nice smile. As if on cue, my phone vibrates with a text. It's from him: *Hey. The roads have been a bit rough for riding, but I'm hoping after Christmas you'll come somewhere with me. I have a present for you, but it will have to wait. Can you get away?*

I am tickled with hope and excitement. I simply reply: *Yes.*

In my mind, I shout, *yes, yes, yes!* His text is vague and he doesn't elaborate, but excitement about whatever it is pulls at me.

Christmas is more disappointing than I expected. After Mass, I help package some gifts for soldiers overseas and then go home. Skunk is drunk by noon, apparently still grieving over Petunia. He throws three empty beer bottles at me and thankfully misses each time, the last one just grazing my arm as I flee into the kitchen. I wonder where he's getting the stuff. Though I know from around school there are a few out-of-the-way liquor stores that sell to kids under twenty-one, plus there are the guys that still party with the high schoolers.

Mama hates the humidifier and tells me to take it back. I'm hoping Fat Henry and Stacy surprise us, but he calls in the afternoon to wish us a merry Christmas.

I heat a TV dinner for myself and bring one to Mama.

"Merry Christmas," I say cheerfully.

"Yeah," she says, not taking her eyes off the TV.

I leave the room with quiet tears blurring my vision.

Skunk leaves, presumably to beg his girlfriend to take him back, and I plop on the couch watching *A Miracle on 34th Street*, eating popcorn, and hoping for one of my own.

Chapter Fifteen

Even won't tell me what my Christmas present is. He just sends me a text instructing me to dress warmly. Like, extremely warm, but also to bring a bathing suit. This doesn't make sense, but whatever. I haven't worn a bathing suit in nearly two years, but having lost some weight, I'm happy to see it fits me, barely. It's saggy in all the wrong places, but the truth is, Even will be hard-pressed to get me into it and then into the water at this time of year.

In the afternoon, I drive through the newly snowy streets to his house. I'm relieved to see his father is out. Even doesn't mention Nash at all while he puts some things in his backpack and then juggles some apples before tossing them, along with a thermos, into his backpack. I laugh.

"One of my hidden talents," he says with a wink. He's wearing a knit hat and looks adorable.

"Oh, I almost forgot," I say. I pull the photo collage out of my bag and pass it to him. "I had it printed on smaller paper so you could take it with you, when you go cross-country."

"When *we* go cross-country," he says, correcting me.

I'm nervous to take the motorcycle-license test. There's a class, but I have to get parental permission since I'm still under eighteen. I have a feeling Mama won't go for it given the fact that it would likely remind her of her ex-husband, my father, and his penchant for motorcycles. Even reasons that, with his instruction, I'll be better off waiting until I'm eighteen and just straight-up taking the test, so the countdown is on; it's just under a week until my birthday when I'm eligible, but a three-thousand-mile trip on a bike sounds impossible.

"I love it. Thank you," he says. He pulls me into a one-armed hug as he looks at each of the photos carefully. He rests his head against mine. "And here I just thought you took these for your Facebook page."

"I don't have a Facebook page. I closed my account last year after—well, never mind." I don't want to tell him about how a bunch of kids, who still haven't owned up to it, hacked my account and posted photos of pigs dressed in costume with my name underneath and the words "Sugar, World Champion Porker." They were totally Photoshopped, but still, it was ugly. It hurt. Then the paper airplanes on the day we had the fire drill sail into my mind. It was probably one of Hillary's crew or Brandon. Even stashes the collage in his room. When he comes back, he has a set of keys and twists them around his finger.

"So, what's your plan? You're being so mysterious," I say, nearly flirting.

He winks, his blue eyes sparkling crystalline like the fresh blanket of snow outside.

"Wouldn't you like to know?"

We tromp down the stairs and through the deep snow. When he pulls out the snowmobile, I realize it's a good thing that it snowed for the last twenty-four hours, in one giant storm. I guess I got my wish, just a bit late.

"Surprise!" he says, flashing another winning smile. Even hands me a helmet and says, "Get on and hold on tight."

At different times, out riding on the Harley, I thought he went fast, but I suppose that, without police enforcing speed limits, there's no risk of a ticket on a snowmobile. Whizzing across the snowy trails, nearly at ground level, is a lot different than speeding across asphalt. I feel closer to the earth, the world, and Even.

We go over a couple of jumps and Even whoops. I haven't seen him this happy since we went to the ocean, though that was a trip tinged with melancholy because that's when he told me about losing his mom and having to move away from the place he called home.

He slows when we go by some houses. I have no idea where we are. After about twenty minutes of winding along a trail buffeted by trees, I see an opening up ahead. An icy white lake spreads before us. Even lets off the gas, and we stop.

"Fun?" he asks.

I nod, my helmet bobbing up and down. I've bundled up in gloves, a ski jacket, and Skunk's snowmobile bibs, which are enormous but do their job of keeping me warm. After I take off the helmet, I put on a hat.

"You look cute with that pom-pom on top of your head. Come on," he says, bonking it and then taking my hand.

Even leads me down to the lake.

I slide onto the ice in my boots. For a moment I'm afraid I'll crack it, but then seeing all the people skating makes me realize I've believed that all the jokes, crude comments, and offhand remarks about my size are true.

It's slippery, and I've never skated, but wearing boots and not blades makes it surprisingly easy. We glide around the wooded perimeter, passing summer lake houses nearly hidden behind drifts of snow. On the side opposite where we parked the snowmobile, a crowd of unfamiliar faces gathers around a fire on the bank, warming their hands. Kids toast marshmallows and chase each other with snowballs. Around these hooded and winter-wear-clad strangers, I don't feel quite so awkward and self-conscious. We all look like colorful polar bears with all this clothing on. Even pulls the thermos out of his bag and offers me cocoa.

"I made it myself."

I smile. Not even Mama has ever made me cocoa. The best she used to do was tell me to heat up chocolate milk in the microwave. I savor a long sip of the steaming chocolate then pass it to Even. We warm ourselves around the fire before boot-skating back to the snowmobile.

"So how'd you find this place?" I ask.

"The Internet. Google. And the cocoa recipe."

"You're a modern man," I say, laughing. "And thoughtful. This is fun."

"Isn't it, though? There's nearly nothing I love more than being outside. I suppose that's why I like motorcycles, snowmobiles, and camping. I told myself I'm going to try surfing when we get out west. Funny how I never tried it when I lived by the ocean."

I realize that with Even's influence I like being outside, too. I never thought of it much, but since that first walk we took in the woods, we've spent most of our time outdoors. Before that, I spent ninety-nine percent of my time inside.

"Next stop. Hop aboard," Even says.

We take off, through glades and enchanting glens with snow-frosted bows of hemlocks and other evergreens. For the moment of a breath, I realize I'd rather be out here enjoying this than eating frosting, fudge, or any other sweets for that matter.

The faraway winter sun nudges toward the tops of the trees, and its last rays make the snow glimmer like jewels. I feel wealthy, rich with friendship and freedom. As the sun disappears behind the trees, Even puts on the headlights as we meet up with a well-worn trail. A while later we arrive at a log-cabin-style lodge. Even parks among a dozen other snowmobiles. From outside, the light through the windows looks warm and inviting.

"May I ask what you would have done if it hadn't snowed?"

Even smiles. "You asked for snow. I didn't doubt that it would fall. But we would have come on foot."

I give him an "Oh really?" look because we seem a million miles away from town.

We go up the stairs and into a warm room.

"Anderson, two for dinner," Even says properly, even though the hunting-cabin-style lodge and everyone in their snow gear doesn't suggest formality.

"Right this way," answers a woman with a brown ponytail, mukluks, and a hand-knit sweater. She brings us to a table set for two by the large stone fireplace.

Even excuses himself to the men's room. I suddenly fear he and Allie are going to jump out with a camera, make pig noises, and laugh their butts off.

Hot tea arrives at the table while I read the menu. Even returns. I crack a smile, relieved that the only laughter comes from a couple of burly woodsmen by the bar.

"So, you might have to order for me. If it isn't packaged in plastic or a box, I'm not familiar with it," I say self-deprecatingly.

"This is a hunting lodge that they convert to a restaurant for snowies on the weekend. I work with the owner's brother. They catch all the game they serve here. He said they also grow the vegetables in their home gardens and then put them up in the summer. Cool, huh?" Even explains.

Grandma Boo had a garden, but now it's nothing more than overgrown weeds tangled up with an odd bucket, a broken resin chair, and some other junk.

The waitress comes over and introduces herself as Wayne's niece. I learn he's the guy Even works with at Vin's. They chat for a minute, and she makes some friendly recommendations from the menu.

Before he places our order, I tell Even I want nothing reptilian, which leads into the story about the snake. In no time, Even and I are warm, laughing, and munching on complimentary fresh-baked dinner rolls while we wait for our entrées.

After we eat what I can only call a proper meal of vegetables, potatoes, and some gamey meat I nudge aside, Even settles back in his chair, clasps his hands behind his head, and stretches his long legs. He looks like time is waiting for him; there's no rush, no urgency. He looks content and sleepy.

"Delicious. I could go for a nap," he says as the warm glow of the fire lights up his eyes and they twinkle. "I'm not big on actual gifts; you know, the kind you wrap. I never know what to get. I suppose that's another by-product of being my father's son. I used to get him little things at the school Christmas bazaar and he would nod, mutter a thanks, and toss it aside. After that, I told myself that if I ever had someone worthy of a gift from me, it would be a time to remember. An experience."

I say the only thing that comes to mind. "You, Even Anderson, are an experience."

His lips turn up. "So far so good?" he asks.

"Better than good."

Even pays and leaves the tip. We get up from our table, and Wayne's niece directs us down a wood-paneled hall toward the bathrooms. "Follow me," she says.

We arrive at a door with a flowing fountain burned into the wood. Even opens it. Inside, there's a queen-size bed with a purple-and-yellow quilt. Hunting paraphernalia and framed needlepoint decorate the walls. An accordion privacy screen stands in the corner. Across the room are French doors that open to a deck with a bubbling hot tub.

"I figured we needed to get out of our lives for, oh, fifteen hours or so. I'd go for twenty-four, but I know your Mama needs your help. I hope she can spare you until morning."

I want to cry. I'm terrified and so deeply touched at the same time. I haven't slept away from my house since I used to have sleepovers with Hillary. What if Mama gets mad or worried if I don't come home? Or what about Skunk? What if—but my inner doubts are frozen when Even tugs off his sweater and starts to unbutton his shirt. I've only imagined what's underneath his clothes. He is my very own version of a Greek god—muscular and bronzed. I swoon at the thought, but I must look alarmed. He's just in his T-shirt and jeans, reminding me of when we met.

"Bathing suit?" he asks before ducking behind the screen to finish changing.

Oh good Lord. What am I going to do? I turn to the bathroom.

Inside is a Jacuzzi encased in wood, the walls are wood, and I am deeply in the woods. No one but Even knows me here. I tell myself he wouldn't have brought me on this secluded getaway if he didn't like me, maybe not like a girlfriend, although that lone, queen-size bed sitting expectantly in the center of the room tells me otherwise.

I take off my sweater and then my shirt and am down to my bra. *Oh, Sugar, you fat, miserable piece of*—I stop the script in my head, the one that has played for as many years as I can recall. I think of the broken mirror in the bathroom back home.

I straighten up a little taller and put my shoulders back. I lift my chin. I whisper, "You are not fat and miserable. You are a good person and—" but the tears threatening to gush from my eyes stop. I hear Even on the other side of the door.

"You almost ready? Meet me outside."

"Be there in a minute," I say, hoping my voice doesn't sound like I'm crying. This is my chance. This is like an answer to my prayers, to be normal for just one night. To do something a normal girl would do with a boy. I mean, he's not just any boy. But when I look at myself I see a girl who isn't worthy of any of that. My shoulders slump. A draft from beneath the bathroom door cools my feet. I assume he went outside. I've never been in a hot tub. A thousand conflicting thoughts play in my mind while I mechanically tell myself how to put on the bathing suit: first a foot, then a leg, now the other, arms through the straps. If I don't instruct myself, I'm afraid I'll stay in here forever and ruin the night.

Then I open the door, with the bath towel wrapped around the front of me because it won't make it all the way around the back. Now it's one foot in front of the other, robot-like. I pad across the wood floor to the door. The bubbling water of the hot tub reaches Even's shoulders.

"There are steps right over there," he calls, lifting a steamy arm and pointing. The cold shock of the air semi-distracts me from being nearly naked and about to show my bathing-suit-clad body to a boy. I ascend the steps and then very carefully lower myself in as I remove the towel. It's painless. The warm and fizzy water envelops me. Actually, it's divine. I sink in up to my neck.

Even wears an enormous grin.

"Great, huh?"

I don't answer, just smile with my head tilted back. The stars above blink, and for once, I don't need to make a wish.

We lounge in the hot tub, chatting about this and that. I tell him about Brittany and my suspicions about Mason. I talk about Fat Henry and Stacy and how I think he let go of his second job at Dunkin' Donuts because he's saved enough for a ring and how I think he might possibly propose on New Year's Eve. When I feel like I've run out of things to say, Even matches my silence for a moment.

"You've told me about some of the other people in your life; now how about you tell me about you?"

"What's there to say?"

He gives me a look. "You're nearly halfway through junior year. Plans after you graduate next year? What do you do all the hours when we're not together? I know you sew; tell me about that. Or about what your dreams are or what book you're reading or I don't know. I just want to hear about you."

I let myself sink completely under the bubbles. I've never been sure if you can cry underwater, but I just learned it is possible. Even's words cut right through the fascia that holds together my battered self-confidence to the little girl who has yearned for someone to show an interest in her. She is the same girl who wanted her mama to hang her paintings on the fridge, no matter that they were scribbles. And the girl who wanted a daddy to dust off her knees when she fell down, and then help her back up. She's the same girl who, because of the absence of care, concern, and kindness, put on a shield made of donuts, cookies, and cakes to hide from the pain of dismissal, of being told that she is less than valuable and that she's utterly unlovable.

I rise to the surface.

Even guesses at the roller-coaster of emotions I'm riding. He grapples in the water for my hand and grazes my boob. I let out a giggle through a hiccup.

"Sugar, I see a beautiful, creative, and intelligent girl. Yes, I see what you look like on the outside, and it isn't what little girls growing up see in magazines or movies or what girls like Hillary and Allie look like either, but if we all looked just alike or worse, acted alike, this world would be a boring place. You've got curves. But all of you makes you who you are, and I like that girl. In fact, you're my favorite person in the world. You have confidence in there, but sometimes I think you just misplace it."

He gives my hand a squeeze that lasts and lasts. I hope he'll never let go.

An owl hoots in the surrounding darkness, and I think I might have feathers too, for how light I feel right now. "Thanks, Ev," I say and mean it.

After this, we talk for hours, lounging in the hot tub until we're both pink-cheeked and our fingers shrivel into raisins. I discreetly arrange it so he gets out of the hot tub first, and then, trying my best to wrap the towel at least in front of me, I follow him back inside. I rinse off in the shower and then, after putting on my clothes, sit on the end of the bed. Even takes a turn in the bathroom and then comes out.

"Well, you can't sleep there," Even says, pointing to the end of the bed. "I hope this isn't weird or anything," he says as he pulls the covers back.

I climb in on one side. He's wearing boxers and a T-shirt. I want to freeze-frame this moment to imprint the details forever in my mind. The way his hair hangs when still damp, the little grin he's worn all night, the way the bone in his right wrist juts out, how he's already filled out, not overly muscular, but strong. He pads to the light switch and turns it off. I shimmy out of my jeans in the darkness and feel the bed shift when he gets in. His arm wraps around me and our bare legs touch.

"Good night, Sugar. Sweet dreams." He kisses my cheek and then nestles close, his face buried in my hair.

A wave of something like electric, molten lava surges through me from the place where his lips touched, through my chest, and to the spot below my belly button. He settles, and, in a short time, his breathing becomes deep.

I've never been more comfortable in my life, but something eats at me. It isn't that I missed my usual midnight snack or the utter strangeness of sharing a bed with a boy. No, it's what he said while we were in the hot tub. Everything he said was right, except he was wrong about one thing. It was about what I look like; in other words, my fat does not make me who I am. This layer of extra flesh hides the real me, even from myself. It conceals emotion and truth. I take this with me as I drift away on a bed of water, out into my memory of the ocean on that blustery day in October, and then I am asleep.

Chapter Sixteen

When I wake up, Even sits in a leather chair across the room, gazing out the window. The sun washes him in pale light. He's so stationary, for a moment, I'm not convinced he's real. Then he takes a sip of coffee from a white mug, and our night rushes back to me like a pinch on the arm.

"Morning, sleepyhead."

I look at the digital clock on the bedside table. It is 7:22.

"I wanted to wake you for the sunrise, but you looked so peaceful."

"Sorry I missed it."

"At my old house on the coast, the sun would stream in through my bedroom window every morning. Bright and promising. I've never missed it coming up since."

I slide to the edge of the bed and, using the covers to conceal my legs, slide into my jeans.

After we're washed and are ready to go, we help ourselves to breakfast in the dining room where we ate dinner. Even fills his plate with eggs and toast. I follow suit, adding a couple slices of melon.

I hang on to each breath as we sit at the table by the fire, the same one as last night. I don't want to let this feeling, freedom, companionship, and nourishment, of a sort I never knew existed, slip away. We chat idly, exchanging smiles, and after some more coffee, we're back outside and breezing down the trail on the snowmobile. Even takes a different route back because we don't go by the lake but stay on a well-packed trail until we reach a crossroads where I recognize a farm on the edge of town. The magical fantasy of the night shrinks away as slush and familiar buildings take shape in the surroundings. We continue until we reach Even's apartment.

We're both quiet as we anticipate returning to lives we don't want. Even pushes the snowmobile into the shed beside his motorcycle. I turn to leave, but he takes my wrist and pulls me into a hug. I return with a tight I-never-want-to-let-you-go kind of hug. Then I'm in my car and pulling up in front of my house, which looks sorrier than ever against the somber clouds and dirty roads.

After I stash my bag, I check on Mama. She tears her eyes from the television and glares at me from the bed. "Where you been? Skunk said you ain't come home last night. I want to know, what creep were you sleeping with, you slut?" She practically spits at me as she shouts, her face growing purple. Then she erupts into a fit of coughing.

"Mama. Stop. You're upsetting yourself. I just went—" but I don't tell. I'm afraid by describing my wonderful night I'll somehow sully my memory of it. "I went with Brittany to a party. It was late and I was too tired to drive, so we just stayed. I'm sorry if I worried you." Why has lying become so easy? God, please forgive me. She looks convinced, but only for a moment.

"I heard that girl got herself knocked up. I don't want you hanging around with her no more. Don't want you to get any ideas and find pudgy little Sugar-babies running around here."

Heat builds behind my cheeks. I'm surprised that Brittany is actually pregnant, but more surprised that Mama knows. But what really gets me is hearing how little Mama thinks of me. I'm smarter than that. I go to church. I'm a good Christian girl. I know how the plumbing down there works, and I have plans for my life. Big ones. I'm not sure what they are yet, but I feel myself getting treacherously close to discovering that they are not going to unfold in this falling-down house in this crap town.

"Nothin' to say? I thought so. Now go get me something to eat. I'm half-starved."

I retreat, but not because I don't have anything to say, but because I boil over with anger. Before I realize what I'm doing, I've got a mixing bowl filled with cake batter and am spooning it into my mouth. I look down in the bowl. I feel like drowning in it. For all the force of the thoughts I had in Mama's room, I'm now equally defeated. I had intended to make this cake for Mama later, to make up for not being here earlier for her and for upsetting her so bad, but now here I am, a helpless little girl stuffing away her feelings with sugar, sugar, sugar. The sound of my name in my head blends with Mama calling it from her room.

"Coming, Mama." I bring her a plate of microwaved chicken fingers and tater tots and then go back to baking the cake. I whip up some frosting and think about Even and me gliding through the snow. I think about sitting in the hot tub under the stars. After I set the timer, I go to my room and take out my boxes of fabric. I root around until I find a square of clean white polyester. I find a similar shade in linen to go underneath. I sketch an idea: snow, stars, magic, and layers.

I think of hopes and dreams and then smell cake. I rush down the stairs and get the pan out of the oven just before it begins to turn too brown. I let it cool while I return to my room to begin to cut and pin together the pieces of fabric.

Downstairs, the front door slams, indicating Skunk has come home. I hurry back to the kitchen so he doesn't eat the cake before I have a chance to give it to Mama.

Before I get to the living room, Skunk and a few other boys cackle. When I pass the living room, they all have beers and are crowded around the TV. There's more laughter, and then Skunk shouts, "Hey, Sugar, bring us some snacks."

I consider telling him to get them himself, but after being gone last night, I don't want to ruffle any more feathers. I grab a bag of cheddar-and-sour-cream-flavored potato chips and a box of Cheez-Its. I bring them into the living room. The image of a woman only in her underwear, licking her lips and walking on her hands and knees, blazes across the screen. I stop midstride, appalled. Not daring to get any closer, I toss the food to Skunk before skittering back to the kitchen.

He shouts, "Aw, come on, Sugar, it's just a naked chick." Then he says, "It must be hard for you to look at her, though, since she's so hot, and you're not."

The guys laugh.

Butterflies knock around in my stomach as I become increasingly uncomfortable. When I bring Mama the cake, she has a cigarette up to her mouth, but as if her body is unsure whether to take a drag or cough, she does both.

"What's this?" she asks.

"Well, it's been so gloomy out I thought I'd make you a cake."

"Nice excuse to eat one yourself, I bet. Though with all that weight you lost I think maybe you're living off rabbit food."

"Mama—" I start to say.

"Bring it here. What kind?"

"Chocolate with vanilla icing. Your favorite." I bring it over to her and pull out the paper plate and fork I have on the bottom. As I'm doing so, she stubs her cigarette out in the middle of the frosting.

"Mama!"

She glares at me and then, before I realize what's happening, she takes the back of my head and pushes my face down into the icing. I struggle to get out from beneath her grasp, but she has me by the hair. I twist my head to the side and shout as I wriggle away.

"Little bitch," she says.

I dash to the kitchen, wiping my eyes, and toss the cake, which I held all the while, into the trash. I have to go back through the living room to get upstairs. It's hard to see, but I do well enough to glimpse that the woman is still on the television screen, another has joined her, both naked, and they writhe together, kissing. At the sound of my steps, the boys turn to me and laugh.

"What, Sugar, you couldn't inhale the cake fast enough? You had to stick your whole head in the thing?" They make other mean comments that I don't hear as I run into the bathroom.

I grab a musty towel and wipe my face. It's no use, so I get in the shower and let the water wash away the frosting and humiliation. When I turn the faucet off and dry myself, all I'm left with is anger. As I pull aside the shower curtain, the door to the bathroom opens. I let out a sound of surprise.

"Hey, there you are. I thought you might be done in here by now." Caleb, one of Skunk's friends, stands in the doorway. He has a smear of pimples above his upper lip and greasy hair. He stands with one boot on the toe of the other and leans on the doorjamb with his arms crossed. "I've always liked you, Sugar. I don't think you're as bad as your brother says. You just ain't understood. Anyway, I like a girl with a little meat on her bones."

I clutch the towel tightly around my body and pull the shower curtain to cover the rest of me. Just my head pokes out. "Uh, OK. Could I have some privacy, please?" I ask.

"You don't need no privacy. I just thought I'd come in here and we could, you know, get to know each other better."

My mind races. That porn movie probably got him fired up. I'm not interested. At all. "I don't think that's a good idea."

He takes a step closer.

I stiffen.

His eyes are glazed from the beer and probably pot; I could smell it on them when they came in.

"Aw, come on. I just want to have a little fun," he says.

"You need to leave now." I look around for something to poke him with if he gets any closer. In this house full of junk there's nothing more than a couple magazines, a toothbrush, and some empty cups and shampoo bottles within reach. "I mean it. I'm not interested."

"I hear your friend Brittany is easy. She screws that boyfriend all the time. Come on. You'll like it."

Nervous sweat mingles with my already wet skin as he steps closer.

"I want you to suck my cock," he says forcefully, unbuckling his belt.

"No. Listen, Caleb, you better leave now. I'm not joking. Go on. Leave."

"Nah. I don't think that's what I want to do," he answers. "I bet you've never been with a guy. It'll be so good, you'll want more."

I can hardly breathe and my limbs feel like liquid granite.

"I'm warning you. I said no. Go."

He gives me a dirty look, his fingers still on his belt.

"*Skkkkkkunk*," I scream in my loudest imitation of Mama's bellow.

"You didn't need to do that." He turns to the door.

Surprisingly, Skunk bounds up the stairs, perhaps out of reflexive habit when he hears Mama's voice. Only she hasn't been up here in forever.

When he reaches the door, Caleb stands in the hall, the bathroom door hanging wide open with me still behind the curtain.

Skunk realizes his mistake. "What does she want?" he asks Caleb.

No answer. His lips vanish with a greasy flick of his tongue and he flashes something I wouldn't call a smile.

"Tell your stupid friends to stay away from me," I shout.

"What, were you messing with my sister? You dog."

"No way, man. She's uglier than a mud duck," Caleb says. Laughter follows them as they barrel down the stairs.

I slowly step out of the bathroom. Making sure the coast is clear, I pass into my room. I lock the door and lean against it, sliding to the floor. I don't care that I've never been with a boy. I couldn't give two shits about Skunk and any of his friends. But I'm scared to leave my room lately, to even be in this house, but I have nowhere to go. I can't sleep in my car.

More laughter and hooting filtering up from downstairs hushes my sobs. I pull on some sweatpants and a shirt. I want to leave, but when I think about where I'd go, there's no answer. I can't go to Brittany's or Even's, and that leaves pretty much no one. I'm alone.

I pick up my stitches on the dress I'd started earlier and tears fall onto the thin fabric. For a moment, they look like glistening snow.

The only thing that breaks the monotony of the next couple of days as I try to avoid Mama and Skunk in our ramshackle house is a text from Even that says: *Miss you. Birthday plans?*

I reply: *You, too. None.*

I don't hear back from him, but while I fix Mama's lunch, she and Skunk argue loudly. I hesitate bringing her the fried chicken, biscuits, and pierogies I warmed up, but if she doesn't get her lunch, it'll only make things worse. As I carry the plate down the hall, Skunk moves to slam her bedroom door, but it catches on something blocking the frame, and all it makes is a whooshing sound. They must have had a disagreement; he probably asked her for money, something I've overheard him do a lot lately. He knocks my shoulder as he passes me. All the food slides off the plate and onto the floor. I follow the five-second rule and scoop everything back up, pulling a strand of hair from a pierogi.

I bring Mama her food, and she lays into me. Her cough is like a dog's bark.

"Now don't you be messing around with any of Skunk's friends. They're good boys, and I don't need you corrupting them."

I feel my face squeeze into a look of perplexity.

"I'm serious, Sugar. I don't trust you around them no more. Not after I've heard all about Brittany. You stay away from them, you hear me?"

I'm about to protest, but the front door opens and loud voices fill the hall. I nod and wait outside Mama's door until they've all passed into the living room. I'll have to go by them to get to my room, but I step quietly so they don't hear me.

I close my door slowly, otherwise it creaks. I return to the solace of making the dress. I have it entirely together and am now working on the tiered ruffles that cascade in tidy layers down the bodice. The skirt drops to below the knee in a smooth slide of sheer pleated fabric. The ruffles have scalloped edges that I imagine are like drifts of snow. Or like the edge of a frosted cake.

Nasty whoops of laughter from downstairs interrupt my peace. I blink my eyes, trying to rid my mind of Caleb's slimy glare, the way he licked his dry lips, his commands. I swallow hard, pushing away the churning in my stomach.

I worry about Caleb coming back up here and bothering me.

A car drives by, its tires making a squishing sound in the slushy street. The headlights beam through my window. I stand up and lock my bedroom door. I put away all my fabric and tell myself I'll finish the dress another day. I fold it up neatly and stash everything in my closet.

I grip my phone, as if by holding it I'll figure out whom to call or where to go. It vibrates in my hand with a text from Even: *Birthday surprise. See you tomorrow? Another overnight. Hope that's OK. This one is gonna blow yr mind.*

The promise of Even's message soothes me. *A birthday surprise.* I wonder what it could be. The next day can't come soon enough. Rough laughter booms from downstairs. I grip Boo's sharp sewing scissors tightly under my pillow just in case.

Chapter Seventeen

As I dress, I realize a shirt that was too snug on me at Thanksgiving now, about a month later, fits. It's probably not much, but I'm pleased. If I keep at it, I'll be down to my freshman-year weight before long. Never mind Mama's diet pills; I'm making this happen with good old-fashioned exercise, mostly walking, and eating better, most of the time. I think of the cake. I'm awash with shame, but I shove the thought away. It's a new day, I tell myself. Today I'll be good and nourish my body with healthy foods, I hope.

I feel better in my skin already, ready to spend time with Even. I grin widely with pride until I find Skunk and a couple friends, including Caleb, passed out downstairs. There are two cases' worth of beer cans, in various stages of crushed-ness, littering the room.

I've filled my backpack with overnight items this time. As I grab a granola bar from the cabinet, Skunk saunters into the kitchen, scratching his crotch.

"What are you doing up this early, dipshit?" he asks.

"It's eleven a.m."

"Oh." He opens the fridge and chugs orange soda from the bottle.

The rumble of a motorcycle approaches. A lump rises in my throat. Heavy boots clomp from the living room. I hope it isn't Caleb. Without looking, I make for the door. This time I don't care if Skunk or anyone else sees me leaving with Even.

I get on the back of the Harley and wrap my arms around Even. I make a quiet wish that we're going far, far away.

We pass out of town and head south, up over hills, and toward the highway. We pull to the side of the road and put on helmets before we cross out of New Hampshire.

"How are you?" Even asks.

The answer to this question now is *great*, but just hours ago, *frickin' awful*. But I don't want to tell him any of this and ruin the moment. "Wonderful. You?"

"Same. Glad to get out of there. It's like as soon as I'm a measure away, I feel like me again. I swear that town has some kind of negative magnetism that makes you feel about as lousy as you can."

Even speaks the truth, but the only times I've noticed it are when I've been away with him.

"So where are you taking us this time?" I ask.

"Do you want to be surprised?"

I chew on this. "Hmm. If you tell me, I'll be excited with anticipation."

"Well, it's your birthday present, so I'll let you choose."

I waffle, but, standing on the shoulder of the road, I'm getting cold without the press of his body against mine. "OK. Tell me," I say.

He does a drum roll with his mouth. "New York City," he says, and smiles.

My mouth falls open and I say, "But it's New Year's Eve."

"Exactly. I might never be back to the East Coast after this spring. I thought it might be a once-in-a-lifetime opportunity. Plus, I couldn't think of somewhere better to ring in the New Year and celebrate your birthday. New York City, the city of golden dreams, the Big Apple, the Crossroads of the World. Not to mention, just like you'd hoped for snow on Christmas, I hoped for a warmish day for us to do this. Wishes granted . . . Is that OK?" he asks. Suddenly, concern creases his forehead.

"Yeah. I just never thought I'd be going there. It's so big. There are so many people. Especially tonight. Where will we stay? What will we eat? What about the Harley? I thought you liked being outside?" I feel myself hesitating, worried what all the cosmopolitan people will think of the big fat country girl, but then I think of the alternative. Even stands before me, jittering with excitement. "Duh. Of course," I say. "It's going to be great. I'm just being silly."

His smile returns and his eyes light up with relief.

I get the sense that he is just as eager to get out of town as me. Of course, we each have our own reasons.

As we get on the highway, I stretch one arm toward the sky and let out a whoop. Even lets out a smiling laugh.

As we head farther south, the landscape changes from rural with bare trees and is replaced by buildings rising up on either side of the highway. I read signs naming businesses, look at billboards, and am nervous as the traffic gets heavier, feeling especially vulnerable being on the bike as we whiz by tractor trailers. But the sun is high above us, and the air warms the farther away from New Hampshire we get.

We go through tolls and eventually cross the biggest bridge I've ever seen. I don't like heights, but glance at the slate-colored water below and realize, with a sudden shiver, that this is all real.

New York lies before us like a feast for the eyes. I survey from the ground up and then scale the buildings from rooftop to rooftop, struggling to take it all in. Even slows in traffic. The mixture of exhaust, something nutty roasting, and the cold winter air excites my senses.

There are so many people crossing streets and it's so bright with signs and traffic lights and shop windows all aglow. Even pulls to the side of the road, consults a piece of paper in his pocket, and then maneuvers back into traffic. We crisscross through streets I recognize by name only from television shows and books. It's one thing to see New York City on TV or imagine it as an author brings it to life on the page, but it's another thing entirely to be in the midst of the action and energy. It pulses out of every crack in the sidewalk, from signposts, and from mortared bricks. It's like everyone who's ever been here left a little bit of themselves behind, making the city itself a living organism.

Eventually, we pull up to a hotel. Even descends into an underground parking lot. When we emerge onto the street on foot, without the protection of my helmet, I feel the city up close. I practically feel the pulse of it on my skin, as a dog yaps, horns honk, and shoppers bustle.

We go into the hotel, and Even checks us in at the desk. The lobby is nicer than any building I've ever been inside in my life. It's grander than anything I imagined. I'm in a fairy tale. Chandeliers glisten, large potted plants stand lush in corners, and the posh furnishings look brand-new.

"All set. Let's go leave our stuff up in the room."

We ride the elevator up a dozen flights. As we exit into the hall, I smell new carpet.

After Even slides the key card in the slot and opens the door, I practically skip into the room, twirl around, and plop down on the lone king-size bed. Even smiles and crosses to the window. I look around his shoulder and see more buildings, some with lights on, others dark. I couldn't be happier.

"What do you think? Wait, never mind; I think I know," he says.

Without thinking, I throw my arms around him. "Thank you. This is wonderful."

"Happy birthday. Almost. Let's see. It's nearly four. Should we go exploring and maybe check things out before the masses descend for tonight?"

I nod with glee.

"That smile," he says.

I take a moment to fix my hair and freshen up after the blustery ride.

I'd have figured Even for a country bumpkin like me, but once back outside, he charges straight ahead like he knows what he's doing and where he's going. All I can do is stare up, up, and up.

"First stop, the Empire State Building."

We hoof it to Fifth Avenue and arrive at the colossal skyscraper. As we ride the elevator up to the top deck, Even gives me a shy smile, like if we were strangers we'd still get off at the same floor, we'd still end up together at dinner, and then find ourselves back in the hotel room at the end of the night.

When we unload at the top floor, I see clear across the city in every direction. The buildings look like Lego blocks standing on end surrounded by splashy puddles. Even though they're each engineering miracles, they remind me of inspiration and play and how everyday people do the impossible. And in this moment with Even, on top of the world, I realize anything *is* possible. The sun begins to set, burning fiery orange in the distance. I don't even care about the height; I feel safe, especially with Even at my arm.

"I wanted you to see the whole city, but this is the best I can do in one evening. What do you think?" he asks, as awestruck as me.

"It's amazing," I say. "Truly. I am nearly speechless. After looking at the same shabby buildings for most of my life, I had no idea of the magnitude of the world beyond our small town. I feel filled with possibility." These words feel strange on my tongue, yet true, like they could, in some other dimension, really belong to me.

"I know exactly what you mean."

After we watch the sun set and are completely shivering from the whipping wind, so high up, we take the elevator down and are soon back out on the street.

"I want this to be your day. Is there anywhere here in Manhattan you've ever really wanted to go to or see or do?"

I am utterly overwhelmed. I pause, spinning in a circle and catching the coattails of a street performer, a mother with five, possibly six, kids, and a homeless person with a shopping cart heaped high with bags. "Being here is enough, but you know how we went boot-skating last week? Well, I've always wanted to go ice-skating. I've been scared, because of, you know—people making fun of me, jokes about me breaking the ice, but no one knows me here and so—"

A hint of sadness crosses Even's face, but then he smiles in a way that lights up his blue eyes. "I know just the place."

This time we walk up Sixth Avenue, still taking in all the smells, sounds, and sights as we pass decorated store windows, street vendors selling sugared cinnamon peanuts and cashews, and chicly dressed city-dwellers. I'm struck with the fact that although Even arranged this special evening away for us, what's going on around me happens all the time. Twenty-four/seven. It's my own life that often feels like it's screeched to a halt, but really, New York continues to spin its city stories.

When we arrive at Rockefeller Center, the giant Christmas tree I see on TV every year is still lit up, larger than life.

"Boy," I say, taking in the tree from bottom to top. "This makes up for Christmas, too. It was sad with no tree, though we haven't bothered to put one up for a few years," I remark. We gaze at it for a few minutes, and I continue to absorb my surroundings with childlike wonderment.

Even and I rent skates, and wobbly, like a new foal, I struggle out onto the ice. Even offers his arm, but I'm afraid if I fall and take him down with me, he'll get hurt. I hold on to the side of the rink, and after he insists, in the most gentlemanly way, I finally consent to link my arm in his. Together, we make it all the way around once, then twice. By the fifth time, I feel safe to skate on my own, but I hold on to Even's arm just because it's so nice, like we're a couple. My princess fairy-tale fantasy continues as we glide beneath the lights.

When we're both exhausted, Even asks about dinner. "Anything you want. This city has a restaurant for any and every kind of food in the world. We could have Thai, Italian, um . . ." He looks around. "There's a burger joint over there, and Chinese. French or Mexican. We could have dessert for dinner and dinner for dessert. Or we could check out a coffeehouse with live music, or we could do karaoke. How about sushi? Have you ever tried that?"

I need him to slow down. I've seen loads of restaurants in New York featured on shows on food and cooking channels, but now that I am here with all of these options, my mind is blank.

We return our skates and warm up with some coffee while I consider what I want to eat. The notion that I am here, in Manhattan, to make this choice isn't lost on me, but it's overwhelming nonetheless.

"I can tell you what I *don't* want. Anything they sell at Od Town."

Even laughs. "Yeah. That's one nasty outlet food shop . . ." Even looks around as we walk around the plaza. "Dinner theater? Or hot dogs from a vendor? Pizza? Moroccan? Greek? Indian? Have you ever had Spanish tapas?"

"I think you've named every kind of food there is." I'm just not sure. "How about we continue to walk and see where our feet take us?"

"Ooooh. My favorite kind of plan."

We set out away from the hubbub of Rockefeller Center and onto a quiet cross street, and our hands, wordlessly, join.

"That was fun," I say, slightly distracted by the feel of his palm in mine.

"Yeah. Way to go not falling."

"I concentrated hard."

"The first time I learned to skate, I had a bruise the size of a grapefruit on my butt for a little over a month," Even says. We joke, comparing bruises and scars, safely away from their sources, but then the smell of garlic and basil interrupts our laughter and entices us to cross the street to a small restaurant with a red awning. The lighting is low when we enter. The hostess seats us in a private booth with a view out the window.

Bread drizzled in garlic oil is brought to us along with lemon water. I browse the menu, never having seen, at least in real life, so many complex and delicious-sounding options.

There is antipasto, caprese salad, penne with winter squash, roasted tomatoes drizzled with a balsamic reduction. My eyes flit across sumptuous descriptions of carbonara, gnocchi, and pasta e fagioli.

"Get anything you like; it's your birthday dinner," Even says as if reading into my uncertainty as I continue to peruse the menu and notice the price tags. This is no Od Town.

I settle on fettuccini Alfredo with chicken and asparagus. He orders us gorgonzola garlic bread and shrimp scampi with linguini for himself. A candle burns between us on the table. Our salads arrive with Parmesan-peppercorn dressing and, for good measure, a waiter offers us still more freshly ground pepper and Parmesan cheese. It's all lovely. I feel like a princess or a grown-up or a grown-up princess.

"This has been wonderful," I say, not knowing how else to express how extraordinary it all is without sounding corny.

"And it's just beginning."

A dark shadow of a thought intrudes as I think about having to leave the next day and return to the house with Mama and Skunk.

Shame, anger, and sadness fill me, but as I stuff another piece of cheesy bread in my mouth, the flavors lighting up my tongue, I try to forget it all.

After dinner, we sweep back into the streets toward Times Square to secure places to watch the big ball drop at midnight. Even puts a warm arm across my shoulders as the growing crowd jostles us.

We got lucky and managed to get a standing spot within view, though just barely, of the stage where the big acts will perform later. Hordes of people scream and cheer around us, waving foam fingers and pom-poms. Even looks at me, our faces pushed close because of the undulating crowd around us. We're in a sea of humanity, and never have I been so gleeful.

"I love to see that smile." He moves closer, our lips inches apart. Then the sound of a guitar screeches. We look up to see a band starting their set on the stage. Colored lights flash and we sing along, lost to our worries and troubles back home. We're free, for just this moment.

The rest of the night moves by as quick as a blur. The momentum slows when the amplified voice of Ryan Seacrest announces it is nearly time to watch the ball. I gaze around at the crowd. The countless beautiful faces craning up to see the glowing orb stun me. I'd never known people could be so outstandingly gorgeous, but it isn't the classic New York look I'd seen in magazines or on TV, but just people, together, joyous, and celebratory.

I join in. As one, we begin to count: "Ten, nine, eight, seven, six, five, four, three, two, one."

Blasts and cheering explode around me, and then Even's lips are on mine. We kiss sweetly, desperately, and wholly. After it feels like time stops and then starts again, we pull apart. Confetti comes down all around us like snow.

"Happy New Year," we say at the same time.

"Happy birthday," he says.

It takes us ages to pick our way out of the revelers. I'm in no rush. I wish the night would never end. But all too soon, we arrive back at the hotel, and still clothed, we both collapse into the bed. Even lies on his side. I'm on mine and we face each other. He takes my hand, smiles, and then closes his eyes. The glowing numbers of the clock indicate it's nearly three a.m., and that's the last thing I remember.

When I wake, I expect Even to be at the window, watching the sun greet the city, but he is beside me, lying on his belly, with one arm down the side of the bed, the other tucked by his chest. I've never seen someone look so perfect. And like last night in Times Square, I realize it isn't in the "Oh, he's so hot" kind of way. He looks innocent and peaceful. Tears come to my eyes as I'm struck with wonder, with a sense of how bittersweet and fleeting life is. All we have is this one moment, really. I wipe my tears away as his blue eyes open. I don't want him to think I'm sad or anything.

"Who's the sleepyhead now?" I ask playfully, thwacking him with a pillow.

"Happy birthday," he says.

"Rabbit, rabbit."

"Huh?"

"Whoever is the first to say that at the beginning of a new month—"

Even interrupts, "Wins a prize?"

"Actually, I don't know. You just win because you're the first to say it," I say.

He clobbers me with his pillow. We romp in the bed, my hair frizzy and his with bedhead, and then we drop back, hand-in-hand, and I count our inhales and exhales until he rolls over to face me.

"Where to today?" The previous night, in all its detail, races into my mind, and, once again, I lose my ability to make decisions. "Central Park? A museum? Both?"

"Sounds perfect," I answer, relieved he thought ahead to come up with something. I'm so overwhelmed, I feel clueless.

After breakfast in a quintessential New York diner, we take a cab to the Upper West Side. The evidence of the night before in all its messy chaos and revelry still litters the streets. The taxi drops us off in front of the Museum of Natural History. I've never seen this classic building in old stone, with massive pillars and the statue of Theodore Roosevelt on horseback greeting us on the steps. I'm in awe.

"Remember that from *A Night at the Museum*?" Even asks, pointing.

"The night at the what?"

"You know, the movie with Ben Stiller. Everything comes to life? He has a battle of wits with the monkey? The statue that says, 'Dum-dum'?"

I look blank as we take our tickets. "No?"

"I think we have a movie to watch in our future. It's hilarious. I can't believe you've never seen it. It was my favorite when I was a kid. I think they made a sequel, but I never saw it. We'll do a double feature," Even says.

I quickly wonder where we'd watch it. Skunk and his friends seem to have taken over ownership of our television with illicit videos. And Nash? I just want to stay clear of him.

I'm not paying attention to where I'm going, and then an elephant, frozen in time amongst its herd, its trunk raised triumphantly, rises before me. I forget my anxious thoughts. It's enormous. It is beautiful. I'm instantly in love. It's not alive, of course, but I identify with its beautiful face and its immense body that almost seems too big to be allowed. I detect the faintest of smiles on its wrinkly lips. Either way, I know then that someday I'll see an elephant in real life instead of someone rudely commenting that I'm as big as one. We ask a museum patron to snap a photo of us in front of the display.

We stroll through the museum, and the day escapes us. It's midafternoon. I know we'll have to leave soon. A desperate urge to tell Even to just stay here and never go back pulls at my heart. No one will miss us. We can get jobs and find a place to stay. We have our lives ahead of us. Then I think of Mama. How would she get along without me?

As we exit the museum, the wooded haven of Central Park spreads grayish-green across the street. I didn't notice it earlier, distracted by the impressive museum building.

We cross to the park and continue to stroll, leisurely, purchasing a small bag of roasted chestnuts from a vendor, watching skaters, and ending up by a fountain.

Even pulls some change from his pocket.

"Want to make a wish?"

"Right now, I don't have anything I'd wish for except for today to go on forever. But I guess I have a wish for the future, though."

I hold the coin in my hand tightly and then toss it in.

We return to the underground parking garage where Even stowed the Harley. We tug on our helmets. After I'm securely on the back, I say goodbye. Tears moisten my eyes as the sun sets behind the skyline.

Chapter Eighteen

There is no mention of our New Year's Eve kiss as we make the trip north back to New Hampshire. We don't kiss again either, which is fine by me because, for a first kiss, ours was outstanding. I'm still dizzy from it. I went from a big fat loser to a girl who's had her first kiss with the nicest and cutest guy she's ever known. I can hardly see straight.

Even leaves me at the curb in front of my house. I turn to go in as he pulls away, but then I pause on the porch. I watch his motorcycle until he's beyond the reach of my vision on the lamp-lit street. I don't want him to go, and I don't want to go in.

The house is silent. I half expected Skunk to have burned it down or to be waiting at the front door with a shotgun, but maybe he doesn't have the need to antagonize me as much as I'd thought.

When I get in my room, I close my eyes. I can almost feel Even's lips on mine from the night before. He tasted woody and minty at the same time, but I also detected salt and coffee. He was delicious. I fret over my performance, but he seemed satisfied. I hope for another moment like that soon. My lips turn up into a smile at the thought.

I trot downstairs to get something to drink, and my footfalls must cause Mama to stir because she calls my name as she coughs long and hard. Fug. I hope Skunk was still drunk in the morning when he saw me leave and didn't say anything. I don't feel inclined to endure her harassment.

"Hey, Mama. Happy New Year," I say when I duck my head into her room.

"Where the hell did you think you were going? I know you didn't come home last night. I bet you've been partying with Brittany and those losers over in the trailer park. Damn scum is what they are. You stay away from them, you hear me? You'll start up with that twitchin' and then there'll be nothing left of you. They start using that shit and get all skinny. Nasty business, Sugar. You hear me? I have the mind to ground you."

I have nothing to say to this. I did leave without permission, but she's never made clear what I'm allowed to do and what I am not. Sometimes I think Mama makes things up as she goes along or to suit her aims. It goes unwritten and unspoken that I am to look after her, make sure she has food, make sure she is cleaned after she goes to the bathroom, and make sure she's relatively OK. I have the idea of what she wants and doesn't want me to do, but she doesn't impose rules on Skunk, so I assume the same goes for me.

She starts coughing again when she lights up a cigarette. The smoke as she exhales obscures her for a moment, and I wish myself away.

In my mind, I drift out of the stuffy bedroom with its clutter and smoke. Even and I whiz through the snowy fields, then we're ice-skating, and then, as if we're two pieces of the same cozy puzzle, I remember how we fit together on the back of the motorcycle.

"I see that smirk on your face, young lady. Now don't you—" A cough interrupts her lecture again, and every part of her shakes.

Then I realize today is still my birthday. I'm eighteen. I may still be a "young lady," as she says, but it also means I'm free—legally an adult. No one in this house can actually make me do anything. When her coughing dies down, she speaks again.

"Listen, Sugar, I need your help. I hate to admit it, but Skunk don't do nothing but cause me more trouble. I can't get along without you. I need you, Sugar, and you need to help me or else I might not—" Her voice gets quiet. "I've lost your father and my sons. You're all I got. You ain't much, but I need you." She practically whimpers and looks up at me with beady eyes. I try to see the beauty in her face as I did in all those faces late last night seeking hope and possibility in the sky as it turned to a new year. I search her for authenticity and love.

She can't force me to do anything, but it wouldn't be right of me not to help her. "Whatcha need, Mama?"

I rush out to the drugstore and get some cough medicine; she still refuses to see a doctor. When I get back, I go to the kitchen and get her a box of corndogs and French fries. I fry up some bacon. The house fills with its enticing smell. My mouth salivates as I pull a box of cake mix from the pantry and begin to add the ingredients, one at a time, mixing away the lumps. I shovel heaping spoonfuls into my mouth. If I am going to endure this life with Mama, I need something to take the edge off. Sugar, sweet sugar.

I spoon the batter into the baking cups of a cupcake pan and begin to mix the frosting. I shove a piece of bacon in my mouth; it mixes with the remnants of the vanilla cake. It tastes surprisingly good together. I dip a piece of bacon directly into the icing. Then, opening my mouth like a baby bird fishing for a worm, I swing it into my mouth. It's a taste explosion. Sweet and salty goodness.

While everything cooks, I go to Mama's room and clean it up a bit, shoving food wrappers in a trash bag along with old magazines and other garbage. It's amazing what a mess she makes in just a few days from her stationary place on the bed.

The ding of the microwave brings me back to the kitchen. I consider chopping up the bacon real fine and adding it to the cupcake frosting. I wonder if Even would like it. He had bacon at breakfast. I stop in my tracks. We were just in New York City today. It seems like a lifetime ago, or maybe that's just the magnetic pull of returning to this sorry town and this sorrier house.

Mama has me running, as usual, retrieving her ketchup and soda. Then she has me fetch mayonnaise. Finally, I finish making the cupcakes, adding the bacon to half of the frosting just as an experiment. I put a candle in one that really puffed up on the top. I light it and then quietly hum "Happy Birthday" to myself. I make a wish as I blow out the single, flickering flame.

Mama makes no mention of my birthday, but Even's thoughtful trip fills every crevice in my heart. I eat one cupcake, with the bacon added to the frosting, then two, and I can't help myself when I have the third. They're so delicious. I save one in a small box I find, wrap it in string, and plan to bring it to Even the next day at school.

Even and I sit together at lunch on Monday. He gives me the thumbs-up after he takes a bite of the cupcake. As a crumb falls from his lip he asks, "Bacon?" I nod and he shakes his head in a way that tells me it's unexpectedly good.

He has a project due in physics, and intends to skip lunch the rest of the week because he needs to use the science lab and can't stay after because he picked up more shifts at work.

When I get to my locker, there's a Post-it Note stuck to it. The letters spell out the message "Try Anorexia." I tear it up as my eyes tear up and then slam my locker and consider leaving for the day. But leaving is akin to admitting defeat. *I can do this*, I tell myself. *The rest of this year and then one more. I'll make it.* Then the vicious voice in my head asks, *And then what?*

On Tuesday, I bring Even another cupcake, this one with caramel and bacon. Since I forgot he wouldn't be here to enjoy it, and I had one too many, I toss it in the trash with the rest of the cafeteria slop. I eat by myself, pretending to be busy on my phone, answering all my emails, texts, and keeping my social media up-to-date because I am so popular. Not.

On Wednesday, Allie laughs when she passes my table at lunch. Not thinking fast enough, I make the mistake of looking up and making eye contact.

"I see Even has abandoned you. What, did you steal all his food? Leaving him hungry? Wanting more than a girl like you could give him?" I want to retort with something witty or snarky even, but she swishes her long hair and sits at the table by the window, joining in some critical conversation about ending the injustices in the world. Not. They're probably either laughing at me or something else insignificant.

Near the end of the week, I'm up to my elbows in homework and helping Mama, and growing ever more melancholy as gray skies hover overhead. After I've made sure Mama has her dinner, I dig into a Lean Cuisine meal. I'm determined not to be the source of amusement for the entire student body at Johnson Regional anymore. My phone rings; I don't recognize the caller, but it's local, and I answer.

I hear breathing. "Hello?" I ask. I'm about to hang up when I hear a squishing noise or slurping or something, I can't quite tell, and the breathing gets heavier. Then I hear laughter. The caller hangs up. Yeah, that was hilarious. Prank calls are so clever. Not.

I block the number from calling again and turn to the TV. I treat myself to a package of chocolate mint cookies I picked up from Od Town the other day. The Thursday night lineup of comedy entertains me until nine, when I dip into my homework, feeling extremely unmotivated. At ten, I drag my feet upstairs and collapse on my bed and fall deeply into a sugar-induced coma.

Friday blurs by with assignments due, and no Even on the walk home, but he promises we'll go Monday after school and get my motorcycle license. Having this to look forward to carries me through the weekend of laundry, cleaning, tending to Mama, church, where I see Fat Henry, and then my routine grocery shopping at Od Town.

On Sunday night, as I pick the mini chocolate peanut butter cups out of a pint of ice cream while watching a cooking show, the power suddenly blinks out. Mama panics. Fush.

"Sugar. Help. I can't see. Who turned out the lights?"

"Darned if I know," I say, though she can't hear me. I wade through junk in the living room and stub my toe as I make my way to the kitchen. I paw through a drawer trying to find a flashlight. My hand lands on one, but the batteries are dead. I use my cell phone to find a new set and then make my way to Mama.

"Do I need to find the fuse box or something?" I ask.

"It's in the basement. Go on." She swipes for the flashlight.

"I'll need the flashlight," I say.

"Oh no. You ain't leaving me up here in the dark."

"How am I supposed to see?"

"Find another one."

I sigh. I flick on my phone and dial Skunk. He doesn't answer. I text. Still nothing.

After unsuccessfully trying to locate another flashlight, I go to Mama's room to see if she has stashed some in there for just this kind of scenario. When I come up empty-handed, I dial Skunk again as Mama complains.

He answers with an annoyed "What?"

"The power has gone out. What do I do?"

"Hell if I know. Ask Mama," he says grouchily.

"She doesn't know either. Do you have a flashlight in your room?" Although I don't dare go in there without electric lighting. Mama starts talking as I try to listen to whatever it is Skunk tells me. A headache comes on. He must hear Mama squawking in the background.

"Dammit, Sugar. Do I need to come there?" he asks.

"Yes, I think you do."

"You owe me. You know that." He hangs up.

I don't owe Skunk a darn thing. If anything, I've kept him in house and food for the past nine months that Mama has been off her feet. I tell her Skunk is on his way.

"That good-for-nothing twit? And what do you expect he's going to do? Sit around in here and wait for the lights to come back on? I'm gettin' cold. You realize without electricity we ain't got no heat." I leave Mama to complain, but am powerless to do anything. Back in the kitchen, I dial Even.

"Hey, sorry to bother you. I have a problem. The power went out. I'm not sure what to do," I say.

"Has it gone out in your neighborhood? Check out the window," he instructs.

I split the vinyl blinds and see lights on in the other houses. I tell him.

"Did you pay your bill?"

I let out an insulted sound.

"Hey, I had to ask. Just like if the toaster isn't working, you always check to see if it's plugged in. Where's your electrical panel?"

"In the basement. Skunk said he's on his way, but he doesn't know any better than I do how to get it back on. Mama's flipping out because she's getting cold. I wish I paid more attention when my granddad was alive; he always knew how to fix things."

"Sugar, it isn't your fault. I'll be over in five minutes."

I hear his door slam and his feet hitting the wooden stairs outside his apartment as his breath comes in little bursts through the earpiece.

"You don't have to do that." The Harley starts. "It's snowing. And what about Skunk?" I ask.

"I'll be there in three minutes."

"Seriously, you don't have to. I'll get it figured out. I can call an electrician."

"It's late. I'm sure it's just a switch."

"Fuse box."

"OK, a fuse. I'll be there in two minutes."

"I don't want to inconvenience you."

"I can see your dark house."

"Did you bring a flashlight?"

"Of course." Then he's knocking on the front door.

"Skunk, is that you?" Mama calls out. Mama's high-pitched, yet somehow gravelly voice, probably from all the smoking, embarrasses me, but I'm thankful for the dark because Even can't see how hideous our house is.

The beam of the flashlight bobs up and down, casting shadows on all the boxes of junk and discarded memories in the basement.

"Lead the way," he says. I know I've seen the fuse box before, but never really paid attention to it. I take a moment to orient myself. The clock is ticking. I don't want Even to be here when Skunk gets back. That could get ugly. We walk over to the freezer and then the washing machine. To the right, my granddad's old workbench is exactly as he left it, in the corner, little baby-food jars of screws and nails lined up neatly. If he could see this house, he'd roll over in his grave. He was fastidious about taking care of it; he even enjoyed maintenance projects, as if the house itself was the son he never had.

Even sees the box on the wall before I do, and flips the door open. He says, "Hmm," and then roots around the shelves of the workbench.

"Aha," he says, after a moment. I can't really see what he's doing, since he's working so closely with the light shining directly into the box, but there are some clicks and then the freezer hums to life, followed by the appliances on the floor above.

Even turns, looking triumphant in the glow of the dim flashlight bulb. I wrap my arms around him.

"Thank you for saving the day."

"I wouldn't want to find a Sugar Popsicle, all frozen up in here, tomorrow morning. But I should probably get going—don't want Skunk to get an inferiority complex or anything," Even says.

"Thanks. You're the best," I say, thanking him profusely and keeping up a constant flow of dialogue to try to distract him from the mess and dilapidation of the house as we make our way through the hall and kitchen. Even slips out the door, and moments later, the back glass slider jerks opens as Skunk battles to get it to move.

"What the fuck?" he says, laying into me. "I thought the power was out? You called me all the way back here in this snow to what is clearly a house with the lights on?" He stumbles closer to me, nearly falling over an old filing cabinet he dragged out of the attic a couple of years ago. "Sugar, was this some kind of prank?" He reeks of beer and sweat.

"No. The power really went out. You heard Mama." As if on cue, she hollers.

"Skunk, is that you? Did you get the power back on? Well, I'll be. You know your Mama has to watch her shows. Sugar, bring me some more soda, would you?"

Skunk's voice gets low. "Did you have that pretty boyfriend of yours come over here to fix it? What? You thought I couldn't do a man's job?" He grabs me by the shoulder and holds me firmly at a distance as if he's getting ready to slug me.

I try to wriggle away.

His face is red and he's breathing heavy. His lips bunch together tightly.

"I better get Mama her soda," I say quietly.

"Yeah, you had better, you fat turd. Oh, and you got a call earlier?"

I'm confused.

"We dared Caleb to call you and jerk off into the phone." He laughs like it's the most hilarious thing in the world. "Did you like that, you nasty slut? Or are you going to run to your boyfriend and tell him big brother and his friends are being mean?"

"Shut up, Skunk."

"Oh. Sugar told me to shut up. I'm scared," he says.

"You act like you're six, you know."

"*Suuuugarrrrr,*" Mama calls.

With the roads plowed and the skies a continuous sheet of gray, the only thing that brings relief for the fatigue I feel from a nearly sleepless night, as I continued to argue with Skunk, is the sight of Even waiting for me at our usual spot the next morning. I thank him again for his help and we fall into our easy routine as we walk to school and back again at the end of the day.

We hop on the Harley and go to the DMV that afternoon while Even has someone filling in for him at Vin's Garage. I print my name in block letters on the form, make the correct little ovals dark, and pay the application fee. I'm prepared to take the test, but my sweaty palms betray my anxiety. It's one thing to scoot around in the parking lot with Even, but another under the scrutiny of the examiner, who, with his pleated khakis and cardigan, doesn't look like he's ever ridden a motorcycle in his life. Then again, I probably don't look like a prime candidate either. He determines whether I pass or fail. My palms continue to sweat.

Even takes my hand, smooths my hair behind my ears, and says, "We're going to do this. I can see the finish line. Ride like the wind." He kisses me tenderly on the lips.

The first item on the test is to identify the various parts of the motorcycle. I pass with flying colors. Even smiles, but there's more to come.

The examiner tells me to move through a course of orange safety cones, to turn and stop. This is easy. Then I move into traffic with a testing vehicle behind me giving horn signals for when to turn onto other streets. I am freaking out. What if I screw this up? What if I fail? We cross over the main road into town, and although

I'm familiar with my surroundings, doubt plagues me. Was I supposed to let the other car go first? Am I allowed to make a right on a red? Why have I completely forgotten the rules of the road? Taking my regular driver's test wasn't this stressful. Up ahead, I see a familiar Toyota Corolla. I wonder if Allie is with Hillary. I envision myself crashing in the road, going up in flames, and there, that's the end of the fat girl. Happy, ladies?

But Even's back at the DMV, and some part of him is counting on me. Even though I don't believe I'll be traveling cross-country with him on motorcycles—it sounds like something out of a movie—I can't let him down. I take a deep breath and almost laugh when I pull alongside the Corolla. I'm focused ahead of me, but I imagine their faces seeing me sailing by on a motorcycle. *Fat chicks can ride, too!*

I can't take my eyes off the road. I take a smooth left on the green arrow, and the Corolla waits for the solid green to go straight. After a few more stops and turns, I am triumphant as I pull back into the parking lot with the orange cones.

Even rushes out of the building and gives me a big hug. We both look at the examiner. He gives a quick nod. "Woo hoo! You did it!" Even doesn't shrink from full-fledged enthusiasm. "OK, now I just need to find you a bike. Any preferences?"

He hurries to work, but later that night sends me no less than a dozen texts about what kind of motorcycle I'd like. Of course, it'd be a cheap one he has to fix up, but he sends photos of examples. I like his bike, the Harley, but that's because I'm used to it. Finally, I tell him I trust his judgment and am sure it will be perfect.

• • •

Thankfully, Skunk makes himself scarce over the next few days. As we near the end of the week, sans porn in the living room, prank phone calls, and his butt hogging the sofa, I can't help but wonder if he took up with his girlfriend again.

The weekend arrives too slowly, and motivated by my general boredom, I've managed to come up with a plan for Even and me for Saturday night, his first weekend off in a couple weeks. I dip into my savings and buy us tickets to a motorcycle show at the civic center down in Massachusetts. I don't have the most vested interest in the event, but given the fact that I am now a licensed rider, and motorcycles are probably his favorite hobby, I expect it'll be fun.

We travel in my car because the weather sloshes between rain and sleet. "So where are we off to?" Even asks once we're en route.

"This time I get to surprise you. But it's no enchanted lodge in the woods or New York City on New Year's Eve."

"I'm sure it'll be great," he says with anticipation. "I hope this turns to snow. I'd hate to see the trails ruined before the season's over. I'm going snowmobiling tomorrow—meeting up with some guys from work. I hear your brother has been out there, causing havoc."

"Skunk on a snowmobile? I thought he sold his. Whatever. I haven't seen him for a while. Thank goodness." That's probably what has kept him away lately; he replaced his dirt bike with a snowmobile.

When we pull up at the show, Even practically jumps out of his seat. "No way! This is awesome. I didn't realize it was happening this weekend. Thanks, Sugar," he says, pulling me into a hug.

We walk in, hand-in-hand. I've never seen so much chrome and leather in my life. It's a motorcycle lover's paradise and Even is a kid in a candy store. He points out his dream bike and some kit he'd like for his accessories, and we listen to some old-timers swap stories about the good ol' days.

Once back in my car, Even can't stop talking about his plan to head west on bikes. I'm beginning to warm to it, if only slightly. As we drive back north, his hand reaches for mine in the darkness. Wherever life takes us, I don't ever want to let go.

We get home late, and as I leave Even off at his apartment, the road is turning to ice. He leans over and gives me a kiss on the lips. We linger there, letting our lips and the minutes do a trickling thing that makes me forget what time it is, where I am, and even my name.

"This was nice. Thanks," he says softly. We're both chilled in the car.

"My pleasure," I say, happy to have done something for him.

"You know, you really are the best. I'm lucky, Sugar." I think, *No, I am*, but he goes on, "Listen, drive safe. OK?" I nod, and he dashes up the stairs in the icy rain. I want to go after him and sneak into his room, listen to music, and fall asleep in his arms, but the door opens and closes, and he is gone.

Chapter Nineteen

January is the cruelest month. Aside from the constant twilight—with the days never quite fully revealing themselves with a flash of sun—the rain, sleet, and snow are enough to dampen anyone's spirits.

I go to sleep Sunday night not having heard from Even. Which is OK; we're not married or anything. He doesn't have to check in with me, but we usually text at least a couple times a day. After the show, I was expecting motorcycle madness, with more texts of potential bikes. Nothing. I worry Allie got her talons into him, but no, he went snowmobiling, probably against better judgment, with the guys from work. The icy rain and cold temperatures have coated everything in a slick frozen layer. I sleep fitfully with worry.

The next morning, I wait at our spot. And wait. My frozen toes beg me to get a move on to school, but my heart wants me to linger, just one more minute. He's coming; I'm sure of it. He's late. I count ten cars go by. Not wanting to be late, myself, and endure Mr. Hammons's wrath, I finally start to walk.

When I settle into my chair, I notice, oddly, that everyone else has already taken their seats. The raucous mood that usually persists until the bell is absent—it's somber, quiet. The bell rings. Mr. Hammons bows his head. The principal's nasally voice crackles over the intercom.

"Teachers and students," he begins. "I regret to make this announcement, but we have lost one of our own this past weekend."

In the pause, I know. A chill works its way over my skin.

"Even Anderson died in a snowmobile accident yesterday. He was new at Johnson Regional this year—" Whatever other kindness the principal offers is lost to me.

I cry out. Through vision blurred by tears, twenty faces stare at me, including Mr. Hammons's. Something blocks my throat. I can't breathe, but the sobbing still comes. The principal asks us to take a moment of silence. I can't be silent. I rush out of the room, not caring that I trip over someone's backpack. I don't know where to go. I need to get away. This can't be right. There must be a mistake.

I leave the school. I walk and walk. I don't want to walk, but I put one leg in front of the other. I find myself in front of my house. I go in. Mama calls my name. I ignore her. I turn on the television. The news is on. There's footage of a newscaster, reporting at dusk the night before. She wears a winter coat and stands on the side of the road in front of snowy woods. The lights of emergency vehicles swirl, casting eerie blue-gray light on the ice-covered ground. Someone at a live news desk appears on the screen and says something about tragedy and loss, a young man, and then the name Even Anderson. I refuse to believe it.

"You're lying!" I shout. This can't be right.

Mama calls again, but it is as if she is somehow far away, too far for me to answer.

I throw the remote control at the television. At the spot it makes contact, the screen briefly turns blue, and then I pound up to my room and throw myself on my bed. I cry and gulp for air.

How could anything have happened to Even? He's solid. He knows how to ride a snowmobile. He's careful. He is smart. He is beautiful. He's mine. It can't be possible he's been taken away. "No, no, no," I say through fits of tears. My blanket is damp beneath me.

I picture him, tall, strong, blue-eyed, always generous with his smile. My friend. My Even. *No, no, no*, I replay moments we shared and then, *no, no, no*, and this repeats until I've exhausted memories, and I know nothing.

• • •

When I wake up, it's dark. My damp bed and aching eyes remind me why I've been crying. I look on my phone for the time. It shows a couple of messages, one from the school and one from Brittany. I don't want to listen to them, but hanging on to the sliver of hope that there's a mistake, I press play: "Mercy, this is Ms. Barrows, the counselor from JRHS. I understand you were friends with Even Anderson. In light of this tragedy, I'd like to invite you to come into my office tomorrow. Thank you."

I can't imagine going back to school. Ever. I listen to Brittany's message: "Hey, Sugar. I heard. I'm so sorry. Call me."

I don't want to talk to anyone but Even. I want Even. My stomach grumbles. I've missed lunch and dinner. Downstairs, I find Skunk on the couch, playing a video game.

"Hey, chubs. Heard about your boyfriend. Too bad. How sad."

I don't detect a hint of sympathy. I ignore him. I hate him. I go into the kitchen and root through the pantry. There's nothing to satisfy me.

I go outside without my jacket. The cold car reluctantly starts, and I drive, in a trance, to Od Town. When I enter, the lights overhead are too bright.

The cashier calls out, "We close in five. Hurry up."

I sleepwalk to the candy aisle. I grab Skittles, Twizzlers, and Swedish Fish. I wander to the Hostess display and fill my basket with three different kinds of cakes. Then I walk down to the dairy section and get reams of cookie dough, one in each flavor, and a carton of ice cream.

I pay and leave. When I return to the house, Skunk starts in on something, but his voice sounds distant, just as Mama's did. I take the two plastic grocery bags to my room. I open the cookie dough, and using my fingers, I dig in. The chocolate chips crunch amidst the soft dough. I mash a couple Twizzlers into my mouth. Unable to decide which kind of cake to have, I open all three and have a bite of each and then another and another. I anticipate the calm I feel when I eat sweets, but it doesn't come.

I go downstairs to get a spoon.

Mama calls, "Sugar, is that you?" She coughs. "I'm thirsty; bring me some soda."

I open the fridge and my hand is on the plastic bottle. I take a chug. I pour the rest into a cup and bring it to her after getting a spoon.

"What's the matter with you? Why haven't you been answerin' me?"

"Sorry Ma—" The scene on the television screen interrupts me. A school photo of Even wearing a blue button-down sits serenely in a square in the upper right-hand corner. The reporter says something about snowmobile accidents becoming more common. Then she's interviewing an expert on snow safety. I'm crumbling.

"Stupid kids get drunk and go too fast. I told Skunk to get rid of that thing. Do you think he listened? Nope. He was out there that night."

A dim light goes on in my mind. I slip out of the room and enter the living room. I plant myself in front of the TV, where Skunk continues his game.

"Move it, fat shit."

I stare at him and search his face for recognition.

"I said out of the way, Sugar."

"Skunk, were you there last night? Did you see Even?"

Skunk leans back on the couch. He wears a nasty look; his eyes are like two black beads set in his thick face.

"There were a lot of people out last night at Cripple Canyon; there's a jump there that skirts the gulch."

"Did you see Even?"

His eyes are hard.

"Answer me." I ball my fists, one still clutching the spoon. "Skunk, did you see Even?"

"Yeah, I did. And you know what? He's a jackass," he says. "He's a fuckin' idiot. I told him to stay off my trails and he ignored me. I pointed him out to Caleb. Told him that Even was the boy you liked. Well, we were just having a little fun. A little game of cat and mouse. Listen, if he knew how to handle a snowmobile, nothing would have happened, but he's a tool and—"

I roar. I lunge at him, but he pushes me to the side, and I roll to the floor. Tears spring from my eyes.

"And now he's gone, Skunk. Gone." I can't believe my brother. Did he really have some part in this? "Did you tell the police?"

"Fuck no. Why would I? There was craziness down there last night. No way am I getting involved."

"But you just said you were chasing him."

"Yeah, but I didn't cause him to run into that tree. He shouldn't have been going so fast."

"But you were after him?"

"We was just fooling around. We didn't make him go so fast or drive into a tree. The fucker did it to himself. I probably did you a favor. I bet you were ready to give it up to him. Slut."

I feel ill. I want to stab Skunk with the spoon, with a fork, with a knife, with anything. I want him to disappear. My body quakes with nausea and disgust. It's so brutal I don't imagine it ending. Ever. I bend over and overturn the coffee table in a rage. I scream and run up to my room.

"You'll just have to clean it up later, fat face," he calls after me.

I jam the spoon into the soft ice cream. I eat bite after bite, hoping for that hit of relaxation, the cessation of nerves pinging dangerously, emotionally, despairingly over the loss of Even. I tear into the candy and dump it in my mouth. I chew until my jaw aches. I return to the ice cream, practically pleading with the sugar to erase my emotions.

I am beyond sad over Even. I am beyond angry at Skunk. I don't want to feel so much. Tears come. I hiccup and burp. I hold half of what is left of the roll of sugar-cookie dough, the plastic torn. I look around at the mess on my bed; it looks like a starving animal came in here, tearing through the wrappers and containers, hunting for something other than food. I take a hunk of dough on my finger and bring it to my tongue. The oblivion I'd hoped sugar would bring me doesn't come. I pull my finger from my mouth. I am overly full, and yet I'm starving. I long for Even.

I step back from my bed and survey it. Skittles form rainbow polka dots, there are cake crumbs everywhere, and the ice cream has melted onto the comforter. I'm disgusted with myself. I crumble to the floor in a big heap. I am intensely aware of every inch of fat in my body. I cry. I cry and cry. I'm upset with myself for eating all of this junk. I am shattered that Even's been taken away. I'm furious at Skunk for his callous attitude and possible part in Even's death. I can't think through all the tears, but for these simple facts. I can't begin to untangle the ways in which they are interwoven.

Without getting off the floor, I reach around on my bed for my cell phone, mashing my hand into the sticky ice cream before landing on its plastic case. I click it on and find a photo of Even, a close-up of the two of us at the beach. I stare at it and force myself not to cry, because the tears would blur my vision. Then, once again, I fall asleep.

Chapter Twenty

I whisper, "Rabbit, rabbit." I wish with everything I have that Even will appear in the bed beside me, just as he was on the first of last month. At school, I may as well be a zombie. I plow through crowds commenting about my puffy eyes, bloated face, overall unacceptability, and, of course, Even.

It's no secret that Even and I were friends, ate together at lunch, showed up together at school, and then walked home afterward. His attractiveness didn't stem the bullying when he was alive; apparently, being friends with someone like him didn't move me up the ranks of popularity. Nothing changed now that he's gone. Hillary is abysmal when she hugs Allie in the hall; her shoulders shuddering in time with her dramatic tears. The look she gives me reminds me of daggers, but my glare is worse. Hot knives. I'm still shoved in the lunch line and hear someone whisper that I'm going to take over as lunch lady when Mrs. Nichols retires.

There have been a few gestures of condolence: a math nerd from the AV club pats me on the shoulder, several familiar faces offer smiles when passing in the hall. In the morning, Mr. Hammons asks me to stay after final homeroom to talk. It's what I expect;

he's sorry for my loss and asks if I'm OK. I just nod and shrug. He's probably concerned that I haven't said a single word since the principal's announcement. I've taken him up on the moment of silence he'd requested, the one I interrupted.

When I get outside, I pause to wait for Even by the brick wall, out of habit, but then realize he won't be meeting me. Twin tears form in my eyes and drop, one and then the other, down my cheek. Reluctantly, I walk home, taking my time. I should have driven, but I'm not ready to let go of the ritual that still connects me to Even. I'm desperate for him to materialize.

As I cross over to my street, grimy slush sprays me. I blink grit out of my eyes. My skin prickles with cold. When I rub my face clear, the taillights of a black Corolla turn the next corner. Hillary and Allie have no reason to hate me that much. It was probably just an accident. If I weren't standing there, it would have sprayed my neighbor Natty Gimbal's forsythia bush.

When I get home, I run a hot shower after bringing Mama her food and soda. As the warm running water soothes my frozen skin, I think about seeing Mama's enormous body spread out on the bed, immobile and helpless, and it reminds me of my binge the night before. I think of how I tried to stuff down my feelings with food, and how I've been doing that most of my life. This time, my feelings won't let me bury them. Even was too significant to be lost to candy and cakes.

The slow drain causes water to pool around my ankles like the tears that will not relent. I cry as I get dressed. I cry as I plop into my bed. I cry as I beg my body to offer some relief, even if just sleep. But my heart is persistent. It won't let me forget.

Forget what? Even? That he was the only person in this town that was nice to me, including myself? That he offered me hope and allowed me to dream? That Even liked me, my smile, and accepted how I look. I can't even offer that to myself. I'm ugly, worthless, and turn into a blubbering mess with endless tears.

I hear the bullies at school and the bully in my own mind. It's crowded in there, with loud voices vying for the cruelest insults, the bitterest truths, and how it's obvious now that I didn't deserve someone like Even. I listen to this assault for hours as the sun sets, my homework goes undone, and Skunk and Mama argue. My name accompanies the words "stupid" and "piece of shit." Mama calls me. Skunk slams around. The loss and the nastiness that play through my mind paralyze me. I don't respond or move.

The principal announces a memorial service for Even the following week. All day, it's as if I am carrying all however-many-hundreds of pounds of myself in my own arms. When I zip up my backpack at my locker, Ms. Barrows snares me in the hall and asks me to follow her to her office.

I take her invitation to sit down in a pleather chair opposite her desk. A kitten hangs on to a bar on a poster behind her with the message "Hang in there." I've been hanging in there my whole life, and just when someone came along who made it so I was doing more than just hanging in there, he's gone. I'd rather do whatever comes when you stop hanging in there and let go.

I don't say this to Ms. Barrows; she'd probably have me committed.

"I know this must be hard for you, Mercy," she says. "Loss is never easy."

I wonder if she knows this firsthand or if she's memorized one of the pamphlets on her wall.

Then she asks, "How are you feeling?"

Something about this question erases the snide comments I'd been preparing. I open my mouth to answer, but there isn't one. How am I? I swallow. I want there to be an answer. Her face looks soft and her lips are certainly not wearing a smile, but they're not *not* smiling either.

"I know some of the kids call you Sugar. Do you like to be called Sugar? Or would you prefer Mercy?"

My mouth parts, but still no sound comes out. She doesn't look impatient or like she has something better to do. Like her face and lips, her eyes are soft as if she's inviting my response. I think about how I got the name and about how much sugar I've eaten in my life. I think about how Even pronounced Sugar, like the *g* twirled a baton or dazzled with sparklers, and how he'd sometimes call me Shoog. I don't want the name Sugar, because of some associations, but I *do* want it because that's the girl Even knew.

"Is Sugar OK?"

Back to that question. Or does she mean is it OK to call me Sugar? I'm confused. I feel like a child and not because she's condescending, not at all, but almost like I'm at the beginning again, like I've been broken down to all of my basic parts and am figuring out how they go together. She continues to look at me openly, warmly.

"I know how to swim, but I feel like I'm drowning," I finally manage to say. A wash of relief comes over me when she rises to her feet, walks over to my chair, takes me by the hands, and holds me in her arms. I begin to sob into her wavy red hair. Her hug is warm and soft—yet firm—like nothing, not even a seismic shift in the earth, could move her. Like Even.

"I will be your life raft for as long as you need me to be," she says, but in my head, I hear Even's voice. We return to our chairs. The lights of the main office outside hers flick off. "I've got all night. If you'd like, you can start at the beginning."

I'm not sure if her offer is within the job description of high school guidance counselor, but I take her up on it. I tell her about my family and the bullying, but leave out a few key parts, not wanting to get anyone in trouble. She asks about my father, but there's nothing to say. I tell her about how I eat and then about Even, and how he was like a ray of sunshine or just a really good dream.

She listens all the while, asking questions here and there.

When my voice gets hoarse, she asks me, "Will you come back tomorrow, after school?"

I nod. As I walk home in the frigid darkness, I feel about one hundred pounds lighter, until I walk into my house.

Mama's voice crushes me as she shouts my name and coughs at the same time. I want to pretend I don't hear. I discover she's messed herself and is starving. I do my duties, give her cough medicine, and then disappear into my room. I cry myself to sleep.

The following day, I resume the confessional with Ms. Barrows. It's as if, overnight, she set several missing pieces of my puzzle into place. She asks me about Mama, and I mostly tell the truth. She asks me about the bullying, and I name names. She asks me about my diet, and I tell about the sweets, the binges, and about how the calm they used to bring has vanished.

It's dark when I leave again. As I walk home, I'm suddenly worried I said too much, like I betrayed Mama and ratted out the kids at school. Something heavy sits in my stomach . . . guilt or maybe betrayal.

I creep into Mama's room. The TV is on, but she's snoring. She rustles when I near the bed, but she's groggy from the cough medicine she's finally taking. "John, John?" she says, her voice a rasp.

"No Mama, it's me."

"John," she repeats.

Or maybe she said *Juan*. I'm not sure. I press my hand to her forehead, but she doesn't have a fever. She must be dreaming.

"I didn't mean for everything to fall apart—" As usual, a cough interrupts her. "Can't put it back—together."

I quietly get her a glass of water from the bathroom, leave it on her night table, and turn off the TV.

The next day, which almost feels like one long night, I feel like I have a target on my back. I'm afraid that, at any moment, someone might come up to me and thank me for getting them into trouble with a big punch to the face.

I return to Ms. Barrows's office a third day. The last, I promise myself with building anxiety. As before, she invites me in with a warm smile.

"Sugar, I've been thinking a lot about you over the past couple days," she tells me. "I feel honored that you shared so much of your personal life with me. I got the sense that you really needed to unload it all, but I think speaking to someone else might be more effective. You see, I'm just a high school counselor, and I get ambitious about helping you and everyone else here at JRHS, but I think you have more to say and perhaps more to hear. I have someone in mind if you'd be willing to see her. Her name is Juliana Collins. She's in Keene. I've spoken to her, and she'd love to meet you."

I'm a combination of betrayal and confusion. "A shrink? But I thought you could help me?"

"Haven't I?" I want to be mad at her, but I can tell she doesn't mean this in a patronizing way.

I want her to be the one. I want to find a reason to dislike her, to replace the disappointment I now feel.

"Please go see her, Sugar," she says. "I'm certain she can help you."

I've never thought about myself as a person who needs help. I do the helping. Ms. Barrows repeats this back to me almost verbatim. I take a card with "Juliana Collins" written in embossed script across the middle with contact information beneath.

"Can you promise me you'll call her?"

I think about the target I had on my back all day. I'm afraid.

With trepidation, I leave her office while it's still daylight. When I get back to my house, I turn the card over and over in my hand. I think about how good it felt to tell Ms. Barrows everything. What she said about how I have more to say and hear echoes enticingly. I memorized the phone number and the email on the card.

I leave the house and drive to the library. I have an email account, but usually access it from my phone since we don't have a computer at home, and I hardly ever use it because typing a long message on my phone is daunting. Who'd I write anyway?

I log on and type Juliana Collins's email into the address bar. I enter, "Recommendation from Ms. Barrows at JRHS" as the subject line. I proceed to write an impossibly long email, repeating everything I told Ms. Barrows. I finish with "She said I need help" and my name. I log off, meeting the same feeling of lightness followed by fear as I did earlier. Am I supposed to be telling anyone this? I imagine consequences involving humiliation and bruises.

Mama used to say, "Don't air your dirty laundry in public," but then our dryer broke. *But the laundry was washed, clean,* the voice in my head counters. *Right, but if it is out to air, it was dirty before; everyone knows that.* I argue with myself all the way home.

The following day at school, the entire student body gathers for an assembly. I assume it has something to do with Even. I tremble, fighting back tears. I take a seat on the end of a row in case I need to make a quick escape. My hips spread off the hard folding chair and overflow into the space by my neighbor. *Not now. I don't need the body-hate now.*

The principal steps up to the podium and tests the microphone. He reads the school's policy about bullying and then turns on a video meant to discourage it. When it's over, to my horror, Ms. Barrows stands at the podium. I pray she doesn't bring attention to me or mention anything I told her. I'm frozen. I don't blink or swallow. I'm not even sure I'm breathing.

She announces that it's anti-bullying week across America and then launches into an inspiring speech about how when she was younger she wore glasses, had braces, and her red hair made her stick out like a sore thumb. She goes on to explain how she was different, picked on, and what it felt like. She's younger and more stylish than most of the teachers in attendance and therefore probably more attractive and therefore acceptable in the eyes of the target audience for this presentation. A peculiar thought skates into my mind and then just as quickly leaves. *Maybe she likes herself the way she is. Imagine that.*

I listen to her story and, in places, it mimics my own. She catches my eye. Again, I hope no one notices. She implores us to stick together, to make this a safe community, and reminds us that bullying won't be tolerated at JRHS. There's polite applause.

I duck out of the auditorium while trying to think of where I might hide. I decide to leave, so I go to my locker. I'm thankful there wasn't a stampede, but I fear they'll all know I'd tattled, just like they did when in third grade I knew who broke the classroom computer and told the teacher after she'd threatened to take away pajama day, which was sure to be chock-full of delicious sweet treats.

Ms. Barrows catches me in the hall on my way out the front door. She asks if I've contacted Juliana. I look down at my shoes with a feeling of shame brought on by letting her see right through me to my weakest spots, revealing that I do need help—prompting her to lead an anti-bullying assembly and recommending me to a shrink.

"Sugar? Did you make the call?"

"I sent an email."

"Wonderful. Would you like to come into my office?"

I shake my head. I watch her shoulders lifting with each breath. I can't meet her eyes.

"If you change your mind, I'll be in there for the next couple hours." She turns and her heels echo as she clicks down the hall.

I breeze out the front doors of the school. I plant myself on the wall, as if Even will come. Then the reminder that it isn't the end of the day and Even isn't coming, now or ever, storms into my mind like the gathering clouds overhead.

I plod through the slushy streets back to my house, but before I enter, I turn back and bring myself to the church. It isn't Sunday, but I pause on the stone steps, unable to go farther. I turn my back and gaze at the sky, the color of sour milk. I clasp my hands before sinking to my knees. I shout, "Why?" Tears spill. "Why?" I moan.

I sob until I can't see clearly. I close my eyes, asking God why he took Even away. Why dim the sun? Why ruin everything? Why the cruelty? In my mind I scream and tantrum and beg, gripping my hands together until they're red and cold. I collapse, unable to hold myself up. I'm tight with anger but can't bring myself to leave. I stay there until my tears freeze on my face.

Back in my room, I thaw and continue to let the tears fall. I repeat this for the rest of the week: school, tears, and more school. Almost as notable as Even's absence is the lack of laughter, comments, and jokes at my expense over the next couple of days. Maybe Ms. Barrows's assembly worked.

That night, when I bring Mama her dinner, I see a news report on TV about how a girl in Alabama took her own life because she'd been harassed about her speech impediment. I've never really thought about that, except maybe in the cool water of the river last summer, hoping for a snakebite, but that was more like escape, not death. No, that's not my fate.

As the chirpy newscaster tries to sound somber and Mama huffs over her with comments and intermittent coughing, I know what Even would have wanted from me. Without a word, I walk up to my room, lost in thought, hardly noticing Skunk and a couple of friends in the living room devouring chicken wings.

Even wanted me to travel cross-country with him. He wanted me to laugh, smile, and live brightly. Then, in another fit of tears, I dissolve.

I scrape myself out of bed for the memorial service the following day. Bleary-eyed, I tear through my clothes, finding plenty of black, but nothing worthy of this particular occasion. Maybe the idea came to me in a dream or maybe my consciousness has fractured, but I don't want to wear typical mourning clothes. I imagine myself in something bold and beautiful, maybe involving chrome. I can't even summon a laugh at my ludicrousness and throw my closet door open. Hanging there are a dozen hand-sewn dresses, even a floor-length gown. I settle on a dress with lace along the arms and chest, sewn into a fitted bodice and flared skirt. The color is between pink and coral: the sky at dawn.

I shower and brush my hair, suddenly sodden with grief. The dress remains on the hanger. The only color for the way I feel is the darkest, most starless, and deepest of nights.

Almost the entire upper class turns up, as well as teachers; a bunch of mechanics, as evidenced by the line of grease under their nails; and, of course, Even's father and family. Father Caplin offers a eulogy and the principal says a few words. When he's done, the priest asks if anyone would like to say something. Utter silence.

Through a veil of tears that I don't try to resist, I approach the microphone. As I turn to face the group, I wish myself invisible. I spot Allie and Hillary, Will and Nash. I clear my throat. I didn't plan what I'm going to say.

"I may not have known Even as long as some of you, but he knew me better than any of you. I feel a hole in my life and in my heart. He was the kindest person I've ever known. He acted like a mirror, showing me the best parts of myself, things I didn't see and I'm sure you don't either. He was unmatched in his generosity with words and gestures. I can't imagine life without him. I don't want to—" I pause, on the verge of a breakdown, but will myself to continue. "But he would want me to. So right now, I call upon the very first day Even and I met, and every day thereafter, and welcome him fully into my heart, a place for him to rest peacefully, and I hope for you to do the same." My voice cracks and tears fall, but I call out, "I miss you, Even."

Chapter Twenty-One

After the service, with soggy feet and a tearstained face, I wander aimlessly. I'm numb and feeling everything acutely at the same time, as I retrace all the steps Even and I ever took.

I find myself on Birch Road. My toes are frozen. The driveway is empty. I slip as I go too fast up the ice-encrusted stairs to Even's apartment. I knock and knock on the door, calling out his name. Little white clouds of desperate hope accompany every "Even? Are you there? Are you home?"

I jiggle the handle. It turns. I push the sticky door open. When I cross the threshold, dirty dishes litter the messy kitchen. I run my hand along the counter, realizing Even hasn't been here to clean up. Even's gone. I turn the water to warm, keeping my hand under it until I'm satisfied with the temperature and my fingers thaw. I clean every dish, spoon, bowl, and pot. I sponge down the counter and sweep.

I tidy up the living room, stopping at a dusty family photo. There's young Nash and a woman who must be Tansy, Even's mother. Her hair is the same color as Even's and a little wild. When I wipe away the dust with my sleeve, I realize the photo of the baby,

Even, was stuck behind the glass to make the picture whole; to look like a family with a baby. Tansy never held her babies, Even or his twin. I set it down. Tears trickle from my eye.

I save Even's room for last. When I enter, his distinct smell makes my knees weak. I sink to the bed and rest my head on his pillow. I cry into it until it's damp and the grays of winter dusk prompt me to reach my hand over to the night table to turn on the lamp. My hand brushes against a book. Even's journal. I clutch it to my chest.

When I flip through the pages, his great adventure, his dream to bring his mother's ashes to the sea, floods my thoughts. Then I recall his tempestuous relationship with his father and don't imagine he would take kindly to me pilfering through his late son's room.

Just as I am about to turn off the light, I notice a wooden box on Even's dresser. Pressed into the top, in what looks like opalescent seashell, is the name "Tansy Anderson" and her birthdate and the date she died. I take Even's pillowcase and the journal. I descend the icy stairs carefully. Just as I'm about to head down the driveway and walk home, I have a better idea. I go to the shed and back Even's motorcycle down the ramp. I straddle it, start it up, and rumble back home.

When I pull up next to the Honda, my stomach sinks. I have nowhere to hide the Harley. Skunk will see it if I park it in the driveway and will probably vandalize it. Nonetheless, I turn it off and sit there to think. The familiar curve of the cool metal and sturdy handlebars reminds me how perfectly Even and I fit on it together.

I spot my reflection in the windows of the garage door, which is brimming with old junk. I open up the bay. I rearrange some boxes, an old plastic swimming pool, and some other stuff. It'll fit in, and then I'll conceal it again. I go about this endeavor, praying that Skunk won't appear or, if he's already home that he won't hear me. When I'm done, the only sound that greets me is Mama's holler.

I bring her dinner and another bottle of cough medicine. She asks why I look so wet. I don't dare tell her it's sweat. A car drives by in the slush.

"Sprayed by a puddle," I lie, asking God to forgive me.

"Stupid. Why didn't you get out of the way? Always in the way, Sugar. I remember when you were a little girl, you were always underfoot—"

I don't stay to hear the rest.

When I return to my room, I check my email on my phone and see the therapist has written me back with an encouraging note and her availability. I reply, confirming an appointment for Monday. Then I dive under the covers and crack the first page of Even's journal.

For a moment, I hesitate. Is this intruding on his privacy? Would he want me to read this? Then a slip of paper falls out. When I flip it over, I realize it's a photo of the two of us, not the collage I gave him for Christmas, but another; it looks like one he snapped one night when we went out for pizza and took turns playing our favorite songs on the jukebox. He must have printed it out. I begin reading his mother's entries, and just when I reach the end, I doze off.

I wake in the morning, and the journal is open, resting on my chest. I mark the page where I left off, the break between Tansy's writing and Even's, with the photo of the two of us.

After church, as I linger, enjoying the familiar smell of extinguished candles and letting the Holy Spirit bring me to my knees to pray, I think about Tansy. She wrote about becoming a mother and her hopes and dreams. I felt her love for her family in her words, stretching through time, her legacy for her son. I kneel and bring my hands together. I think about Granddad and Boo. Sometimes when I pray, I get the sense that God has opened up the lines for me to talk directly to them.

In my prayers, I confess that I've hidden a motorcycle in the garage and promise Boo that I will get back to my sewing. I tell them about Mama and Skunk and how I'm afraid I'm failing them, but as soon as these thoughts cross my mind, I am overwhelmed by the feeling that I'm failing myself more than anyone. I slide back on the pew and sit there, just thinking, until the setting sun illuminates Jesus's feet in the stained-glass window.

The next day, after school, I take the Honda to Juliana Collins's office up in Keene. It's inside a house painted salmon-pink with green trim, almost a Victorian, but not quite. When I enter the office, the smell of lemon and sage greets me. I know this only because Boo loved the combination. Juliana's head peeks out from a closet, and she lifts a smile on her lips when she sees me.

"Hi, Mercy. It's nice to meet you," she says as she puts down a folder and extends her hand. She shakes mine with a firm grip. She is old enough to be my mother, but her legs look strong, sturdy, as does her jaw. Her hair is short, but not poufy like many women prefer when they reach a certain age. She moves efficiently, and her voice has deliberateness to it.

"Since I've already read your backstory in the email and learned a bit about you from Rebecca—I mean, Ms. Barrows—I think the best thing to do would be to jump right in, with both feet, and get things sorted out. What do you think?"

We spend the next two hours with equal floor time, as she asks questions and I answer. Like a tangled piece of yarn, we unravel my story into one long strand of events, thoughts, actions, and consequences, so that I can see them all clearly stretched before me. Then she helps me spool it all back up again, neatly, in a way that makes sense.

When I leave, I have that same lightness as I did after that first night with Ms. Barrows. Along with it, I have a sense of what could be, more so than I did when I just poured out my heartache to the school counselor.

Juliana commends me for walking to school and back, and not at all in an insulting way. She recommends I keep at it, and suggests that I take a walk when I'm feeling stress or anger instead of reaching for a sweet. She seems hopeful and not at all judgmental about my body or situation but sees the relationship between the two. More than anything, she urges me to prioritize my health, both physical and mental. This sounds a lot like permission to take care of myself—not everyone else, including Mama and Skunk. She tells me something revolutionary: *I'm worth it.*

When I get home, Mama says, "You seem cheerful."

I don't want to tell her what I've been up to, but then I have a flash of inspiration. "Mama, I'm getting help."

"What do you mean?" She eyes me suspiciously. "You haven't been taking drugs, have you?"

"No Mama, with my eating habits and my, um, situation."

Her eyes alight with flame. "What, this ain't good enough for you? You have some kind of problem? After all I've done for you, this is the thanks I get, you telling me you've got problems. No, Sugar, I'm the one's got problems, namely you and your brother." She carries on as I back out of the room, knowing now that I don't have to listen to this and seeing very clearly how she simply won't listen to me.

I heat a dinner from the freezer and retreat to my room. I rub the heart-shaped seashell between my fingers and then open Even's journal again, starting where I left off. Almost as if in answer to his mother's entries, Even outlines his trip west with passages of his own. I imagine him there beside me, just as he was when he first revealed the journal that day on the beach. I almost feel his warmth radiating. I close the journal and cry over loss—over my loss of him but also over his lost opportunity to take his epic trip and be free.

Over the next month, I go to school, manage to keep up with my work amidst tear-filled afternoons, which only abate when I visit Juliana on Mondays and Wednesdays. She helps me work on rebuilding my self-image and confidence. I can't help but superimpose this against the backdrop of heartache, but Juliana is so earnest in her belief in me that I don't tell her how much I hurt for Even.

April sweeps out March, and drizzle and downpours replace sleet. Spring is in the air. On afternoons when the sun manages to show itself, I smell the earth thawing. Salt and sand border the streets where the slush has dried up. A sliver of hope knocks on the door of my heart as I take my evening walk. As I set out, I notice Natty Gimbal's forsythia bush is keen to bloom. Little golden buds dot the slender branches. I remember a poem by Robert Frost.

Tears come to my eyes. I'm stricken with the paradox of beauty and impermanence. I held on to Even so briefly. Gold. Now he's gone. Forever. Everywhere I walk, something reminds me of him, but if I take those memories away, there are others: darker memories of belittling, bullying, and when Mama was still on her feet, public humiliation. Now I just carry the shame on my own, but it haunts the streets and shops, and crawls insidiously through every inch of the town.

It's nearly dark when I round a corner close to the convenience store. Hooting and loud music issue from a car as it approaches from behind. It speeds by. I dismiss the antics as townies, hot with spring fever. When I get home, though, the same car that sped by sits beside the Honda in the driveway. I hesitate, wondering if I should go in, but I need to make sure Mama's settled in for the night. Juliana urged me to hire a nurse, because Mama's state-subsidized health care would cover it, but when I mentioned it, especially about getting her cough looked at, Mama raised hell.

I slip in the door and tend to Mama. Like a ghost, I keep close to the wall as I make my way to the stairs. I slip past Skunk and his friends in the living room, watching some stupid movie. Relieved, I close the door to my bedroom. I take out my sewing, intent on finishing the details on a couple of the dresses I've nearly completed before starting a new one. I lose myself in the rhythm of my needle: in, pull, up, in, pull, up.

I continue my biweekly visits with Juliana. I've made progress, and all my crying washed away more pounds. As Juliana helps me construct a positive image of myself, it's like a tightly closed bud inside of me softens, hinting at blooming.

My middle-sized pants hang loose around my waist. I can practically see my goal body shape in my future. I still crave sugar, or maybe it's Even. He's never far from my thoughts. When I get the urge to stuff myself with cinnamon buns and pie, I think of what he'd want from me, what I'd want to offer him: a healthy girl, ready to ride to the Pacific. Although that won't be happening now, I still dream about it. He and Juliana have taught me strength and courage.

At school, I receive nearly as many nasty comments about losing weight as I did about being heavier. Brandon now calls me "Jenny Craig" and offers me jellybeans and chocolates. Another kid, one of Hillary's friends, says Mama's eating all my food. The girls default to accusations of anorexia and bulimia, when they're the ones in the bathroom during or after lunch period.

May brings Fat Henry home, also looking slimmer. He comments on my weight loss, saying I look healthier.

"I have something exciting to tell you and Mama and, well, Skunk, too," he says.

The rumor is Skunk dropped out of school, so it's doubtful he cares about much, least of all any news Henry has. Henry's eyes twinkle. He follows me to Mama's room. Something smells foul, but we both act polite and try to ignore it.

"Mama, I have something to tell you," Henry says, practically bouncing.

She flicks her lighter. After she takes a drag of her cigarette, smoke pours from her nose. "Well, you better tell me quick; you look like you might disappear. If you're still with that girlfriend of yours, tell her she better start cooking right or else you're going to straight-up vanish."

Henry's eyebrows furrow. "Mama, actually it is about Stacy and me," he says.

"I don't know if I like that girl. She's that Brittany's cousin? The one that got herself knocked up?"

I start to interrupt that nearly everyone in town is somehow related to Brittany, but button up, wanting to let Henry share his news.

"See, Sugar here, she wants to be skinny like Brittany. Don't you, Sugar? For a while I thought you was trying to starve me or keep me from all the food and eat it yourself, but now I know you ain't doing that. You and Fat Henry here, I hardly know you anymore."

Henry looks dismal. "Mama, I came here to tell you some good news. Why do you have to be like that?"

"Be like what? The way I am ain't never been a problem for you before? What? Has that Stacy girl taken my place? You don't love your Mama no more?"

"Mama, I don't think it's that. Just give him a chance to tell you," I say, trying to make it easier for him. I'm still used to Mama's spite, but perhaps Henry has forgotten how to arm himself.

"Shut up, Sugar. You don't know what you're talkin' about. Stupid fathead. I've always said you were just a pain in my ass. Why don't you make yourself useful and get me some soda," she says.

I bow my head. "Sure, Mama." I go to the kitchen. Moments later, she's shouting, and Henry thunders from the room, red-faced.

"Sugar—Mercy. I want to call you Mercy. That's your name. Or Bella—and remind you you're beautiful. She's a nasty woman, and don't you believe for a minute anything she says to you." Henry's eyes shine with tears. I've never seen him like this. "I came here today to tell you all that I'm getting married. I love Stacy and she loves me. What that woman does isn't anything that could be called love," he says, pointing to the wall that separates the hall and Mama's room.

"She's never loved us, and having been away from her, I see so clearly how messed up she is. She just doesn't want any of us—you, me, or Skunk—to be any better off than she is. I bet she wants you to end up in bed next to her, followed by Skunk and then me. Lying there in misery, letting this house and the weight of unhappiness crush us to death. Just don't forget that you're a good person. Don't let her make you believe otherwise." He lowers his shoulders, and his breathing becomes even again.

"I'm sorry, Henry. That didn't go as planned. I try to help her, but—"

"It's not your responsibility."

"I'm all she's got—"

Henry shakes his head. He takes my upper arms in his hands. "You are not her mother. And if I didn't know better, I'd say she isn't yours either. It's not your job to take care of her. You're just barely still a kid. Be free." He pulls me into a hug.

Juliana says that I am my responsibility; his comments echo this.

"I don't think I'll be coming back here. If you ever want to leave, you always have a place to stay with me," he says, and exits.

I watch him walk down the path and get into his car. He pauses before he starts it up. I don't dare go back to Mama's room until she cools off.

At midmonth, as I take my evening walk on the dirt-bike trail, I remember Even honing his riding skills on it before he fixed up his motorcycle. I remember that sunny day when we searched for his wallet. I am lost in Even-land when a dirt bike comes toward me. I jump out of the way. The rider doesn't stop, but I see his dark eyes. Caleb. A few others follow in his dust. At the next break in the woods, I get off the path and hurry onto a main street. I walk until it's nearly dark and the mosquitos nibble at me.

When I get home, Skunk, Caleb, and some of their friends are on the back deck, drinking beer and taking shots with a BB gun at the empty cans. I slide upstairs unnoticed and go to my room to finish my homework.

After I've finished my Spanish and history, I look at my phone, click to Even's photo, and then turn off my light, holding his image in my mind as I drift off to sleep. After a time, I feel breath close to my face. The covers suddenly whoosh up and cold meets my arms and legs. Someone slides in next to me.

"Hey, Shoog," a voice slurs.

"Huh? What? Please don't call me that," I say, confused, but very quickly I am wide-awake. I shimmy to the other side of the bed. The guy grabs my arm in a tight grip. Futz.

"Now come on. I know you're lonely now that your boyfriend's dead."

Heat rises to my face. "Caleb? Let go of me."

"C'mon, it'll be fun."

My courage puddles toward the floor. But I force a deep breath and remain firm.

"Sugar, I'm going to fuck your brains out," he says.

I taste bile in my mouth. "No. Back off."

He pulls me toward him. The sickly smell of stale beer fills my nose.

"Yeah. I think you want me. I saw you on the trail. Were you looking for me?" He grabs for my pants. I feel ill. I scramble to my feet, wriggling away. "Now that you've lost all that weight, I want to bang you even more. Come on, Shoog."

"I said don't call me that. Leave now." The streetlight shining outside my window reveals his unfocused eyes. He crawls across the bed, closer to where I stand, trembling.

"Get back on the bed. Unless you like the floor, you dog." His lips are an invisible line.

"Shut up!" I scream at the top of my lungs. I don't know why I expect anyone to come. "If you don't leave right now, I'm going to call the police."

"My cousin is one of the officers. They're not going to believe you. Plus, why the hell would I try to fuck a fat chick? Get in the bed. If you don't, I'll make you." Very slowly, I've rounded to the side of my room with my closet and sewing materials. I didn't put them away the other day, and my scissors are resting right on top of my thread box. Caleb follows closely. His proximity makes terror pulse inside of me.

He reaches for me and brushes my breast. I back away, but he's quick and clutches my arms. As he gets close enough to put his lips on mine, I grab the scissors and put them between us. In the dim light, the metal gleams menacingly.

"I said to leave *now*," I say through gritted teeth.

He backs away, his arms up in surrender. "You wouldn't really, Sugar." He wears a mixture of fear and defiance as the dim streetlight shines across his face. Then, in a blink, he's dark again. My door opens, the hall light shines brightly for a moment, and then it closes, leaving me alone in the dim room.

Caleb clods downstairs.

I sit on the edge of my bed, shaking. I'm not sure what to do. I can't sleep here with the scissors under my pillow again. It's not safe. The numbers on the digital clock creep by. No one comes for me.

I put all my sewing materials in their bin and neatly fold all of the dresses I've made and place them on top, but I keep the scissors handy. I shove all my schoolbooks in my backpack and then take a bag and fill it with clothing. My fingers tremble as I put Even's journal, his mom's ashes, and the pillowcase in my shoulder bag. I make sure I have my phone and keys.

I stand on the inside of my door and listen. Hooting comes from the back of the house, telling me Skunk and his friends are still out there. The hint of wood smoke in the air suggests they have started a bonfire. A firecracker booms and then a dog barks in the distance. I wonder if anyone is still in the house. Do I dare go downstairs? Should I wait until morning? What about Mama? I sink to the floor. I glance around my room. So many memories of these four walls, the shabby paint, and the threadbare rug. I take a breath. No, I have to leave. I have to risk it.

I can't stay here with Caleb lurking around, with Skunk and his nasty friends partying nearly every night, and Mama. What about Mama?

She'll have to let a nurse come. She will just have to. I stand up, turn the doorknob, and exit into the hall with my bags in hand. I slip down the stairs to the living room. My heart pounds in my chest. Through the smudged sliding glass doors, the silhouettes of heads darken against the blazing fire. My quickened pulse rushes in my ears. I go through the hall and pause near Mama's door. It's quiet.

No, I have to put one foot in front of the other.

I continue to the kitchen. Behind me, I close the front door. I draw a breath. I let the cool air inflate my lungs. I rush to the car, toss my stuff in the back, and escape into the night.

Chapter Twenty-Two

I drive away from the house without looking back. I don't know where to go. My stomach churns about leaving Mama. I find myself in front of the twenty-four-hour Dunkin' Donuts attached to a gas station near the edge of town. I order a mixed dozen plus a Coolatta, anything to quench the searing fear that slices through me every time I think about what I'm doing.

In the nearly empty parking lot, I chew a jelly-filled donut. I worry that I've done the wrong thing. I lick the powder off my fingers from a Boston Kreme. Then there's Skunk; what will he do to the house? I let the glaze on a chocolate donut melt in my mouth. But what about Caleb? I fear the worst about what he might do next. I lick the cream out of an éclair. Where will I stay? I can't very well sleep in my car. I eat a pillowy glazed donut, conflicted about school.

A man in a flannel shirt fills the tank of his Dodge in the yellow light of the gas station. I slurp my drink. I think about the motorcycle. I'll have to go back for it at some point, but a big part of me never wants to return. A part of me feels like I'm on the back of the Harley, the wind in my hair, almost free.

The door to the convenience store opens, and a group of kids from school with the midnight munchies walks out. I slump in my seat so they don't see me. I'm still shaking, but not only from flight; the donuts and Coolatta have given me the jitters. I close the box and put it on the backseat. What am I doing? Where am I supposed to go? Less than a month left at school until summer break. I'm eighteen, so I can get my own apartment and finish senior year. Where? With what? How will I support myself? I've saved money over the last three summers, but that won't get me far.

I start the Honda and drive, hoping movement will clear my head. Back in town, I pass the church. I double back and park in the lot. Resting my cheek on the headrest, I gaze up at the building. I wonder if they lock it.

The side door pulls open easily. It's pitch-black, so I use my cell phone to illuminate the square foot in front of me before settling into my usual pew. When I get on my knees, I'm not sure where the room, immense in the darkness, begins or ends. It is a bit disorienting. It doesn't matter, because when I close my eyes and bring my hands together, I may as well be in the cavern of my own heart.

I pray.

I call upon God, Boo, and Granddad. I ask what I should do. Then I listen. Even laughs, warmly, like breath warming my hands, like a whisper of a memory, like seagulls and the rumble of a motorcycle. It's like sunshine and water lapping my toes. Then everything gets brighter; the light within me fills in the dark corners and forgotten crevices. I see myself smiling by the glow of this light. I feel peace.

I slide back on the wooden pew. I take a deep breath and then I remember Henry telling me if I ever want to leave, I can stay with him. I've never been to his apartment, but have a vague idea of where it is in Keene near the university.

I have school the next day. Afterward, I'll call him and see if it's OK for me to go there. It'll be a long commute each morning, but it's only until school is over, and then maybe I'll leave for good. I recline on the pew; lie on my side, pulling my sweatshirt close around me; and drift to sleep.

When I wake up in the morning, I'm staring at Jesús. Not his holiness, but Jesús, the man who cleans and tends to the church.

"*Buenos días,*" he says.

"Hi," I say, my voice rough from sleep.

"*¿Español?*"

"*Un poco.*" I tell him. A little. My grades in Spanish are fair, but I'm certainly not fluent. I'm positive he speaks English, at least *un poco*.

He sighs and says, "*Qué pena.*"

I wonder why he thinks that's a shame.

"Are you hungry?" he asks, in accented English.

I remember the donut binge and guilt crushes me.

He beckons me to follow him.

I ache from sleeping on the narrow pew and stretch before catching up to Jesús.

We walk downstairs to the recreation room and then through a hall into what looks like an efficiency apartment. I wonder if there are more like this and if Father Caplin rents rooms to the needy—now, that being me.

"Come in. *Siéntese, por favor.*" Jesús tells me to sit, offering me a chair at a little round table against the wall, and goes to the counter. He works with his back to me, and after a few moments, the smell of coffee perks me up. He brings me a cup filled to the brim and, on a plate in his other hand, he holds a tortilla spread with beans and cheese.

"Breakfast," he says. "You like?"

I nod.

Jesús's bed is in the corner, neatly made; above it hangs a wooden cross. Also in the sparse room is a bureau topped with several candles bearing the image of Mary. A pair of dress shoes and a pair of boots are lined up underneath.

I roll up the tortilla and take a bite. It's simple, but filled with flavor that satisfies my taste buds in a way that the donuts the night before didn't. He is silent while I eat. We avoid each other's eyes, or rather, I avoid his, but I sense that he watches me intently. I try to ignore it. I wipe my mouth and then take a sip of the coffee.

"*Por favor*, why were you sleeping upstairs?" Our eyes meet. His are somehow familiar. I've seen him at church every week for my entire life, but there's a flash of recognition and then it's gone. I blink. I'm not sure how to answer, and I don't know if I should. Maybe if I say the right thing, I'll avoid getting in trouble. I'm guessing sleeping in the church is frowned upon.

"I had to leave home," I say, carefully arranging my napkin.

"Why? Trouble?"

It takes me a moment to understand what he said, because of the way he blends the letters together. Then I nod.

He looks sympathetic. "We all have that from time to time. I see you here every week. I know you are a good girl." We are quiet for a minute. He must know that it wasn't me who caused the trouble. "You came to the right place, but now, where will you go?"

"For starters, school. Then I will stay with my brother."

"Enrique?" he asks, lighting up.

"Henry," I say, correcting him. He never goes by his real name, preferring the English version.

"I see him here sometimes, too."

I'm surprised he knows who my brother is. "He started going to the church near where he lives in Keene."

"Oh good. He is well?"

I nod. "He's engaged to be married."

Jesús beams. "*Bueno*."

"Yes, *bueno*."

"You have another brother. How's he?"

I don't know how to answer this or why Jesús cares; perhaps he's just trying to fill the silence. I shrug. "He's Skunk, I guess."

"Skunk? I do not know what this means." Jesús looks perplexed.

Skunk hasn't been to church since he was still in the single digits.

"Ernesto. Skunk is his nickname. He's just . . . difficult."

"I see."

But I doubt he does. I say, "I should probably be going—school."

"Would you like to clean? Shower?"

I actually would, though this seems like a strange thing to do here.

"It's OK. I go and wash floors upstairs. You shower there." He points to a door.

"Thank you."

"De nada." He exits.

I find Jesús's tidy bathroom and quickly rinse off yesterday's indignities and put my clothes back on. I'm already a target for insults whether I'm skinny or fat, so wearing slept-in clothes won't really make much of difference, though I could change into something clean from the bag in my car once I get to school. I use my fingers to untangle my hair. I'd like to brush my teeth, but feel weird about using Jesús's toothpaste. The floor above creaks with footsteps. I quickly squeeze out some of the paste onto my finger and run it over my teeth.

I take one last look in the mirror. My eyes reflect clearly back. For a second I think I see Jesús's eyes, too—a ring of coffee-brown, and an even darker hue in the center. I shiver and open the bathroom door. Blocking the doorway back upstairs and shifting nervously, Jesús holds his clasped hands together, as if in prayer.

"Thank you. I feel much better," I stutter.

"Yes. Good." He bobs his head up and down.

I thank him for the breakfast and edge toward the door.

"*Sí*, Mercy Bella, I have something I'd like to tell you." He takes a deep breath and walks over to his bureau.

I'm suddenly nervous and consider bolting. What if he's crazy or tries something like Caleb did? No one knows where I am. I doubt anyone would hear me scream. Then I think about the night before and how no one would come anyway. No one cares. I break into a cold sweat.

Jesús turns back to me and holds an envelope in his hands. "Please sit down. For one more minute." He studies me. "Your hair. Beautiful hair."

I think it's rather limp and disheveled since I only brushed it with my fingers, plus it is still damp. I put my hand up to it and instantly think of Even. He liked my hair, my smile . . . "Uh. Thanks." Jesús stares at me. My stomach does a turn. I should leave. This is getting weird.

"I have this to give to you. *Por favor, lo abres*," he says, handing me an envelope and urging me to open it.

I take it and hesitantly lift the flap. I pull out a small stack of photos and a letter. I look at the pictures. There is one of a man holding a baby and smiling the widest smile I've ever seen. I can practically count his teeth. I put it at the bottom of the pile, and there's another, this time just of the baby, dark hair and eyes wide. The next one is of a little girl wearing a dress, still wobbly on her feet, and the last is this same girl sitting on the front of a motorcycle, the man holding her tightly and smiling over her shoulder. Tears spring to my eyes.

I recognize the man and the motorcycle. I take a photo out of my pocket and hold it up to the one in my hand.

"*¿Comprendes?*" Jesús asks.

"Yes, I think I do."

Chapter Twenty-Three

Time speeds up as it nears the hour I have to be in homeroom, but I have questions and so many blank spaces to fill in. Jesús's smile radiates warmth as I continue to study the photos.

"Yes, that is your *papá*, Juan. I am his brother. Jesús."

I almost choke on my second cup of coffee when he says this. It's one thing to think a life-altering thought; it's another thing entirely to hear it confirmed.

"His brother."

"Yes," he says, grinning. "First we went to Puerto Rico from Mexico to work when we were your age. Then we came here. He met your mother shortly after. Fiery passion."

I cringe.

"They marry before she have the baby. Then trouble, as you say. After Ernesto was born. Juan thinks everything is going to be OK. But Silvia, *tu Mamá*, doesn't want him anymore. She sends him away very angry."

I wonder whether he means my father or Mama was angry. I want to say something so he sees that Mama is a complicated woman, not so much as an apology, but so he understands, though I'm not even sure I do.

"She—"

He shakes his head. "I'm very sorry, *mi sobrina. Ella es una perra.*"

I think he means Mama is a dog, but the way he says it suggests something worse.

"*Lo siento.* She is not good woman. She reported him to the authorities for something he didn't do, and they send him back. He tried to get back to the States, to you and your brothers. He wrote letters every week but could not get here. He stayed in Mexico with our mother, who was sick. You have hair just like her." He's quiet a moment. "She's gone now, but he stayed there, hoping someday to return," Jesús says, looking sad. I don't know what to make of this.

"Your *papá* speaks very good English, better than me. But he wrote that letter *en español.*" He points to my hand. "Maybe you try to read? He wanted to come back to you, but when he couldn't, and it was obvious *tu mamá* would not let him, he write this. I want to give it to you long ago, but no. I'm afraid *la perra* will bite."

"Me, too," I whisper, fighting back tears. I turn the letter over in my hands.

"Gracias, Jesús," I say, when I've regained my composure. He has a generous smile. I realize it's not only his eyes that mine resemble, but his smile, too, generous, open, and warm. When I look again at the photographs in my hand, I see that these traits are from my papa. That must have been what Even saw. "I should go. School."

"You come back. Visit? I tell you stories about your *papá.*"

I nod.

"And you read that letter, *sí*?"

"Yes, I will. I'll read it." I am out the door.

"Mercy," he calls after me and trots to catch up. *"Por favor, no dices nada a la perra."*

I don't intend to go back home or talk to Mama again, at least not for a long time. "I promise."

I rush to school and slide into my seat just as the bell rings. Mr. Hammons doesn't give me the look I'm expecting. I exhale with relief.

I can hardly concentrate with the envelope burning in my pocket; I feel the heat right to my core. During my free period, I take out the letter, but then put it away. I don't want to cry at school and give anyone more reason to pick on me, but I'm dying to know what it says.

The large circular clock seems to have paused as it painstakingly ticks its way to the final bell. I rush to my locker, get everything I need for my homework assignments, including my Spanish dictionary, and then burst outside. I pass the low wall where I used to wait for Even; my jaw trembles. I press my lips together to stop the tears and then walk to the parking lot. When I get to my car, my mouth drops open.

Donuts cover it. Chocolate and glaze melts all over the hood and a chocolate frosted with sprinkles slides slowly down the window. More sprinkles confetti the roof and trunk, along with every kind of donut imaginable: cake, blueberry, glazed, jelly. There are creams and puffs and rolls, sticks and even donut holes dotting the Honda. I peer through the window. My Dunkin' Donuts box from the night before still rests on the backseat. I pull out my phone and take photos from all angles.

I pluck the donuts from the windshield and then get in. The Honda smells like a bakery, but not in a good way. I'm disgusted, but more angry than sad. Someone must have seen me in the parking lot last night pigging out and then went and spent a small fortune on donuts and a good chunk of time defiling my car. For what? Just to have a laugh? Can they see me now? Maybe it was Skunk and Caleb? Or that group that I saw seeking out late-night munchies?

When I pull out of the lot and into the bus loop, a crowd has gathered in front of the school, including Will, Hillary, Allie, and a bunch of their friends. Then I understand. I'm the senior prank. Familiar faces, all seniors, cheer and hoot. They yell things like "Hungry much?" and "Don't let that one fall off; you might want to save it for later."

I'm about to drive away, but then stop and put the Honda in park. The calls from the crowd get quiet. As I take a deep breath, their voices fade away. I open my door. Someone calls, "I knew she couldn't resist. Don't forget to share, Sugar." Someone else adds, "Yeah, why'd you have to go and clean out Dunkin' Donuts? Next time leave some for us."

It doesn't matter what they say.

I walk around the car to the passenger side so I face the crowd. Just as I did with Mama, I try to see the beauty in their faces. I try. I clear my throat.

"I feel sorry for all of you if your idea of humor is insulting the way someone looks. Yeah, I may be different, but in addition to my pity, you also deserve my gratitude. Going on four years, you have all done a solid job of teaching me who I am, but it's not who you think. I'm a good person, and I am going to do great things." I pause, but decide to leave it at that.

"So, see ya around and—" I smile my beautiful smile and lift my arms in victory. Staring into the crowd I loudly say, "Fuck you!"

My words stun. If someone dropped a pin we'd all hear it. Something shifts inside, and I feel relief. I get in the Honda and drive away from Johnson Regional High School, away from Mama, and away from the pathetic town. I meant what I said to them. In some kind of twisted way, all the darkness they showed me guided me toward my own inner light. I'm sure it would have been better had they just been nice to begin with, and I had some friends to hang out with on the weekends, a boy to invite me to the prom, or even just a day free from harassment. That would have been refreshing. But that isn't how it was, and there was nothing I could do to change myself that would change the way they treated me. Juliana told me that one. The best thing for me to do is accept myself and move on.

I'm not sure I'll be going back to my therapist either, though if I stay in Keene with Henry and Stacy, I'll be closer to her office. I want to leave it all behind, everything except me. I want to say *adiós* to Mama's abuse—that idea came from Juliana, too—and good riddance to Skunk as well. Juliana explained that there is physical abuse, the kind when they'd hit or shove me, but the emotional abuse did as much damage. Even's words echoed this truth.

Mama's weaknesses are clear now—unfortunately, she's passed her problems on to Skunk. She doesn't like herself. She taught me the same, but I don't buy it. I'm bound to find my own strength, and the first step is simply stepping away from the past. It's time to leave the bullying at school. I don't deserve it, and I don't have to take it. I see now that the world is bigger than Od Town; I've felt just as stuck here as I have to the stickiness of the sugar and junk food I've stuffed myself with.

When I've driven out of my hometown, I pull over to the side of the road and call Fat Henry. I don't know why I still call him that, not to his face anymore, but just in my mind. Maybe it's like embracing the name Sugar. It's part of who I am, maybe not a proud part, but it's shaped me. Denying it would be denying part of me, and that doesn't feel right.

He's still at work, but arranges to get out early to meet me at his apartment. I follow his directions. He won't be back for about an hour, so I park in the lot and take a walk. I think about the past twenty-four hours and how wrong everything went but then, taking a deep breath of late-spring air, realize that actually, everything went right.

I met Jesús, found out about my father. I'm not only who I thought I was, but so much more. I stood up for myself in front of almost the entire school. I feel freer than ever, which is saying a lot since up until recently Mama and compulsive eating imprisoned me. It's as if everything Juliana and I have been talking about finally clicked. Or I cracked.

I stop on a bench and pull Even's journal out of my bag. I gaze at his smiling face in the photo of us. Tears slip silently down my cheeks.

"And where do you fit into all of this?" I ask. What direction has my life gone? His appearance in my backyard that day was the catalyst. I didn't know it at the time, but since meeting him all those months ago, I slowly started to crawl out of my own personal hell. *Or shell,* I think as I rub the heart-shaped shell from our day at the beach between my fingers. And now what? A bird flies high above me, circling. It's an eagle. It dips past the tops of the trees and out of sight.

Balancing Even's journal on my knees, I trace his route west with my finger. My tears turn to sobs and I start to shake. The journal slips to the ground. I leap to the sidewalk to retrieve it and find the back cover has come loose. I try to adjust it so it fits together correctly and then notice the inner lining rubs up against the binding. I open the book all the way to discover the inner lining is actually a flap. I peel it back to reveal a few pieces of the journal paper folded and tucked inside. How had I not noticed this before?

I carefully remove them and flatten the first one. Across the top in Even's handwriting it says, *Dear Sugar.*

I gasp.

I've wanted to tell you this for a while, but didn't have the nerve. I saw you before that first day when I was looking for my wallet. You served me ice cream once at the Scoop and Sprinkle. Maybe you don't remember, but I do. You said, "Sprinkles? They're free. Would you like some?" For some reason I think you were expecting me to say no, and when I said, "Rainbow, please," your face lit up in a smile I will never forget. Something about it pulled at me. I kept thinking about you. I went back to the Scoop and Sprinkle a few other times, but you weren't there.

When school started, Will and Hillary filled me in on all the cliques at Johnson. Hillary made it clear how uncool you were, but I didn't care. It's so lame anyway. Sometimes I wonder if you should just go to a different school. I'd go, too, and then we could just avoid it altogether. But I've never known how to talk to you about this. I could see Will and Hillary were right in some ways, you didn't really have any friends, are the topic of ridicule, and you just take it. I want to talk to you and make things better, but it's awkward. It's like if I bring attention to it I'm just . . . I don't know. Making it true? Validating those idiots who don't even know you? I'm not sure what to do, but it just doesn't seem right. I don't know what I'm saying here. I don't know what to say to you other than I really like you. Maybe that's something.

-E

Tears stream from my eyes. Even, Even, Even. There's a hole inside me that longs for him, an emptiness that hurts with his absence. I want him to appear, so we can talk about it. I'd tell him about the donuts and my big speech. I wished he'd talked to me about this back then. Maybe none of this would have happened, and maybe we'd still be at JRHS as a couple who'd gone to prom together—or somewhere else.

The voice in my head that used to be hateful toward me nudges with a persistent *pssst*. I know what it wants to tell me, but I don't want to hear it. I want my fantasy back. The voice is louder than make-believe, so I have to listen. I'm not at all glad Even died, but before I read this letter, I was happier and freer than I've ever been. Staying at JRHS, no matter what the circumstances, would have prevented me from feeling that. No, if he were still with me, we would have found a way. But still, the ache.

I slouch on the bench. I pull out the second letter.

Dear Sugar,

I'm going to try again. I wrote you another letter, but didn't really get my point across. It didn't come out right. I've never had as much fun with anyone as I have with you. Especially not a girl. You make me laugh, you make me think, and ~~even though everyone at~~ I think you are beautiful. There I said it. OK, wrote it. I'm not sure I could say it aloud, I might turn every shade of red, but I want you to know how pretty you are. I love to see you smile, your eyes light up. Your hair is so soft and smooth and smells like sunflowers. You're special and forget whoever says you're not.

I can't wait for Christmas. I've thought up the best plan. Just hope for snow. It will be unforgettable. Maybe even magical. I hope. A boy can hope. Hang in there, though. I know things aren't always easy for you. Someday, it will be different. I'm sure of it. So even though I didn't give you that other letter, I'll sum it up. I like you. A lot. And you're pretty. Bella—your middle name, right? See, someone knew what they were talking about, you just ignore the others.

-E

I can hardly feel my body. All I am is head, and heart, and the hands that hold this piece of Even. I'm not sure I am breathing. As happy as I am to know Even's feelings for me and to have these pieces of paper to remain connected to him, they punctuate how very gone he is. I don't know if I can handle it. I put the second letter back without taking out the last one. I close the journal. I close my eyes. My conflicting emotions confuse me—freedom, happiness, grief, loneliness.

I put Even's journal back in my bag. I walk back to Fat Henry's as Even's words, in Even's voice, dance around in my head, making me feel a little drunk with love and a whole lot alone.

Fat Henry's car pulls in when I get back to the parking lot. He slides in next to the Honda and pops out.

"What the heck?" he says in alarm at the sight of dozens of donuts dotting my car. Like my own when I first saw the spectacle, his mouth hangs open. I open the rear door and pull out the box from the night before.

"Want one? Help yourself."

He shakes his head. "Explain."

"Apparently I, Mercy Bella Legowski-Gracia, aka Sugar, was the senior-class prank at Johnson Regional High School. Pretty spectacular, huh?"

Chapter Twenty-Four

Henry runs upstairs and grabs a paper bag for all the donuts that managed to remain affixed to the Honda. When he returns, we pluck each one off.

"Stacy insists we compost, so into the bag they go." When we're nearly done, which doesn't take long, Henry says, "I'm so sorry. What assholes."

I shake my head. "I probably wouldn't have said this last week, but it's OK."

"*OK?* Hardly. Want to go to the principal or the police? . . . I have a baseball bat. Cracked windshields will be sweet revenge for this mess."

"How about the car wash," I answer.

While he sits in the passenger side, pointing the way, I start to explain my last twenty-four hours.

"So Skunk's buddy has been harassing you. Like, sexually?"

I nod, somewhat embarrassed.

"That's fucked-up. Stacy may have taken the fat kid out of me, but she didn't take the fight. And you, Sugar, are my sister. You're Skunk's sister. What's the matter with him? If you want—now,

I'm totally serious—I will go beat the living crap out of that kid. Whatdya say his name was? Caleb?"

I smile. Now that's the Fat Henry I remember. The bruiser. The fighter. Sometimes a bully, but I'm sure Stacy has gotten that part out of his system.

"I know you would," I tell him. "But I don't plan to go back there. In fact, I've been thinking. Well, first there's more."

"More?"

"Yep. Hold on tight," I say. I tell him about going to church and meeting our uncle Jesús.

We return to the apartment, and when we're inside, I pull out the envelope. Henry drops onto the couch. Very slowly, he shuffles through the photographs. His face is unreadable. He holds his forefinger up, giving me the one-minute signal, and goes to another room.

The apartment is neat and tastefully decorated. A large bookshelf filled with novels and texts takes up nearly half of one wall. A black-and-white print of Paris hangs on the wall above the couch where I sit, and the bases of the two lamps on either side are wire renditions of the Eiffel Tower. On the coffee table are a few magazines, mostly food-related, and a block with photos on each side. I pick it up and see different snapshots of Henry and Stacy, all smiles. It reminds me of the collage of Even and me.

When Henry comes back out to the living room, his eyes are red. He hands me another photograph. Our father stands in front of our old house, holding Henry's little hand. They're both grinning—identical smiles, my smile. Henry takes a deep breath.

"I thought he was dead or in jail. I never thought Mama drove him away. Why would she do that?"

I shrug. "Beats me. There is also this. Maybe it will tell us more. But I'm afraid my eleventh-year Spanish won't quite translate it in its entirety."

Henry grins. "I may have been a pain in the ass when I was younger, but I never forgot the Spanish Papa taught me. It was the only subject in school I did well in. Looking back, I clung to it. Did you know I met Stacy at a weekly conversational Spanish group at a café in Keene? I know it sounds weird, coming from me, but it was my only tie to our dad. You know? If Mama ever heard me utter a word that wasn't in English, she'd tear my hide, but now I can speak freely. Stacy minors in Spanish at Keene State, and we speak it all the time. Or, to be more accurate, Spanglish." Henry's expression is an exact mixture of happiness and sadness.

I've never thought about how our dad being gone affected my older brothers, who actually remember him, especially Henry.

"I can probably read the letter," he says.

I hand it to him, afraid of what I might hear and afraid of what I might not.

"A mis queridos hijos," Henry says. His voice falters. "To my dear children."

"It's OK." I have tears in my eyes, but never in a million years did I expect this moment. Henry reads the letter aloud in Spanish first. I catch the gist. Our father tells us how sorry he was to have to leave, how much he misses us and loves us. It was exactly what I hoped, in my deepest heart, to hear. I'm crying buckets by the end, and Henry is, too.

"Now in English. Papa tells us that he fought to stay in the U.S. He didn't want to leave, but someone reported he sold drugs, something easy to pin on him because he was foreign. He says he never ever did any of the things they accused him of. Nonetheless, when questioned, it appeared that Mama did her best to make him look guilty. He did everything he could to remain with his family, but because of the shame he brought upon us, he thought maybe it was better he was out of our lives. He writes that his brother Jesús kept an eye on us and let him know how all of us kids were doing. He said Jesús tried to get Mama to cooperate, to tell the authorities that she'd been fabricating the truth so he could come back. When that didn't work, he'd even saved enough money for us to go visit him in Mexico, but Mama said if Jesús bothered her again, she'd report him, too."

"If Papa is anything like Jesús, there's not a mean or law-breaking bone in his body," I say, appalled at what I've just learned.

"He goes on to say that his mama, our *abuela*, became very sick and he had to take care of her. Apparently, we are Mexican and Polish, with some cousins in Puerto Rico," Henry says lightly. "Mama always said we were Puerto Rican, but Juan and Jesús went from Mexico to Puerto Rico and then came here. Anyway, he continued to try to gain access to the U.S. via the Mexican authorities, but they forbade him, because of his record. And now he's there, waiting. He says he hopes to see us someday, that we are always welcome to visit him. He regrets everything that happened and prays for us every day. He adds that he will send money if we need it for passage and that, more than anything in this life, he loves us."

I push myself over on the couch and put my arms around Henry, who is crying just as much as I am. I never thought we'd share this moment, but it's comforting, raw, real.

"Who knew? I never expected this," I say when I've finally stopped sobbing.

"What I can't grasp is what the heck is the matter with Mama? Why would she do something like that?" he asks.

"I think she's sick, and has been for a long time. For a little while now, I've been seeing a therapist and she's explained a lot of things to me, has helped me see myself within the context of our lives in that crazy house and, now, outside of it. She's helped me to see myself differently." I pour this out and Henry listens with interest. "Also, a friend of mine, a dear friend, perhaps my only friend, once told me I was full of confidence; I just misplaced it. Turns out, he was right. Mama did a job of helping me hide it real well," I say, pausing a moment to process all of this before I go on.

"So that brings me to a couple things. I'm wondering if I can stay here for a while, just until I figure out what I'm going to do. I have a few weeks of school left. I am going to find out if I can finish up out of the building and still pass this year. I hope so. There's also the matter of Mama. I took care of her, but I can't do that anymore. Her cough, it's so bad. She needs to see a doctor. And Henry, she really needs another kind of help, not just someone to yell at and bring her more soda, clean up after her mess, and take out her frustrations on. Juliana, my therapist, said that a nurse could go and look after her; it'd be covered by her insurance. When I told Mama originally, she refused of course. But I'm not going back there. Well actually, there is one thing I need to go back for." I proceed to tell Henry about Even and the motorcycle.

"*You* ride a motorcycle?! My little sister? Shut up. It's a good thing I lost all that weight; otherwise I'd probably have just had a heart attack. Seriously?" He braces himself on the couch as if all this new information might carry him away.

I pull out my license. He studies it. "Dang. So you and this boy, he taught you to ride? You own a motorcycle?"

"Well, it's stolen, actually." I realize I've been talking about Even in the present tense. Based on what little I'd said about him, Juliana assumed correctly at our last session when she'd told me that I hadn't digested my grief—leaving me hungry and hollow. I'm not ready to let go of him. I remember the notes in the journal and Even's sweet confessions.

Henry stands up, sits down, and stands up again, incredulous.

"Please sit; there's more." Through choking tears, I tell him all about what happened to Even. I also tell him how Skunk was possibly involved, though I learned from Mama that the police questioned him and found him not at fault. He probably had Caleb's cousin vouch for him.

After Henry's consoled me, he says, "You'll have to talk to his father. You can't just drive a motorcycle around that isn't yours.

There's insurance and all that. You'll have to get it straightened out. OK? And as for the Honda, that's registered in Mama's name. I know you've been keeping up on the bills, but rightfully, it's hers."

This is becoming too complicated. I want to U-turn back to the bright hope I felt when we were talking about possibly meeting our father. The heaviness connecting me to my old life makes extricating myself from it more difficult. But I'm ready for something new, a fresh beginning; though, like a tether, the past draws me back, forcing me to have closure before I snip the cord.

Together, Henry and I hatch a plan, but before we're able to move forward, Stacy comes home. I watch as she holds Henry in her arms for a long time after he fills her in on everything, well almost, that he just learned. She leaves us to talk for a few more minutes while she starts to make dinner.

"I promise, it will be the best meal of your life. She's a wizard in the kitchen," Henry says.

From the other room, she laughs good-naturedly at his comment. After a few minutes, clanging of pots and pans, and a spicy yet smooth smell fills the kitchen.

"You can stay here as long as you need to," Henry says.

"Thank you."

"I'm going to make a few phone calls in the morning, and you'll have to settle up about school, OK?"

In under an hour, Stacy, Henry, and I sit around their small maple table. We say grace and then she dishes us up a plate of *migas*, a dish with onions, garlic, chili peppers, eggs, tomatoes, avocado, and corn tortillas. It's colorful, and when I take my first bite, the taste is intensely flavorful. I wonder how I ever ate shrink-wrapped food or gobs of packaged sweets.

"This kind of food got you to lose all that weight?" I say in disbelief. Henry nods.

"We don't eat anything processed, just about. Everything is fresh and natural," Henry says with a mouthful.

"Will you teach me?" I ask without thinking.

"I'd love to," Stacy says. We spend the evening chatting and then watch a movie while Stacy does some homework.

My night's sleep on Henry and Stacy's couch is the deepest and best since I spent the night with Even in New York. I wake up feeling refreshed and renewed. Stacy pulls out a container of sunrise muffins that she baked.

"They are a complete balance of protein, fiber, and nutrients to start your day," she tells me.

At first, I'm not so sure. They're brown, and not because they're chocolate. But I try one for breakfast along with lemon-infused water and a cup of coffee. Again, I understand how easy it has been for Henry to get healthy with Stacy preparing this nourishing food, not to mention her gentle manner. He calls in late to work, but it's too early to start making phone calls, so he suggests we go for a run. I laugh.

"Have you ever seen me run?"

"OK, how about jog? Or yog? With a soft *j*." We both laugh at a reference from the comedy we watched the night before.

"I can't jog or yog." Then I think back to that morning when I'd discovered Skunk had slashed the tires on the Honda. I recall that unusual sense of lightness I experienced as I ran to school.

"I bet you can." He goes into his room, grabs a pair of sweatpants, and tosses them to me. "Come on, we don't have all day."

I stuff myself in the gray cotton sweats and am sure to pull my T-shirt down over my ample behind. I wrinkle my brow. Juliana asked me about the thoughts, the mean little voice, I have in relation to my body and if I would ever say those kinds of things to a friend. She suggests when I hear it, I say the words out loud.

"Pull the shirt down over your ample behind."

"Huh?" Henry says.

"Sorry. It's an exercise the therapist suggested I try. When I hear nasty comments in my head, she said I should say them aloud.

Then if they sound like something I'd say to the person I love most in the world, then they're fine, but if they're at all questionable or insulting, she said to reframe them. Something like 'I hear you saying I have an ample behind, but I love and treasure my body and all the amazing things it does for me.' Stand up to the bully, but sorta in a loving kind of way."

"I see." Henry looks somewhat puzzled, but goes on, "Well, for a second you sounded like Mama. You know she used to say nasty things to me about my size. I've never understood it, though, because she's always been bigger than us."

"That's just it. She's never liked herself, so she imposed her self-hatred on us; in fact, she went so far as trying to make us worse off than her, but you see where that got her."

In my sessions with Juliana, she explained many things to me, but it's only now that I am with Henry, serving as a witness to the past, that I can apply these new ideas so that I fully understand them. I smile at the two of us, both on the path to health and wellness, outside in the sunshine and about ready to run. Or maybe just walk.

"We'll start slow. Stacy and I go every other night or morning, whatever we can squeeze into our schedules. It's important to get the heart rate up with cardio."

"Who are you and what did you do with my brother?" I say with a laugh.

We start at a slow pace, practically walking. Henry can go faster, but he hangs back with me. We follow the sidewalk and then cross the street into a residential area. When we near the end of the road, I can't help it, I lengthen my stride, I pick up my feet, and I'm running, only this time I'm not trying to escape myself. Henry flashes a grin. We loop around, and when we reach the sidewalk back to the apartment, I let out a whoop. I'm out of breath and red-faced, but I don't care.

"You're a winner, Sugar. You did great. Way to go!" He high-fives me.

I playfully shove him. But he's not wrong.

When we get back to the apartment, I shower while Henry calls the insurance company about Mama. Apparently, he's her proxy or something. He'll report that she's no longer able to take care of herself and refuses the help of family. The way he understands it, after doing a bit of research online, they have to step in, whether she likes it or not.

After I'm dressed, I pop my head into their home office, which is really just the spare bedroom.

"How did it go?" I ask.

"I did my best to explain everything, and they said they'll send someone over tomorrow."

"Good?" I ask, unsure.

"We'll see. I told them Mama might not make it easy. The nurse laughed at that. Your turn. Good luck with the school stuff," Henry says.

Henry goes to the shower. I practice what I want to say. First, I call Ms. Barrows. She answers on the second ring, sounding chipper. I'm happy to tell her the success I've had with Juliana, but then reveal the trouble at home and then the senior prank.

"Yes, I heard about that. Measures are being taken."

"I don't really want to get anyone in trouble. It's just that I don't think I can finish out the last few weeks there. To tell you the truth, I don't feel safe, because of my brother's friends and the bullying." The worst that can happen is she says no, but that won't change my stance.

"Yes, I completely understand. You surprise me; you're so . . ." She hesitates for a fraction of a second. I'm afraid she's going to say something cruel. "Unique, resilient, and"—she laughs—"you're a little bit rebellious, in a way. I admire you. I'm sorry all this has happened. I thought maybe that we could head it off with the assembly. You're really advocating for yourself, Mercy, and I respect that. I'll see what I can do for getting you finished up here. And your plans afterward?"

"I'm not sure yet." This isn't completely true. Over the last day or so, I've gotten closer to knowing exactly what my plans are, but I'm not quite ready to let them surface. Ms. Barrows promises to get back to me by the end of the day. I may have to return to the school to get homework and fill out paperwork, but she seemed positive that they'd find a way for me to complete the year. Mama's care and school—two down, one to go.

Chapter Twenty-Five

In Henry's wake, the apartment is quiet. Too quiet. I have the urge to pilfer their cupboards for something sweet to occupy myself with but instead do another exercise Juliana taught me. I wait fifteen minutes. First, I take a few deep breaths and then chew a piece of gum. After that, I walk around the apartment just to move, but that isn't enough, so I go back outside and find myself on the same bench as I was yesterday when I found the notes in Even's journal.

I slide the first two out and reread them. In tears, I unfold the last one. The handwriting on each of them is the same: solid, angular, and purposeful. I read Even's note. The only difference is this one is dated. Even wrote it the morning of the day he died. My face tingles and more tears gush from my eyes.

Dearest Sugar or Mercy, (Sometimes I want to call you that or Shoog or darling or babe- Lol)

For some reason I couldn't get up the courage to give you the first letter I wrote or the second one either. But I realize why now. I wasn't saying everything I meant or I wasn't saying enough I guess. I've come to realize over these months since we met, went to the lodge together, then to New York, those big moments and then all the other little ones in between, that you and I fit together like two pieces of a puzzle, maybe the most important pieces. Maybe that isn't the best analogy. Two peas in a pod? Nah, I don't really like peas. But I really like you. You know that night in the lodge, I couldn't stop smiling, but it was like I wasn't only smiling on my face, it was my whole body. Then when we kissed in New York, I just knew. I knew that I love you. I am in love with you. How many ways can I say it? Or why can't I say it? But I will. So now that you've reached the end of this note, I'm going to be brave and say it. Please look up.

And that is it. But he isn't here to say it. I see how he wanted this moment to unfold—passing me the note, me reading it and then—but he's gone. My lips tremble. "I love you, too," I say.

In the periphery of my vision, a shadow moves across the sun, and that is exactly how I feel. Happy beyond happy and at the same time the saddest I've ever been. I look up expecting to see the cloud-covered sky. I want to shout *why*? But the eagle's there. It circles once, twice, and then flies off. "Oh, Even, I love you, too."

I fold the note and replace it in the journal. Now, more than ever, I know what I am going to do, what I'm meant to do. I return to the apartment, and call Juliana. Thankfully, she has time for one last session, saying she had a cancellation for her eleven o'clock slot.

I flip through some of Stacy's magazines to pass the time, and then log on to their computer and gather some information. At a quarter of eleven, I drive across town to the salmon-colored office. As quickly as possible, I outline everything that's happened, and what I'd like to do.

"This is a tough one, but I think if you approach it delicately, preferably in the morning, before he's had a chance to, um, get bombed, as you said, he might be willing to listen. There's a good chance if you are tactful and explain he'll understand. Maybe this time, he'll be more compassionate. Sometimes the heart can surprise us, even the ones that seem the coldest," Juliana says.

"And what if he's not?"

"There are other options, of course. I can see you really want this to be the one, but be patient, open, and trust that things will turn out exactly as they're meant to. In many ways, they already have. You are a different person than the one who came in here a few months ago; you're a woman now, actually. A person healing, ready to shine."

I thank her for all she's done to help me.

"You've really impressed me, Mercy. You were ripe for change, but if you ever need to talk, please don't hesitate to call. My door is always open for you."

I spend the afternoon in a café finishing a book I have to write an essay on for English, and then go to meet Henry. Stacy gets home and has me help her in the kitchen, showing me how to cook for real. It's fun, and I'm happy to have her for a sister—well, I will be once they get married.

After we eat, Henry says, "So, are you ready?"

"As ready as I'll ever be." Stacy bids us farewell, and we go in the Honda to Mama's house. I'm jittery with nerves as we near town and absolutely shaking when we pull up to the house. Nearly all the lights are on. From the outside, it looks like any other house on the street, weather-beaten, neglected, but lit up as if there's life inside. As I know, all too well, it is actually filled with just a slow, creeping, and cruel death.

I lean my head back on the seat. "Are you sure about this?" I ask.

"This was your plan. Are *you* sure about it?" Henry asks.

"Yes. I doubt it'll be easy, but yes. Let's go."

As usual, the front door is unlocked. We go in, and I immediately feel seven years old. Helpless. Fear nips at my ankles.

Hopeless. The smell of something burning bites at my nose. The kitchen is a wreck and the garbage can overflows onto the floor.

"Whoever comes tomorrow will have a real thrill," I say.

"We're not going to tell Mama this part, but they're also sending someone from social services. As you said, it isn't only medical attention she needs," Henry whispers.

I open the door to the oven and a black cloud of smoke billows out. I turn it off and open a window. Henry shakes his head, hurrying down the hall to Mama's room.

I take a quick survey of the kitchen, making sure the place isn't going to burn down with us in it.

From the gloom in the living room, Skunk appears. "Well, eff me. Look who's here."

It isn't clear whether we're alone or if any of his friends lurk in the house. Sweat beads across my forehead. My legs tremble.

"It must be so easy for you to just wipe your hands and walk away from us, huh?" he says, gusting me with stale beer breath.

"No, Skunk, it hasn't been easy," I say evenly, daring myself to be bold.

His eyes dart over every inch of me like his vision alone has the ability to slice me to ribbons.

It doesn't.

Licks of rage burn away my sweat and fear.

"I've been here, lookin' after Mama, trying to keep shit together. Doin' what you couldn't. Stepping up and being a man." He narrows his eyes and nods his head like he's won, like his word is final, but it's not, not anymore. Then he adds, "You're not welcome here anymore, fatwad."

I'm rendered ash and reborn in flame. My indignation is singular. A fist grips my insides with bleeding knuckles for my broken family. I want to shake or punch sense into him. To explain to him how much courage it takes to really live, not whatever we've been doing the last seventeen years. Instead, a slurry of rage pours out of my mouth as my voice elevates from normal to shouting to growling. "You're useless, Skunk. You don't get it. I'm sorry for you." I shake my head to counter his smug nod. "You're gutless." I'm out of breath like I've been fighting for my life. I leave him with my anger and rush down the hall.

The moment I appear in the doorway, Mama launches on me with a snarling, hissing, horrid verbal assault.

"Where the flying fuck have you been, Sugar? You piece of shit, I thought I told you I needed your help. Damn Skunk has had to look after me and you can see he ain't no good."

I take a deep breath. I'm going to say exactly what Juliana and I planned, and won't respond to her insults. "Mama, I have moved out. I'm staying with Henry and Stacy now. One of Skunk's friends acted inappropriately to me, and I don't feel safe here. Also, I want to say that, although I do care for you, I can't take care of you anymore. It's beyond my ability."

She glares at me. "Bullshit. You have to. Who else is going to? What the hell did I have kids for? So they could gang up on me and leave me? You're staying in this house until I tell you you ain't. You hear me?" She shakes with anger and then erupts into a coughing fit.

"It's time a professional comes to help you, Mama. I've arranged for someone to be here in the morning. They are going to make sure you're OK and take care of you now," Henry says.

"No way. Uh-uh," Mama answers. She tries to get up. She's purple with rage. She wears the same expression she does just before she strikes.

"This is the way it is. We're sorry if you don't like it, but it's more important that Sugar is safe and your health is addressed properly," Henry says.

Mama starts in with "My health is just fine. I'm just stressed out, that's all, trying to keep track of this deceptive little bitch and make sure Skunk don't burn the house down."

"That's just it. You can't do either of those things anymore. And neither can we. Sorry, Mama. This is what's going to happen, plain and simple. Sugar is staying with me, and a nurse is coming to take care of you."

Mama flies into a stream of expletives and looks as if she wants to mow the both of us down. When she's out of breath and her coughing stops, I take a step closer.

"Mama, I want to say goodbye. I'm not sure when I'll be seeing you again. But I just want you to know—" The words that I know I should say won't come. I know a daughter ought to love her mother, but I can't utter the words. I know a part of me does, but it doesn't feel true. Instead, something Juliana talked a lot about comes to mind, something I thought about this morning. "Mama, I forgive you. Goodbye." I pat the bed where her leg is and turn to leave.

"Bye, Mama," Henry says, and he follows me through the door.

She curses at us as Henry closes the door behind him. I exhale. Just when I think it's over, Skunk charges down the hall.

"Why'd you go and upset Mama?"

"We were just talking to her," Henry says.

"You think you're gonna come in here and abracadabra, fix everything? You just make things worse, both of you. Why don't you get the hell out of here."

"Gladly," I say, fuming at his audacity.

Henry says, "Sugar is staying with me from now on, and someone is going to be coming here to look after Mama."

Skunk looks as if he's ready to spit bullets. "The both of you look so smug. Gone and lost all that weight. Henry, you stole Sugar here away. I reckoned you've been plotting something. But just know she's a fat slut, always coming on to my friends, so I guess that don't matter now she's gone. The only thing she is good for is wiping Mama's ass."

Henry stiffens next to me.

"You wait and see; you'll find out how useless she is. Why, if you ask me, she's better off—"

"Sugar, why don't you go on outside," Henry says through gritted teeth.

I've already said what I needed to say to Skunk, and I've heard enough. I leave the keys to the Honda on the counter and go into the garage. I unearth the motorcycle and back it out. I almost feel like I want to stroke it affectionately, like a horse. Something close to laughter loosens inside. I get in the saddle and feel instantly invigorated. From the house, there's shouting and then a loud slam. I fire up the bike so I don't have to listen to it. I'm done there. I look toward the west, where the sun just begins to set.

After a few nail-biting minutes, Henry bursts out the front door. When he gets closer, I can see a small cut slices across his cheek. He's ruffled and breathes heavily. Without hesitating, he gets on the back of the bike and, with that, we're off. As I put miles between that old house and my old life, my shoulders relax and I mold to the bike, riding easy.

We walk up to Henry's apartment in silence; I get the feeling he isn't ready to talk. When we get inside, Stacy bounces off the couch where textbooks and her laptop are scattered around her. She rushes to give Henry a hug. When she pulls back, she asks, "What happened?"

"After you went outside," he says, looking at me, "I had a feeling things might get ugly, but first I wanted to tell him about Papa. I explained we'd found him, but he said and I quote, 'I don't want nothin' to do with that bastard.' So, basically, Skunk isn't interested. Funny how it seems we're divided evenly. You and I, Sugar, are welcoming change, health, and healing, while Skunk and Mama are content to wallow in their misery."

Henry's the most upset I've seen him.

He goes on, "I didn't really like the things that he was saying but was willing to let them go. Then one of his friends came in and started hollering at me, some stringy kid who I vaguely remember as Caleb. Before he could say any more, I punched him in the face." He bows gallantly.

I laugh appreciatively.

"Your knight in shining armor. Or brother in shining armor."

"Thanks," I say.

"Don't mention it. I'm not sure he understood why he got one in the face, but serves him right. Anyway, of course, Skunk got pissed and threw a punch, but there wasn't much behind it. Just like I remember. He never did think much, just plowed through. Although, he wouldn't stop until I had him pinned."

"Your face," Stacy says, putting her hand gently on his cheek.

"Trust me; he got the worst of it."

"You two used to fight all the time," I say.

"It was good to know where his weak spots are. I didn't mean for it to come to blows, but that's the language he seems to understand. It isn't my way—well not anymore—but I made my point."

"And I said goodbye," I say, feeling somewhat relieved.

"Good riddance," Henry says.

The next day, I set out early on the motorcycle. I pull onto Birch Road and park beside the pickup truck. I wait, sitting astride the bike, hoping to see some movement upstairs that will urge me in or push me to turn around and leave. After another moment of indecision, I tell myself it's now or never, and I have a meeting at the school in an hour.

I walk up the stairs and knock. Nash isn't expecting me, so when he peers through the blinds I'm not surprised he takes a moment before he opens the door. He looks me up and down and then leaves the door hanging open. I suppose he means for me to follow.

I close the door behind me. The kitchen is tidy. Either he hasn't been eating or he's changed, and if so, that's promising.

"Mr. Anderson, I was a friend of Even's. I came here today to ask you something." In the morning light, Nash looks tired, the lines in his face deeper than the last time I saw him.

"Yeah, I remember you. You said something at Even's memorial serv—" He coughs, and I'm not sure if it's just because he needed to or if the word is hard for him to say.

"That's right. I have something to show you. I'm not sure if you've ever seen it, but I suppose he might have liked you to. Do you mind if we sit down?"

We take a seat at the dinette table. I show him the journal and Even's plan for both Tansy's ashes and his journey out west. By the end, there are tears in both our eyes. Nash looks through the kitchen window into the distance.

"What I'd like to know is if I can have his motorcycle. If you want money for it, I'll give you what I can. He salvaged the thing and rebuilt it, but he also taught me to ride it. He meant for it to take him west, to the Pacific. He wanted it to carry him there so he could release Tansy's—pardon me, Mrs. Anderson's—ashes."

Nash puts his hand over his mouth. His arm shakes beneath his plaid shirt. He takes a moment and then gets up, goes to Even's bedroom and then to the living room. I stare at the floor, as if I might see Even's footprints there. He returns carrying some papers and two wooden boxes. He places them on the table. Engraved across the top of one is Even's name, birthdate, and the date he died. It's almost identical to Tansy's box.

Nash takes a pen from his shirt pocket and then writes a note titled "Bill of Sale." He adds the date and that he's selling the bike to me for one dollar. He has me sign the paper. Then he pushes the box toward me and nods his head.

"Yes. Take them both," he manages to say as he battles his emotions.

"Are you sure, Mr. Anderson?"

He nods.

I'm not sure that we're done, but I see I have five minutes to make it to the high school. I carefully pick up the boxes and put them in my bag. I place a dollar bill on the counter, but he shakes his head. "Thank you."

"No, thank you. Just one thing," he says when I'm at the door. "Would ya do me just one favor. Would you do it at sunrise? That was always her favorite time of day. And his, too. I favor the sunset, but they had that in common. Maybe, if you're able, you could take a photo of it over the water and send it to me. I'd appreciate that."

"Of course." I look around the room, where Even lived, making sure I never forget, and then hurry down the stairs. The wind dries my salty tears as I ride to JRHS. I get to the school as the second period bell rings. I'm a minute late. When I arrive at the secretary's office, she gives me a look and says, "They're waiting for you." I make my apologies, but the principal, my English and Algebra II teachers, and Ms. Barrows don't seem irritated.

The meeting is quick and to the point. They agree to allow me to finish the semester off-campus; though I've never understood why they call the high school a campus; it's just one building. I also have daily online check-ins with each of my teachers and then will return for exams, but I'm not required to be at the school other than that. I agree to this and gather all the materials I'll need. On my way out, Ms. Barrows calls, "Good luck!" I can tell she means it.

Over the next few weeks Stacy and I study and cook together. She really is a whiz in the kitchen. I'm on my way to eating healthy, whole foods and liking it, which I never would have guessed. Over dinner one night, of jeweled rice with lemon, thyme, almonds, and cranberries with a side of baked halibut, the happy couple announces they have something to share with me.

"I've been in touch with Papa," Henry says.

"You heard back?"

He nods.

"And . . . ?" I ask.

"He's so happy. We spoke on the phone earlier. You were out, but he can't wait to see us. I haven't filled him in on all the details; I figured it would be better to do that in person. Well, we haven't picked a date yet for our wedding; we were thinking we'd put it off until Stacy graduates, but now we are thinking we might go to Mexico in August for our honeymoon. We decided we're going to have a private ceremony and a party here for friends and family, but of course Papa won't be able to come, so what better way to include him in our plans than to go there afterward? We won't spend the entire time with him—it's a honeymoon after all—but we want you to be there, too."

My smile matches Henry's. "Of course," I answer with happy surprise before I think of logistics.

"Just call us when you figure out where you'll be, and we'll arrange for a ticket. Sound good?" Stacy asks. I'm glad to hear her say this. Her words tell me that she actually wants me included and this isn't just Henry's idea.

"Yes. Absolutely," I answer.

• • •

I spend the next weeks walking and cooking and sewing and studying. Exam time comes and I make it in and out of the classrooms, unscathed, for English, math, science, and history. My last exam is Spanish. I'm nervous because I know Hillary and Allie will be there, not to mention Brandon.

I have to wade through the rows of desks toward the back to find an empty one. Eyes are on me, but I don't look around. I take my seat. Hillary and Allie laugh. Part of me wants to turn, stare them down, or ask them what gives, why do they pick on me? Then whispering and pointing accompanies the laughter. The proctor gives a five-minute warning for using the bathroom. I get to my feet. As I try to slip by the laughing girls to exit to the girls' room, mostly to center myself before concentrating on Spanish, knowing I'll mostly be thinking about Papa, Allie blocks my path. She gives me an appraising look, up and down.

"No matter how much weight you lose or how many days you skip school, you'll never be pretty"—she pauses—"or cool, or desired." She says this last word in a sexy, husky voice. Her eyes penetrate the layers of courage and confidence I've amassed in the previous weeks. She sees right through to my soft, mushy core. "You'll never be like me." The words hiss like a fuse.

But I'm the dynamite.

I take a careful look at her dyed and straightened hair, perfect upturned nose, painted lips, and narrow hips. "You're right, Allie," I answer, meeting her eyes. It stings. I don't want to be accepted or liked by her, but still, it's mean. I want to tell her how awful she is or at least just call a truce. Instead, I hold her gaze, my chin lifted. "I'll never be like you. And you know what? That's flippin' great, because I'm going to be exactly like me."

Nonetheless, in the bathroom, I brace myself on the edge of the bathroom sink and splash cool water on my face. I think back to the day in the cafeteria when Even bumped into me and I sought refuge in here. When I look up, the girl in the reflection is radiant. That girl is me. There's a discarded tube of lipstick lying on the sink against the wall. I open it. It's bright pink. I ignore the germ factor and apply it, rubbing my lips together. I lean into the mirror and kiss it. "You are beautiful," I say. Next to my lip stain, I write, "Love, Sugar."

I sit for the exam, pink lips and all. Before I know it, I'm on the last question. A chime rings, indicating we have to close our test booklets. Everyone passes them forward, and the proctor dismisses us. I race to the front of the room. There are giggles. I blow them a kiss, a smirk blazing across my lips. Maybe I did have the last say.

I rush out the doors, hoping never to return to Johnson Regional High School. With one last glance at the spot where Even and I used to meet, I get onto the motorcycle in the parking lot and coast through the bus loop toward the street. I lap Brandon, putting along on his bicycle. He calls out, "Ride, fat girl, ride."

Oh, I will. I yell, "Kiss my curves!" I may no longer be fat, but I'm a curvy girl, and I like it. This new body has arches and curls in all the right spots, and is my real body. I have no desire to be skinny, but the excess weight I carried around wasn't mine; it was Mama's, and I'm glad to be rid of it.

That night we celebrate my completion of eleventh grade. Henry raises his glass. "Didn't someone once say something like 'To the best of times and the worst of times'?"

Stacy nods. "I'm no English major, but I did have to memorize that for English in high school. Charles Dickens. It was something like 'It was the best of times, it was the worst of times—'"

I remember it from English, too. I join in, our voices in harmony. "It was the age of wisdom, it was the age of foolishness, it was the epoch of belief, it was the epoch of incredulity, it was the season of Light, it was the season of Darkness, it was the spring of hope, it was the winter of despair, we had everything before us, we had nothing before us . . ."

We sit there for a moment, letting the words cast their nets around us, picking up shards of our lives and holding them as truth and letting others slip through. I imagine Even sitting in the empty chair across from me.

"There's more, of course, but darned if I can remember," Stacy says, breaking the spell.

"Me neither," I say. It means something that Henry wanted to toast using that quote, and both Stacy and I knew it—it speaks to common experience, the good, and the bad. We dig into the ten-veggie stir-fry, my first foray into proper cooking, courtesy of Stacy. They both praise the dish.

When we're done, Stacy brings out fortune cookies.

"A little treat. I bribed the guy at the Chinese restaurant by the university for a few. I figured some good fortune was in order to wish Sugar on her way," she says.

We each crack into the cookies. Henry pulls his out.

"'Good company is as agreeable as a good meal.' Too true," Henry says, reading his.

Stacy goes next. "'You're sitting next to your best friend,'" she reads, beaming. "You've got that right." They share a peck on the lips. "Your turn," Stacy says to me.

I crack the cookie in half and pull out the small rectangle of paper. "'The fortunate make their own good fortune.'" Indeed.

"Right again," Stacy says, laughing.

We enjoy the rest of the evening together, and before I go to bed, I say goodbye. Henry gives me a bear hug and says, "Look after yourself, Mercy."

At dawn, I pad to the bathroom and slide into a romper I sewed especially for my ride. It's the first garment—made by me—I've ever worn. The fabric, against my skin, is fabulous. It looks like a dress, but the bottom is actually a pair of shorts. The zip-up front is hidden by tiers of tangerine and rose, peach and amber: the flames of color that can only be described as sunrise. I will float in the wind, like I have feathers, like a bird. I put on a sparkly, chunky bejeweled necklace. I twirl in front of the mirror, fluttering and shining. Then I look at myself, full-on. I've decided that size does and does not matter. I didn't have to lose weight to grow as a person because the truth is, the girl I see, no matter what I look like, *feels* gorgeous, buxom, and whole.

I slip out of the apartment, and take some time fitting everything into the compartments of the bike. I tuck the two wooden boxes carefully in the pannier bags I added for travel, with my sewing on top. My clothing, toiletries, and supplies go in the other one. I keep Even's journal in my jacket. I tuck my hand into my pocket and feel for the shell he gave me on the beach. It's there, solid and true. I have a photo of the two of us tucked near the handlebars where I can see it, but secure so the wind won't blow it away. I say a prayer and then set off.

At a traffic light, near the state border, I put my helmet on. The sun shines on my back, warming me. I don't look up, but sense an eagle above, circling overhead. Then I get the green light, and I go.

Acknowledgments

To my big and littles, thank you for shining so bright. Dad, thank you for upgrading my MS Word and for the encouragement. I offer heartfelt gratitude to my family and friends for your support. Christine ((C)) for the early read, and Tamar for your cheerleading. Rah! Rah! Rah! Daily hearts to my K-girls for indulging in me.

I thank God for all the blessings and lessons, especially patience.

Tackle hugs are in order for the team at Skyscape. Courtney, thank you for opening that document, reaching out, and taking a chance. If you haven't checked, you may very well have fairy-editor-angel wings! Kelli, you make my words, and me, sparkle. For your dedication to the manuscript, I owe you lunch at Locanda (also, just so we can hang out).

I'm grateful to the amazing writing community on Twitter. You are outstanding writers and people, who not only provided me with the push to focus but also with more than a few laughs and much cute emergency relief.

Readers, for believing in the magical power of the written word, thank you, thank you, thank you.

About the Author

During her teens, Deirdre Riordan Hall traveled throughout the United States and Europe, developing a love for stories and a desire to connect with worlds—imagined or real—on the page. She has written *To the Sea*, *Surfaced*, and the Follow Your Bliss series. When not spending time with her family, writing, or traveling, Hall is at the beach, pretending to be a mermaid.